I0766076

Jacob

Journey of a God

EAMON BLAKE

ISBN: 978-1-7385182-5-8

Acknowledgements

Book 1

This book, **Jacob - Journey of a God** (revised edition), is the first in a series. It tells the story about the amazing life of a teenager who, between the years 2012 and 2016, lived in Dublin, Ireland. For me, writing what I thought was one book, was a labour of love that began in 2016, a love that helped the story morph into a series of five books.

Book 1 - Jacob - Journey of a God

Book 2 - Jacob - Walk of the Messengers

Book 3 - Jacob - War of the End Times

Book 4 - Jacob - Children of the Gods

Book 5 - Jacob - Battle for Olympus

These books would never have been written if it wasn't for the support and encouragement of my amazing family and friends who listened to my relentless telling of the stories and the ideas I had. A special 'Thank You' to you all, you know who you are.

I would like to take this opportunity to thank those who took the time to read and proof-read this book in a genre that, in a lot of cases, is alien to them.

They were the ones who particularly encouraged and cajoled me into taking this epic story to its conclusion. Thank you, a million times, to Teresa Carroll, Rita Foley, Sean Blake, Tom Lillis, Vincent Reynolds, Eamonn Maguire, Raymond King, Marie O'Connor, Thérése McGarry, Paul Cleary, Laura Kelly and Vanessa Keogh.

To my friend Damien Carroll: What can I say. Your regular emails and phone calls were a great help in getting some of my Dublin 'isms' out of the story making it a far better read. I am filled with gratitude.

I am eternally grateful to two groups of very special people, the Poets and Authors in the 'All About Writing Group' and the 'Dublin Writers Forum' for assisting me in getting my book to print ready; this would not have been possible without their valuable critique and editorial assistance, especially with grammar, layouts and storylines.

I would like to acknowledge the staff at Westside Press for their assistance in the publication of the first edition of Book 1, especially in designing its amazing and attractive book cover.

To my amazing niece, Niamh Blake, thank you so much for your wonderful cover designs.

I would also like to acknowledge PerpetuityPublications.com for their assistance in formatting my books and getting them ready for release. Thanks again Perpetuity Publications.

And, finally, to my son, Paul: Thanks for always being there for me. I love you.

Author's Profile

Eamon Blake is from Crumlin, a Southside suburb of Dublin, Ireland, a place he still has a great love for. It was there, between 1970 and 1975, where he attended the local secondary school, Meanscoil Naomh Colm. During fifth and sixth year, he had the pleasure of being taught English by the late Michael Condon, an inspirational teacher who had an amazing teaching technique commanding the greatest of respect from his pupils. Eamon believes that as a result of that teacher's style and perseverance he developed an interest in writing. It was in that same school where he developed his passion for real and classical history. The history and mythology learned during that time lingered in Eamon's mind and those early influences only resurfaced in recent years, inspiring him to pen a series of five fantasy novels recounting the tale of a Dublin schoolboy discovering his extraordinary powers, and who he actually was.

A widower with one son, Eamon, over the years, has successfully navigated various employment roles involving procurement, sales and marketing. His professional journey included delivering marketing presentations to major wholesale and retail chains, as well as participating in monthly sales and planning meetings. He believes the wealth of experience garnered during those years helped him develop his own writing style, ultimately leading to the Jacob series.

Eamon's first foray into writing began with him researching and publishing a book detailing the history and genealogy of his own family in central Dublin, dating back to the 1780s. Motivated by a desire to share this heritage, he produced and published enough copies exclusively for his extended family.

The idea for the Jacob series came to Eamon in the late summer of 2016 after he witnessed a charming yet humorous incident in Temple Bar, Dublin. This event led to the realisation that a fantastical story could be crafted by intertwining major historical events from Africa, America, Europe, the Far East as well as the Near East, linking them, and drawing inspiration from worldwide mythological realms featuring Centaurs, Dragons, Elves, The Gods, The Little People, Mer-Peoples, The Yeti and Wizards.

Contact author:

Email: thejacobsaga@gmail.com

Table of Contents

Chapter 1

Summer of 2016, what a time for Jacob? His sixteenth year! His team winning the schools rugby cup, and his junior exams completed. Travelling was one of his favourite pastimes, especially when with Maria, his ever watchful mother.

That summer they travelled from Rome up to Northern Italy, on to Germany, over to Holland and Belgium, through France, across the Pyrenees and down the coast of Portugal to spend a few days in Gibraltar before finishing their last week on the east coast of Spain.

Maria was thirty six but presented as someone in her early twenties. She was so beautiful she attracted attention everywhere she went. Jacob on the other hand was still a struggling teenager with the associated cheeky attitude, and even so, he too received an equal amount of attention. Those they met never believed they were actually mother and son.

Maria knew big changes were coming and it was no surprise to her that when Jacob left Dublin as a gawky, yet good looking teenager, he would, by the time they reached Gibraltar, have taken on the appearance of an extremely handsome young man. For her, watching her son change made her more anxious until she saw he was still acting like a normal teenager. His phone was more often than not at his ear. His lifelines were Face Time, Instagram and WhatsApp. His earphones became a permanent fixture. She loved it when strangers complimented him as a happy go lucky kind of guy, but she also knew they couldn't see how this was all a facade.

What they failed to see was the horrendous turmoil draining him from the inside out. It was the continuous night terrors that began when he was twelve. Nightmares taking him to places and times that always seemed to be historical in nature or about death and destruction. He'd invariably wake up exhausted, sometimes in shock and more often than not, just numb. They had no way of knowing the difficulty he had leaving his bed each morning to struggle into his bathroom, run some cold water and then, after plunging his face into the basin, wait for relief. When relief came his spirits lifted in anticipation of a call from Shane, his closest friend.

"Hi Scobie," was always the opening greeting coming from his ever happy friend. Shane was the only one who called Jacob by that name.

"Hey Bud," would be Jacob's response and then a never ending pointless conversation ensued.

One particular afternoon Shane had a visit from two other close friends, Davie and Al. Two guys who were also stars on the junior rugby team. All three sat close together to allow for a proper four way Face Time conversation. Davie grabbed the phone and rounded on Jacob, "Mate! I'm pissed, and I could break your neck. You should have been there to have our backs, the embarrassment; the shame. They beat the living daylights out of us. 34 to 7, can you imagine, the worst ever defeat for our school."

"Me and Davie," interrupted Al, "we were placed in the two centre positions and were constantly targeted. We had a crap game."

"You two in the centre?" sneered a smug Jacob, "No wonder we lost but don't worry I'll be back next week."

"That's some cheek," said an unimpressed Davie, "from someone swanning around Europe with his tits hanging out." He turned to Al and Shane, "Time for training, let's face the music, come on, see ya Jacob."

Davie and Al left and called for Shane to follow but he hesitated, he was about to say his goodbyes but decided to sit down again. He got serious.

"Scobie, it's me. Your best buddy. Is everything OK?"

"Yeah," Jacob replied, "I'm having a great time but looking forward to meeting up with you and the boys."

"You look very different. In fact you look stronger, kind of macho, like those guys we learned about in Greek mythology."

"Everyday I feel myself getting broader," said Jacob taken aback that Shane even noticed, "Especially over the last few weeks. My clothes," he tugged at his shirt sleeve, "look! My fucking fingers won't even squeeze up my sleeve and that's since this morning. Everything is getting too tight and it's costing my mother a fortune."

Shane again remarked on his appearance, "You have changed. Your hair is really different, so long and wavy, almost curly. Your face and arms are all bronzed. Jesus, your muscles, fuck sake, I nearly fancy you myself."

"You've got me there," sniggered Jacob, "I'm stuck for words, I can't think of a smart answer," he went quiet for a few moments, "Shane, buddy, I'm worried. I'm really worried."

"Scobie! Have they come back?" asked Shane moving closer to the screen.

Jacob lowered his head, it was obvious he was stressed, "You're the only one I've told, the only one I trust and I can never thank you enough for being there for me. You're such a good listener." His eyes welled up and Shane could see he was getting even more distressed.

"I'd never betray you," said Shane trying to reassure him, "I'd never tell anybody. Listen! I think I can talk my dad into paying for a flight. I'll be with you tomorrow, I'll call you back."

"No! No! Don't!" reacted Jacob, "I'll be fine."

There was a momentary silence, Shane got upset watching tears gather before slowly trickling down his best friend's cheeks.

"I go to bed every night and they're there. I wake in the morning and I find I can't get up. I feel I'm being watched. There's a threat and they're draining me. I try to move my legs and it takes ages before I can put my foot to the floor. I struggle to the sink and have difficulty even plunging my face into the cold water." Jacob goes quiet for a moment, composes himself and then continues, "In the water I see a figure. This time there's no threat. He calls me, repeating I should not be afraid. The water revitalises me and what's interesting is how all the turmoil of the night before is gone. I don't understand. I go out after breakfast full of life, how can this be?"

"Hey man," said Shane. "Are you sure you don't want me to join you?" Jacob just shook his head.

"Do you not think it's time you told your mother?" asked Shane

By coincidence there was a knock on the door, it was Maria who asked as she entered the room, "Is that who I think it is?"

She sat beside Jacob and received her usual cheeky greeting, "Hi Mrs B, you're looking as fit as ever," said Shane.

"Hey prick, that's my mother you're talking to," quipped Jacob

"And a most beautiful mother she is too!" sniggered Shane

"Now now Shane less of the Mrs B, I thought we were friends."

Jacob was getting impatient and insisted his mother leave. He had much more he wanted to say and wanted to do so in private. The door closed and he got closer to the screen.

"Sometimes the dreams are nice and the strange thing is I often feel safe in the places I visit. There's a temple, it's huge and it feels like home. There are times the dreams turn to nightmares, real horror and evil. I feel as though I'm actually there. I feel the pain of the victims and it hurts. I see and the venom of the victors. I reach out and actually touch Hitler, Stalin, the Khan; I see in them their madness. I see their evil and I listen to their malice. I smelt the decay and slip in rivers of blood. It's the despair that gets to me."

He took a deep breath before continuing, "There's more to tell. I'm able to see into the future just like a seer, a psychic. I'm seeing things. I see upcoming events and the latest one is about to happen."

Shane jokingly interrupted, "Hey, send me the lotto numbers." They both laughed

"Write this down," said Jacob getting more serious. "On the 25th October a gathering of warships will be detected in the Atlantic, west of Spain. The aircraft carrier, The Admiral Kuznetsov, will be escorted by fully armed Russian cruisers and destroyers. They'll approach and then pass through the straits of Gibraltar, sailing to the eastern Mediterranean. They plan to assist the Syrian government and will be responsible for changing the course of the war. Thousands will die, many more will suffer and this will be the beginning of the end for the lands west of Mesopotamia. The strange thing is; Mesopotamia is a name we only ever heard of in our history lessons, yet it keeps bouncing into my head. My prophecy is telling me 'We' are witnessing the first signs of the 'End Times'"

Shane was taken aback, "What! What the hell are you talking about? Thousands will die? That's scary!"

Shane feverishly wrote down everything Jacob said and then enquired, "Two things. I forget. Where exactly is Mesopotamia? And secondly, you emphasised 'We'. Who is We?"

Jacob reminded Shane of their history lessons and told him Iraq was always known as Mesopotamia and then said, "The thing is, the 'We' confuses me. I'm becoming aware of how I am part of something big and there are others like me but I don't know who or what they are."

Shane's bedroom door burst open. It was Al and Davie and they were fed up waiting for him to join them. Al whipped the phone from Shane and looked at Jacob, "See ya mate, talk tomorrow; training calls."

Jacob just smiled, shut down his phone and left his room. He did have a lot more to say but he felt it could wait. He went to join his mother and after a short conversation hugged her and prepared for his long run. He left the apartment, looked around then began his warm-ups.

Chapter 2

His run took him all over Gibraltar allowing him to enjoy the tail end of the tourist season. Everywhere he ran he noticed he was being watched, especially by the young girls. He thought of Shanes comment 'you look stronger and more macho' and smiled to himself. He looked at his reflection in the shop windows and saw how he was much broader and more muscular than even a week ago. His shorts and shirt were much tighter than earlier that morning and he felt he was beginning to look ridiculous. He decided to ask his mother to buy him more training gear even though she had only bought him new clothes two weeks earlier, clothes that were already two sizes bigger than when he left Dublin.

He may have felt a bit odd but the admiring looks from the girls helped him feel good about himself. On reaching the end of his run he still felt full of life and decided to walk up the rock where he sat at the highest point to watch the sun take its place in the far west. It was one of those September days that was showing the first signs of autumn but still carried the brightness and warmth of summer.

Little did Jacob know that this day would forever be imprinted on his mind. It was the day his true destiny was to become clear. All the troubled dreams and nightmares plaguing him would by late that night fall into place allowing him to at last understand what was happening to him. Most importantly, he was about to learn who he was, where he came from and why, for almost four years, he had been suffering flashbacks showing him images of traumatic events throughout history.

Right now he was glad to be alone. He felt free which helped him to suppress the sense of terror that had built up in him, especially over the last few nights. He was also very aware how it never took long for the terror to return.

He, in reality, was a sensitive soul, full of compassion and empathy. His strength of character helped him a lot, but today he knew he could no longer battle the nightmares and they were beginning to break him. He rested his head on his arms which in turn were resting on his raised knees, and he began to struggle. The evil images then returned with a vengeance and he battled hard to put them from his mind. He succeeded but it took some time before he calmed. He dried his eyes and turned to look south to the northern coast of Morocco.

While sitting quietly, absorbing the warmth of the now very late afternoon sun, he allowed its heat surround him. He slowly slipped into a deep trance filled with the sounds of entities he had difficulty identifying. A hand emerged, surrounded by a white light, rested on his shoulder and it was then when he heard a voice,

"Jacob, you've always known how special you are. Turning twelve you ignited a spark and as you grew so did your powers, as you aged you grew stronger. Your humility encouraged you to suppress your extraordinary skills but since today all has changed. Today, for the first time, you used your power of prophecy, use it well for it will be your friend and it will help your troubled mind work out what your role in the story of the cosmos will be. Go deeper into your mind and tell me what you see."

Whatever was happening made him feel that he was being protected and surrounded by a calmness he hadn't experienced in such a long time. He travelled further into his mind,

"I see a lagoon. Many friends gathered in my name. There's a quest, the purpose of which is hidden. I can see me as a great warrior. There are many victories but I me suffering many losses. I can't see who I share them with. There's a golden crown and it rests upon my head, is this wishful thinking?"

He tried hard to put some order to the events he was witnessing but was as usual unsuccessful, making this the hardest part for him. He then asked, "Who are you?"

"All will be revealed in time, have patience," replied the entity.

After waking from his trance he was more confused. He reached for his phone and began dialling Shane but stopped himself. He was very proud and more often than not he hated discussing his feelings even though he loved the comfort he got from talking with his best friend. He thought of his mother and decided to take Shane's advice and tell her about the continuous and terrifying nightmares which were now getting so overwhelming he felt traumatised and alone. His instincts told him she was the only one who could help him.

At the very time when Jacob was in his trance, Maria was preparing a late dinner. Sensing Jacob was in trouble, she stopped what she was doing, left the apartment and seemed to know where to find him.

Jacob always knew when his mother was nearby, there was a mind connection, and he sensed she was very concerned about what was happening to him. All he wanted was for her to join him, hold him and tell him that everything would be alright.

When she arrived at the foot of the hill he smiled while watching wives and girlfriends playfully punch their partners who had turned to look at his mother as she passed. To him she was just his mother; to all other men she was something else. He now understood why they kept staring at her. It was everything about her, her figure hugging white blouse loosely hanging over a knee length free flowing skirt, her perfectly fitted brilliant white three strap sandals, her long soft wavy brown hair gently bouncing in the light breeze and her brown eyes that were as deep as the deepest well. Each time she'd wave up at him, her smile showed that even the darkest day can be brightened. He could see she was the most beautiful woman who ever walked the earth. Even from that distance he caught the scent of her perfume wafting in the air, he knew it well. It was a scent created from the Plumeria flower which is considered to be one of the most fragrant of all tropical flowers and it was her most favourite perfume. Its scent always at its strongest at night but its aroma during the day filled a room, cleansed the air and turned the heads of all who walked close by. He strained to hear her footsteps but there were none, she was gliding and at that moment in time, to him, she looked like a goddess.

On reaching him she smiled, hugged and sat next to him. She held his hand and together they watched and enjoyed the frolicking of one of the five troops of Barbary Macaques who occupied this part of Gibraltar. It was an inquisitive troop, noisy and always on the lookout for some advantage over the tourists. Jacob had earlier watched them play as the last visitors headed down to the harbour. The monkeys then gathered together before making their way into the trees to rest for the night. To Jacob's surprise one after another, young and old, they walked by in single file, lowering their heads in a respectful bow as though by instinct they knew there was something special about this mother and son. He remarked, "There's been a lot of strange things happening to me this day but somehow I'm no longer afraid."

"What happened to you today?" asked Maria.

"My body grew again," he said standing to show all his lumps and bumps, brought on by tight clothes. "My shorts were fine when I started running, now they're crippling me and my shirt is so tight it makes me look like a stuffed pig!"

"A stuffed Pig?" laughed Maria, "Ah, but you're my little, I mean big stuffed pig." "That's not funny. I'm struggling and all you can do is laugh, I went into a trance and there I saw my future. Mother, it was strange because it showed me as a king?" He paused and waited for a reaction and when none came, he continued, "Today I shared a prophecy with Shane about a flotilla of war ships heading towards Mesopotamia, or Syria, depending on which time you are in." He stood and turned to face his mother, "look at me! My hair was cut tight two weeks ago and now, it's almost shoulder length. All this is not possible."

He sat again and together they watched the last rays of the now sleeping sun and marvelled at the brightness of the rising moon. Maria looked around to ensure they were alone. "I think it's time for me to tell you the story of your life," she whispered while placing her arm around him, "your two thousand year life!"

He stared in bewilderment. When she said 'Two thousand years.' his chaotic dreams began to make sense. In his mind all the mixed up memories of times past although not in order fell into a sequence he now understood.

"I've a story to tell, an epic story of the Gods, the Underworld and the beginning of my gifted life but most importantly it's a story about the beginning of your journey. I want you to know everything: especially now all the signs of the 'End Times' are growing, evil is all around us, it's everywhere."

"That's not the first time today the 'End Times' has been mentioned." He thought for a moment and remarked to himself as to how he was always relaxed and comfortable in his mother's company, no matter where he was she always seemed to be close by. He thought about his time in primary school, all he had to do was look out the window, up the hill towards the tree line and there she was, just standing, just watching. He never understood how no one else saw her, and from past experiences had decided not to ask, he knew the answer would as usual be evasive. He thought about those times in the junior school playing fields, and the fights with local boys, 'time' stopped and he'd find himself near the school door while the boys he was fighting lay on the ground some distance away, uninjured but wondering what happened. In the distance, there she was, just watching. He thought of his time in secondary school when he made arrangements to meet up with girls, always excuses and then no date. He never understood how his dates were always cancelled. He was by far the most handsome of all his school mates. At twelve he stood at almost six feet tall, broad shouldered with muscles the girls seemed to like. He was athletic, an award winning swimmer, a brilliant junior rugby player and a champion fencer. He often heard the mothers and young girls comment on his looks as he passed through the school gates. He heard them describe him as Adonis. Having said all that, he found it difficult when he saw how all his friends had girlfriends and seemed to be going to the coolest places or just having fun.

His thoughts were interrupted, "I'm your mother and when it comes to events in your life there's not much that'll get by me. I've seen, especially lately, how troubling your dreams are and that's why I'm here. Are you ready to listen to the story of your life? You will need to be open minded, because, by the time I'm finished, all you were taught in your physics classes and all you thought was logical about life will be turned on its head. All I ask is that you hold your questions until the end of the story? Do you think you can do that for me?" She waited for his response and when none came she continued, "You will look at me in disbelief and will certainly be surprised, possibly angry, but the one thing I know is, you will want to meet those I tell you about." She paused again getting upset, "I'm asking that you trust me, bear with me, part of this story really, really hurts me." He still didn't react.

"For the last sixteen years I've hidden and protected you, I did everything in my power to keep you safe but your powers are gathering momentum. The people in Hayden Bridge became very curious about both of us, forcing me to relocate to Ireland. Do you remember your time there?"

"Yes, I liked it there," he said

"You are very special. You have powers even I never imagined anyone could possess. You've been using a muscular strength no boy should have. You've been using healing powers on yourself without question. In your dreams you've witnessed many of the momentous events in human history not realising how your powers were taking you there, into the midst of them, and you've been travelling through time. Now you have the power of prophecy, the most important power of them all, and when you used it I knew we had to have this conversation," She stood, walked about for a moment, "we couldn't have this conversation until I was sure that you were comfortable and somewhat relaxed but most importantly safe. I need you to trust me and listen carefully to all I have to say?" He promised to listen and trust her.

She asked him to look at the wall just opposite from where they were sitting; he looked and there he saw his mother looking back at him. Before his very eyes she disappeared and was beside him again. He leapt up and looked back and forth watching his mother move from wall to wall at an unnatural speed.

"How did you do that?" he spluttered.

She placed her hand on his shoulder and at the blink of an eye took him to Morocco, where they sat under a full moon and a clear and starry night looking across at the bright lights of Gibraltar. Again, she placed her hand on his shoulder, blinked again and they appeared on the second level of the Eiffel Tower in Paris, another blink and they were at the Pyramids of Giza.

The expression of awe on Jacob's face was priceless, he was speechless. Maria smiled.

"You also have these powers and as I told you earlier you have powers even I never imagined anyone could possess, you are far more powerful than I will ever be. I watched the awakening of your abilities over the last three years and started planning for this very night. You should know that I was always aware of you walking about in your sleep. I'd observe your spirit disappear through walls and solid doors. There were times I'd find you wedged against the ceiling above your bed. Some nights I'd hear you scream in your sleep because you were witnessing some terrible event, other times I'd hear you laugh and sing along with the great writers and composers. All this was signalling the awakening of your powers.

Your lessons begin this night, you will have to learn to harness and use them for all that's good. Tell me, have you ever wondered how you were the most athletic in your school or how you commanded the waters to part, allowing you to be the fastest swimmer? Did you ever wonder how you always healed quickly because by instinct you placed your injuries in running water? Did it not cross your mind how you were the most skilful of the fencing class or how you were the best tactician on the rugby field? Your martial arts adroitness enabled you to climb the world rankings so quickly, did you not wonder from where you got those skills?"

"Mother," he replied, "I've always known I could do things others couldn't. I tried time and time again to ask you to explain but you always shut down the conversation, I learned very quickly not to ask. In my dreams I taught myself to do super natural things, wondering if I'd get caught. I always marvelled at some of the things I learned and wanted so much to share them with you but you always rebuked me."

"I was rebuking you," she said, "I was shutting you down for a good reason and I interfered in your attempts at getting together with girls. I needed --"

"I knew there was nothing wrong with me," he said while rapidly pacing back and forth. "I knew girls found me attractive, I just knew it!"

Maria ignored his comment and continued, "I needed to make sure nothing happened between you and any girl. I couldn't risk you getting too involved to accidently call on the 'Light', putting you and me in severe danger."

He went quiet, his mind was racing and after a few moments he asked, "Mother, who's after me and why are we in danger? What's this 'Light' you're talking about?"

She asked him to be quiet and listen,

"You're shutting me down again," he yelled

Maria didn't respond to his outburst and when she saw he regretted shouting she asked him to place his hand on her shoulder and think of where they last stood on the Rock of Gibraltar. Nothing happened. She asked him to try once more and again nothing happened. He wondered was this the start of his lessons and remembered her earlier comment, 'you are far more powerful than I will ever be'. He guessed she was testing him. He closed his eyes, took several deep breaths and as his breathing softened; he relaxed, allowing a calmness to surround him. This time when he blinked it was his power that brought them back to where they started.

On reaching the rock he at first wobbled, then got scared. When his fear abated he got intrigued, then a little arrogant. He wanted to try again but this time travel alone. He knew asking his mother wouldn't achieve anything so he thought of Dublin and blinked. He arrived in Shane's bedroom giving him the fright of his life.

"For Fuck sake," screamed Shane leaping off his bed. "Ever hear of knocking? I could have been doing things!"

"Oh, sorry, sorry, I forgot you have needs."

Jacob saw Shane was shocked and taking time to calm down. He tried to reassure him,

"I took your advice and told my mother, I'm learning more about myself and you're the only one I want to share it with. Come on, I have a plan. Ibiza, I can take you there at the blink of an eye."

He reached across and placed his hand on Shane's shoulder, blinked and materialised in Ibiza, in the midst of a toga party.

"Thank God it's a toga party," whispered Shane, "you do realise I'm in my boxers and they're old ones at that. I feel very vulnerable."

Jacob whipped off his shirt and shorts, "Now we're both in our boxers..... Eh, hello? What are you looking at?"

Shane pointed, "Eh, look around, everybody's looking. Put you fucking shorts back on, your boxers are too tight; every crack and crevice is on view, never mind the fact we can all see the shape of your bits."

Jacob did a full 360 degrees and sure enough, everybody was staring, he felt the sexual tension, smiled at Shane and shrugged his shoulders, "I've nothing to be ashamed of."

"I can see that," admired Shane. "Put your fucking shorts back on. Do it NOW!" Jacob obliged and they both went to join in the fun.

Jacob wondered if his powers would allow him influence the barmen, and was delighted when exotic cocktails drifted in his direction. He and Shane were used to sneaky drinking while hiding behind the school gym but they weren't used to what came at them that night. They quickly became lightheaded. They were having the time of their lives and enjoying moving from club to club. They were two handsome looking guys and everywhere they went they started a male trend of dancing in boxers. They found themselves the centre of attention especially among the boisterous hen parties hailing from many different countries but this wasn't to last.

Jacob sensed danger, something sinister and strange. He looked around and thought he saw shadowy figures staring at him. An overwhelming sense of dread rose up and every ounce of his being was telling him to leave. He discretely made his way towards Shane and blinked them both back to the bedroom.

"Wow, was that a dream?" asked Shane.

"No, Bud, it wasn't. We were really there," he paused for a moment and stared at Shane. Strange emotions were gathering.

"Everything is changing, my powers are growing." He raised his hand and used the power of his mind to shift three books across the room, "That's mild, I can do much more. I have a bad feeling you and I won't see each other again, at least not for a while, and that's not what I want. Never tell anybody about what you witnessed, I sense a danger."

Shane got upset and reached for a hug, "If you go, I'll be lost. I'll have lost my closest friend; we've shared everything since we were twelve."

"No, you're wrong. Our friendship will never end. Right now I'm getting strange visions, you are there. I see you in my future but there are obstacles. You will have a long and happy life, a wife, children and grand-children, and when it reaches its end, I'll be there by your side when that time comes." He kissed Shanes forehead and wiped a trickling tear from his cheek. He slightly turned his head, straining to hear something calling from a far distance and then said, "I'm being called and I need to go, see ya."

Jacob rejoined his mother who was not amused. "I can see you are definitely going to break my heart. You didn't give me a chance to explain how your abilities are to be used. There are dangers you should be aware of."

"I already know the dangers, remember those times you followed me through doors and walls? Did you not follow me when I learned about space and time? I saw others in those spaces, some of them didn't end well, and I thought they were just nightmares. After what happened tonight I now know my dreams were teaching me, preparing me for the real thing. When the dreams first came I started by moving around the house, then moving between my school and the city. I remember being nervous so I never travelled too far. As I got braver I wondered could I travel to the moon, and I did. I got a real shock there, trying to adjust to the lack of atmosphere, but I soon realised I didn't need to breathe when out in space. Mother I'm so happy to be able to talk about this. I came real close to telling Shane but I somehow knew I had to keep quiet."

"I want to let you into a little secret," said Maria gently moving his dishevelled hair back into place. "Tonight was the first time I didn't follow you. Over the last four years when you were dreaming, I knew exactly to where you travelled. I knew there were dangers but I also knew that when you were in the dream world you were safe. If you knew I was following you'd never learn anything. You were learning the ways of a Time Lord and when dreaming you were becoming a master of time. By the way, where did you travel to just now?"

"Ibiza. And it was brilliant. I collected Shane and we made a show of ourselves."

Maria exploded. She leapt to her feet and grabbed Jacob by his collar, "The first time I trust you to travel alone and you put Shane in severe danger. How could you? Did you sense anything?"

Jacob had never seen his mother so angry, let alone heard her raise her voice. He thought back to the club they were in, "Yes, I got uneasy in the last club, there was Darkness, yet lots of light. Strangers were watching me. That's why I decided to leave."

"Did they see Shane?" asked a livid and very concerned Maria.

"No, I don't think so. He was away from me, in his element, chatting up some English girls. I went to my knees and crawled over to where he was, all those around me thought I was drunk. I reached up to grab him then we disappeared."

Maria placed her hand on Jacob's forehead, sought out his memory and found the exact time and the club he and Shane were in. She blinked and travelled to Ibiza, went into invisibility and targeted the clubs security office. She soon located the CCTV tapes and totally destroyed them.

As she was about to leave, the door opened and this obnoxious smell rose up. It was a sinister presence, a Dark Angel, and he too was looking for the tapes. She remained invisible, wondering would her light shine through. It didn't, it protected her. She watched him examining the tapes and saw his anger grow when he realised they were destroyed. She then left and rejoined Jacob.

"Am I forgiven?" asked a chastened Jacob, "Absolutely not, I could break your neck, but I suppose I should forgive you, I love you so much."

"I now know I've much to learn and promise to try and control myself." He paused for a moment and then asked, "Can I do that thing you did to my forehead?" She agreed and Jacob placed his hand on her forehead where he was able to see how she cleaned up his mess.

They both sat in silence for what seemed the longest time. The full moon was now high in the sky and its beams bounced across the mirror-like sea. There was a serene quietness, a stillness allowing you to hear a pin drop. The soft wind that was blowing earlier had died down. It was as though all of nature was waiting to hear the story of Jacob's life.

Maria's temper mellowed and she leaned across to hold his hand, "I think it's time for me to begin your story even though it still worries me that what I have to say will rile you, upset you or worse, frighten you. I'll start by reminding you that you are in your sixteenth year which suggests you were born in 2000."

He furrowed his brow, "Mother, I can do the maths."

"Ah," she smiled, "you may think you were born in the year 2000 but in fact you arrived in that year, as a baby. We were assisted in escaping from the wrath of Zeus. That was almost two thousand years ago."

He stared at her looking bemused; he pursed his lips trying to get the words out, "Zeus?" he exclaimed, "Are you telling me I'm around 2000 years old? What the hell does Zeus have to do with me?"

"No, you're not 2000 years old," she tried to prevent herself from sniggering. "It doesn't work like that, you are actually only in your sixteenth year but you have been moved through time for your own safety and, oh, by the way, Zeus has everything to do with you."

She waited for a reaction but when none came she continued with the story, "Many years ago Zeus was furious with the Olympus Gods, they were having children with mortals therefore creating demigods, some of whom had powers mortals shouldn't have and as a result he decreed that no more children were to be born to any god. He reminded them of how the births couldn't be hidden from him and how he would see to it that the babies wouldn't see their first sunrise. This new decree terrified his wife, the goddess Dione. She was six weeks pregnant with her second child and feared for the life of her baby. She knew how ruthless he could be. Zeus also instructed the council of Olympus to prepare a census of all demigods. He wanted to be sure which ones walked in the 'Light' and identify those who are likely to use the fading memories of the Titan Cronus to bring mankind through the gates of Hell to join the armies of The Darkness. As Dione's pregnancy progressed and the risk of Zeus finding out increased, a decision was made for her to visit her cousins, the Nymph Lords of the northern ice lands. She told Zeus she wouldn't see him again until the snows in the Black Forests had ceased and the first flowers of spring were about to bloom. Dione spent many months with her cousins and just before her baby was due, went to the island of Crete, to a cave on Mount Dicte. It was a cave so protected no birth light could escape. It was there where she gave birth to her baby in the presence of the nymph, Adamanthea. She was the very same nymph who once before concealed the birth of a baby by placing him in a crib, dangling that crib from the highest tree using a vine rope laced with an ancient magic. She suspended him between the earth, sea and sky, making him invisible to the powers of his father. That baby was Zeus. Dione knew the story of Zeus's early life and how he was hidden and then raised by Cynosure, Queen of the nymphs. In gratitude for her protection he placed her among the brightest of the southern stars. Dione looked at her beautiful new baby, wrapped her in the finest silk shawl woven by the cave worms, picked her up and alongside Adamanthea walked out from the cave, she raised her baby towards the southern sky and pleaded for protection. As she brought her baby back into her arms she watched the southern stars dance in celebration. One star shone brighter than all around it until it was seen to rival the light of the moon. As they watched it grow it took the shape of a stork and began to fly towards them. Getting closer its light became blinding yet she could see the bird had landed in the wet sands. When it began to walk towards her it transformed into another Nymph. It was Cynosure, the most beautiful winged Nymph of them all. Cynosure looked at the baby and asked for her name. Dione said, 'My babies name is Aldora, my winged gift.' Cynosure smiled and said she heard the pleas and knew she had to come back to protect a daughter of Zeus. She then said, 'I will change her name to a name much used where mankind now walks. I will call her Maria and will use the same magic as was used to conceal Zeus from Cronus.' At that moment Dione felt that her baby was safe."

Jacob leapt from his mother's side, ran to the other side of the walkway, looked out over the ocean, turned and stared back. He was shocked, yet fascinated, to realise that his mother was the baby in the story making her the daughter of Zeus and Dione and therefore a goddess. Now he understood all the strange things happening in his life, he understood her beauty and why she was not aging.

A lingering silence developed and for the first time ever he realized his mother carried a great burden. He listened carefully when she said, "I've yearned for the love of a mother and father. I've grieved for my lost childhood and the guidance and friendship of my older sister who doesn't even know of my existence. She is your aunt; she is the Goddess Aphrodite, the most beautiful woman in the cosmos."

Jacob shook his head, he disagreed, "Mother, you're the most beautiful woman in the cosmos. Don't you see the way men look at you? I've told you about the way my friends talk about you. Shane is so cheeky he just greets you with 'Hi, Mrs B or hi, gorgeous', even the wild beasts grazing in the fields bow before you."

He paced in a large circle, occasionally looking back at her, eventually he stopped and said, "I know you asked me not to ask any questions until you reach the end of the story but this is big, this is too much. I love you more than anything else and I'm now terrified Zeus will locate you because he is bound to detect my growing powers. Can they be suppressed? I have powers I don't understand. Look at me mother, see how my powers grow as each day passes." He went to his knees and took her hand into his, "Mother, if you're the Goddess Aldora, does that make me a god, or am I a demigod?" When the answer didn't come fast enough he asked, "Mother, who, who's my father?"

Maria got him to sit beside her, she held him tightly then whispered in his ear, "My son, my beautiful handsome boy, you are a god. Your father is the son of a most powerful god. We met by chance when I was out riding with the woodland nymphs. Those nymphs were my friends and protectors. Your father was a charmer, handsome, strong and persistent. We fell in love almost immediately. We began meeting in secret because the nymphs were getting alarmed; they believed Zeus might detect the strong and godly bond developing between us. When I fell pregnant panic spread through the cosmos. My mother, since my birth, and because of the power of the nymphs, never knew where I was but her love for me allowed her sense when major events happened in my life. She sensed the relationship that had developed between me and your father. Although she knew our love was pure she felt she needed to prevent Zeus from detecting us so she arranged for us to be separated. This broke our hearts but as a mother-to-be I'd do anything to protect my unborn baby and your father understood this. We went to the island of Crete, to the very cave in which I was born. We were protected by the power of Adamanthea and shielded by the magic of the cave nymphs. Your father stayed with me for the birth, he kissed you and with tears in his eyes he returned to his kingdom, he kept looking back but he knew this was for your protection, for my protection, for his protection and for another's protection."

"Who is the 'Another'?" asked Jacob. Maria then reminded him of their agreement where he was to hold his questions until the end of the story. She continued,

"For almost twenty years I spent my time under the cloaked protection of the nymphs. It was a special time. The wondrous things I witnessed. I walked under the oldest ring-filled handsome trees and inhaled the scent of the most beautiful of the wildest flowers. Far more importantly the fun and the excitement each day brought made my life so happy. I treasured my time racing the horse lords, and the Centaurs, across the meadows and grasslands of the nymph realm. Having said all that the one thing I desire the most, is to receive just one more embrace from your father. He was so tall and handsome, his long wavy fair hair had a little tinge of red; it was held back by a silver band clasped by the golden leaf of his royal house. I always weaken when I think of him especially our first kiss and how that kiss led to the most eternal love between us leading to us, well you know, becoming one."

"Jesus mother," reacted Jacob. "Too much information." Thinking of his mother having sex was something he couldn't handle. "Eh, do you...do you resent me? Am I the cause of you losing your one true love? Have I......?"

She interrupted him by placing her finger across his lips, "I have and will always love you. I could never resent you. You are my son and a son of the only man I've ever truly loved."

She assured him that she was always happy and it was the nymphs who saw to that. She told him how when the time came for her to bring him forward in time they put in place a plan which included a nymph Lord taking on the image of a man to play the part of a young husband and father. She spoke of how, as they travelled through the centuries, they stopped off in the 1790's and identified a young man who was ill, soon to pass away. She talked about how the Nymph Lord took on the young man's image before they proceeded to the year 2000 to arrive in the small village of Hayden Bridge which was close to Hadrian's Wall in the North of England. She reminded him of how they rented a modest house on the outskirts of the village and how they slowly integrated into the local community where they lived as a happy family known as Owen, Maria and Jacob Baker, running a small bespoke jewellery business based on mythical and Greek imagery.

"Do you remember Owen?" she asked.

"I've never forgotten him and I still see him in my dreams. Why did he leave?"

"His time to return to the realm of the Horse Nymphs had unexpectedly arrived and his passing had to be brought forward. We arranged for the young man back in the 1790's who had just died in his time, to be brought forward to our time. We knew there would be an autopsy so we had to ensure it was a human body not a nymph body that was presented. This ruse allowed Owen to leave without questions being asked."

"I remember Owen's funeral to be one of the largest ever seen in the village. I also remember how I loved him but somehow I was always aware he was not my father and that he would one day have to leave. I vaguely remember crying as I suppose any two year old would cry when someone they love was gone."

Maria reminded him of how they continued to live in the village because her bespoke jewellery business was still very successful. She spoke of the twelve happy years in Hayden Bridge and how people were beginning to notice she wasn't ageing. She smiled when she thought how the local doctor was fascinated not to have met them professionally.

She then told him how she worried when young boys and girls often referred to the way his play or sports injuries healed almost instantaneously, especially when he placed the injuries in water. She reminded him of how his strength became legendary and how he was being challenged everywhere he went, in school, in the football club and as he walked alone through the village.

She asked, "Do you remember your reaction when I told you we had to leave, especially when you saw the 'For Sale' sign over the business and the 'To Let' sign over the house?"

Jacob placed his head into his hands, "Oh God, the tantrums, the doors coming off their hinges, the tractor driven into the river, drinking robbed cider behind the sports hall, smashing the windows and breaking the fences. How come you put up with me?"

"You're my son and I loved you. I understood your anger, losing your friends and moving is always traumatic. I felt we had to move on; your powers at that point were due to show themselves in a more dramatic way. I had to arrange to sell everything, say our goodbyes and spend time trying to convince you that the going to Ireland was in our best interests. In our world Ireland is known as the 'Fair Lands' and I knew it would be there where you would find the calmness. Where there were ancient gods who would watch over you. You fought me all the way even as I tried to buy a house in Dublin and arrange for you to attend 1st year in the local secondary school."

She smiled when she remembered his well-chosen school. It had a great academic reputation and produced some of Ireland's greatest rugby players.

She said, "The most important thing about the school I chose was that for first year students, it offered the classics which enabled you to study the archaeology, architecture, history, imagery, literature and philosophy of the ancient Greek and Roman worlds. A world I knew one day you'd return to. I think, deep down, you know it's a place to which you will have to return."

Jacob thought of his time in secondary school and it brought a smile to his face. He thought of his friends, especially Shane, Al and Davie, he also thought of the girls in the nearby convent school. He thought of his last exam and the plans he and his friends had in place for the Junior Certificate 'after exam' parties especially the one after the results were announced. He was really looking forward to a long weekend of partying.

"When I think about it," he said, "I certainly must have been a nightmare to be around, how did you put up with me?"

"That was easy," she said, "people used to say, 'Jacob is a lovely boy, so friendly and helpful. Always has a kind word to say'. I laughed to myself and my reply always included, 'If you want to know him, take him, or come and live with him'. That always raised a good laugh."

"Go back to the story mother, but before you do, can I say, I'm beginning to feel a resentment build up in me. I want to challenge Zeus. Who does he think he is? How can he threaten to kill babies? They did nothing wrong and can't be held responsible for the actions of their parents. He needs a kicking, and I'm going to give it to him."

Every part of Jacob's being screamed out at him, he wasn't happy with what had happened to his mother. He felt protective of her and was determined to challenge Zeus. He felt his anger grow and hatred build. Within moments he received a vision showing him his immediate future but, ironically, it was taking him back in time to Olympus. He then felt an overwhelming sense of loss and his heart was breaking. He thought of his friends, especially Shane, knowing he wouldn't be meeting them for some time if at all.

"There's much more to tell, but I see you're distracted, so to help you understand your origins, and your powers, we really should go back to a time near your birth. Are you ready to face the risks of such a journey?"

"You bet mother, I'm a bit nervous but I can't wait to meet Zeus."

"Fine, there are several ways you can travel through time," she said trying to reassure him. "As Time Lords the simplest way is to think of where you want to go and then just blink. I'm not prepared to trust you to blink. You've no experience and won't know where to go. The second way is through the dream world which you have been using every night since your twelfth birthday, and the last is with the assistance of an experienced traveller."

At this point and without much more thought Maria asked him to look into her eyes and then into the palm of her hands. As he gazed at her palm her fingers parted and a bright beam of light emitted to illuminate the surrounding rocks and crevices. She placed her hand on his shoulder and they began to spin, slowly at first and then as though a whirlwind had gripped them, they rotated so fast they disappeared.

Chapter 3

It was a bright and warm morning when Jacob awoke. He momentarily thought it odd that he didn't recognise his room. It was quite palatial with stone columns framing the doors and windows, ornate stucco plasterwork adorning the ceilings, and the walls draped with the finest of silk tapestries. He walked across the room to the window and viewed a seascape of crystal clear water all the way to the distant horizon, surrounded on both sides by cascading waterfalls and the most majestic of trees. Trees that store in their rings all the memories of time, trees so old they are protected and cared for by the woodland nymphs supported by a pantheon of elves representing all branches of Elf-kind.

He washed and walked back towards his bed, lifted the clothes left out for him and laughed thinking it strange how he was expected to wear the robe and shawl of an ancient Greek teenager. He dressed and then looked at himself in the shiny shield set on the wall alongside two golden spears. He smiled, admired himself and thought he looked good, walked from his room into a wide passageway leading to the Great Hall.

When he arrived at the entrance he stood in shock. Before him was the awesome sight of marble columns running for 100 meters along each side, and between each column stood the colossal statues representing the senior

Gods of Olympus. Above their heads, hanging from the ceilings, hung colourful flags displaying the crest and motto of each god.

Sitting on a gilded throne, at the back of the hall, was Zeus, the highest of the gods. Jacob looked at him with distain, blaming him for the way his mother missed out on her family and all the trappings of being a goddess, something he knew she was entitled to.

He again looked around the temple and felt so small but he wasn't afraid, he sensed his mother was near. He turned to greet her but instead was met by the purest and blinding of white light. He was taken aback and thought to himself that he had never seen a woman of such beauty. He shielded his eyes just for a moment, and then focused to realize the woman was in fact his mother. He looked across at the statue of Aphrodite and saw her likeness. He turned again to look at his mother walking towards him. Her bright white imperial dress of an Olympus Goddess rustled near the floor and her golden jewellery reflected the early morning sunlight. Jacob could see that she was truly a goddess.

Looking upon her son she knew he was no longer the boy she reared and protected but a young man who was now very assertive. His stature, his muscles, his fresh face and his long wavy flowing hair reminded her of his father, except his father was fair haired and blue eyed but Jacob was dark haired with brown eyes.

"That's the best sleep I've had in so many years," said Maria, "I hope yours was as peaceful?"

"It was," he replied, "strange how I don't even remember going to bed."

"Travelling through such an expanse of Time is exhausting. Anyway, I've brought you back to your real sixteenth year. We've just slept in an Olympus temple and we should really acknowledge the stewards and all they've done in preparation of our arrival. Oh, you look good, Olympus robes suit you."

"Suits me? Mother, I'm underdressed, no jocks, socks or boxers, everything is just dangling; it's a bit embarrassing. I'm curious, how did the stewards know we were coming?"

"It's their task to anticipate the arrival of a god. They wake about two days in advance and start preparing. Have you noticed how many there are?"

"There's at least forty," he said looking around to take a quick count, "and they can't all be for us so there must be others coming."

"I agree," she said, "I feel a little uneasy, not because I fear them. It's because of the impact you are going to have, especially the problems you'll cause."

"I'm not that bad, but trust me, I will challenge Zeus. Nobody hurts my mother and gets away with it. Will he be here as well?"

"Enough of this speculating, let's continue with your story," she said taking his hand and giving him a hug. "When your grandmother left the cave, cradling me in her arms; she knew I was special because my powers were already showing. She didn't recognise them, but knew they risked my existence becoming known to Zeus. She never thought that her baby would have the power of 'Time Travel' and certainly could never imagine that you, for her, a future grandchild, would also be a Time Lord and have even wider powers, allowing you to tap into the strengths of all of the most powerful gods."

"What strengths of the most powerful gods?" he asked.

Maria reminded him of his childhood when he cut his hand on a local farmer's blade and after placing his hand in water how the power of Poseidon healed him instantly. She also reminded him of the time when a wheel fell from their cart and how he lifted the cart using the strength of Heracles.

She said, "These are but two of the powers you began using since your twelfth birthday. You always expressed surprise when you achieved great feats but I was never surprised. I couldn't tell you the reason, you were too young and I needed to be sure your powers would only be used for good and not be attracted by the darkness of Cronus, or detected by Zeus." She paused again, thought for a moment then continued, "There's more to tell but before I do, you should understand all the gods standing here before you. Knowing them will help you understand yourself."

Jacob objected, insisting she continue with the story. She chose to ignore him, and started walking through the Great Hall, "Come," she urged, "let me introduce you to your aunts, uncles, cousins and most importantly your grandparents."

She said on reaching the statue of Zeus, "Here sits the God of the sky, lightning, thunder, law, order and justice. He is the son of the Titans, Cronus and Rhea, and youngest brother to Hestia, Hades, Hera, Poseidon, Demeter and Chiron. He is my father."

She told him again of the birth of Zeus, how he was hidden by the Nymphs and how he grew to be the most powerful of all the gods. She told him of how he trained and built up his strength to challenge his father. Then spoke of the vengeance of Cronus when he was told by the oracles that he will be supplanted by one of his children and how he ate each of his children as they were born. She struggled while speaking of how Rhea, on realising she was carrying another baby, sought the help of the oracles and how between them they devised a plan to protect and hide Zeus, at his birth. How he was hidden from the gaze of Cronus by the magic of the nymphs just as she was hidden from the gaze of Zeus.

She told Jacob of how Zeus, when he reached manhood challenged Cronus, cut his stomach and released his swallowed brothers and sisters who were now fully grown and how Zeus and his brothers then went to war against their father. How they quickly realized they would need the combined force of the Olympians and their Titan uncles. She told of how Zeus located his uncles and discretely arranged their release from the dungeons of Tartarus and how together they slew Cronus, dismembered his body and placed the parts in the deepest and most ancient of the crevices of the Underworld. She went on to tell how, as a token of their appreciation, Cronus' brothers awarded the Thunder and Lightning bolt to Zeus and arranged for the three brothers to split the Heavens between them. Zeus got the Earth and the Sky, Poseidon became Lord of the seas and rivers and Hades became guardian of the gates of both Heaven and Hell to become Lord of the Underworld.

Jacob kept staring at Zeus and folded his arms in contempt, "I look at him, sitting there, all high and mighty and feel hatred grow within me. All these years, how could he? When I see his face all I want to do is challenge and get him to grovel and apologise for what he did to you."

"Always keep an open mind said Maria, "somehow since I came to Olympus, I feel all is not what it seems."

To the left of Zeus stood the statue of Hera, his second consort, and to his right was the statue of Dione, his third consort. "There is another thing that has always bothered me about Greek mythology," sniggered Jacob, "how come Zeus and Hera got together after all they were brother and sister?"

Maria just smiled and shrugged her shoulders, "If that bothers you, wait and see what the other gods got up to."

She looked at Hera and told Jacob of the loyalty and love that existed between her and Zeus and pointed to various statues in the temple that were their children. She then walked over and admired the beauty of Dione, "My mother, how beautiful. She is a Goddess of the Sea with the power of prophecy." She looked at Jacob, "now you know from where you get your power of prophecy. Just think about the love and determination she used to protect me from the wrath of Zeus."

Jacob marvelled at her beauty before stretching up and placing his fingers into her hand, "Thank You," he whispered. He was surprised to feel her fingers move. He stepped back, looked at his mother, looked back at Dione and with great respect bowed to her.

As they backed away they looked to their left and there on a chair of shells, gripping a most magnificent trident, was the statue of Poseidon, brother of Zeus, king of the sea and guardian of the reefs and tides. Jacob was in awe of him, He looked so powerful, so majestic.

"I've seen him before!" exclaimed Jacob, "When plunging my face into the cold water he was there, calling me. I see him and I being great friends. He stands with me many times into the future and will be one of my greatest supporters. He will heal me after many battles."

"Your power of prophecy is becoming very strong," remarked Maria. "Have you noticed?"

Opposite Poseidon stands the statue of Heracles, son of Zeus, gatekeeper of Heaven and averter of evil. "Mother, he comes to me all the time, when lifting that tractor I felt him by my side. He speaks to me of a sense of justice in all situations, he will always be known as a hero."

Maria told him, "All Gods look on him with respect. He's the youngest son of Zeus and the last god to be born of a mortal. Some look on him as a brute, primitive and violent but little do they know that he and he alone caused the defeat of the Giants, and but for him Olympus would have fallen."

When they looked left again, they looked upon the statue of Aphrodite, daughter of Zeus and Dione, sister of Maria, aunt of Jacob, the beautiful Goddess of Love and Procreation.

"The most beautiful woman in the world," said Maria

"Mother, I told you before, you're the most beautiful woman in the world."

A slight tremor rolled through the temple prompting Jacob to quip, "I think aunty Aphrodite dislikes a bit of competition!"

Jacob turned and looked up at the impressive statue of Apollo, son of Zeus, twin brother of the Goddess Artemis. "Another favourite of mine," he said, "my love of music must have come from him, look at his lyre, it's one of the most magnificent I've ever seen. It was created by Hermes. He's known as the God of Music, Prophecy, Healing and the science of medicine. They say he's been instrumental, excuse the pun, in helping man advance medicines to help the poor and sick. Although full of compassion, he also has the power of plague. Mother, he will be called upon near the 'End Times' and will unleash his fury."

Maria said, "He is the most revered of all the Olympians, the Oracles of Delphi speak for him, he has helped in war and has also been known to call for peace. His followers visit his shrines in their thousands."

Turning again Jacob and Maria walked over to the statues of Ares, the God of War and Athena, the Goddess of Wisdom and of War.

"Mother, they don't impress me. I've a problem with that pair. In my dreams, I mean my nightmares; I've witnessed all the great wars, the creation of horrendous weapons, the ruthlessness of generals and the lack of control of their ill-trained soldiers. They've played a part in some of the most barbaric acts of mankind."

"Don't be too hard on them," whispered Maria linking his arm. "Remember, mankind was given a choice, good or evil, right or wrong, war or peace, they alone must face Hades at the gates of the Underworld to answer for their choices."

Jacob absorbed what was said before continuing his walk. The next statues he viewed were those of the most revered Goddess's of all time, Artemis and Demeter. Artemis stood there, proud and beautiful, destined to become known as Diana, Goddess of the Hunt. She is the twin of Apollo and daughter of Zeus. Demeter is the mature sister of Zeus and is the Goddess of the Harvest and Agriculture.

"Mother, I see these two after the 'End Times' battle, they will walk among the survivors, teaching the old ways and bringing back the spring. They will remain until the first harvest and then take their place back among the gods."

Back to their left is the statue of Hephaestus, God of all Craftsmen, husband of Aphrodite and son of Hera. "He," said Jacob "is someone whom I know will be instrumental in the defeat of The Darkness..."

"What do you know of The Darkness?" interrupted a worried Maria.

"I've no idea where that came from, it just bounced into my head. He's the blacksmith, the one who will forge the only weapons lethal enough to smite the serpents."

"Serpents?" exclaimed Maria, "Where's this coming from?

Jacob was now getting distressed, "Mother, it's the serpents 'He' will use. Our arrows will be useless against them. Modern weapons will be made obsolete. The serpents can only die by the sword."

Maria placed her arm around her son showing her concern, "We can stop this, your power of prophecy is now so strong it could consume you, you must stop and rest." Jacob disagreed and insisted on continuing.

Beside Hephaestus is the statue of Hestia, the maiden Goddess of House and Home. She is the chaste daughter of Cronus and Rhea and beloved sister of Zeus.

"Mother, I see her, she is most powerful. She too will walk among the survivors and will guide the architects who will rebuild for the fourth age of man. They will forever carry her flame from town to new town. She will be honoured at all the great feasts. Her eternal flame, taken from the first source Light, will burn in all sanctuary lamps."

Opposite Hestia is the statue of Hermes, Herald of the Gods, his task is to guide souls to the Underworld but he has many other skills. He is known for wearing the winged helmet and sandals.

"He will be your ally with many gifts. He will bring the dream world, confuse your enemies and will challenge the great deceiver with his own deception. He will assist the messengers; he has a love for mankind unknown among the gods. Earn his trust and he will always be there for you," said Maria

Beside him is the statue of Dionysus, son of Zeus, God of Wine and Partying.

"Now we're talking. Mother, I'm in awe of this guy. We're going to have so much fun. His wine and partying will be the death of me but I know I'll die happy. I'm already anticipating some great nights out with him. This is when I'll really miss Shane."

Maria froze and with a disapproving look said, "May I remind you that you are not yet sixteen. If I ever catch you or Shane drinking, trust me, you both might be bigger than me now, but I can still reach places that will make you squeal. NO ALCOHOL."

"Yes mother, as if I would."

When walking away towards the next statue, he thought he observed Dionysus wink only for Maria to say, "I saw that!"

He soon reached Ersa, daughter of Zeus, Goddess of the Dew and Morning Nourishment of all vegetation. "Mother, she will be the lonely one.

She will be my ally by spreading the dew and ushering in the spring. She too will walk the earth and quench the thirst of the seeds. She will usher in the first grasses of the fourth age of man."

They walked to the next plinth and set their eyes on the beautiful Queen of Hell, Persephone, Goddess of the Underworld, beloved daughter of Demeter and reluctant wife of Hades. At the behest of Zeus she's only allowed leave Hell at the dawning of spring. Maria said, "Truly she is most beautiful. I see her walking with Ersa and together they will bring hope and nourishment to man."

Next on the left was Eros, son of Aphrodite and Ares. He's known as the God of Love and his arrow has been known to bring joy to the most unwilling of humanity.

"Mother, this one will cause me much anguish. He'll refuse to wear clothes in places I'll bring him. He, Dionysus and 'Another' will travel to Dublin in 2016 and will have to be rescued. I see them being rescued." He hesitated, thought for a moment before asking, "Mother, that's the second time 'Another' has been mentioned. What does this mean?"

Maria looked uneasy; she knew who the 'Another' was but still wasn't ready to say who it was. She changed the subject, "When I look on Eros, I think of your father. He too has the body of a god."

"Mother, you do realize I'm standing beside you, stop looking."

"There's an old saying, 'It's ok to enter the orchard, as long as you don't touch the apples' even I have needs."

"Ew. Too much information." Jacob turned from his mother and threw his eyes to the heavens.

The last four statues on the right were images of Hebe, Perseus, Chiron and Pegasus. Jacob stopped at the statue of Hebe but before Maria could comment he said, "I have to know, I mentioned 'Another' when we were looking at the statue of Eros, the last time you mentioned 'Another' was when you told me of my father leaving, what's going on?"

"I must insist you don't ask that question for a little while longer. I promise to tell you everything and I will, but not just yet. There's more for you to learn and I need you to wait another few days."

Maria looked at Hebe, "She's a powerful goddess and has the power to grant eternal youth, she's a daughter of Zeus and Hera."

"I think I have her power. I see myself granting immortality but I can't see those to whom I give it. Mother these half-hearted, unfinished images are annoying me."

The next plinth held the statue of Perseus, son of Zeus and vanquisher of the Gorgon Medusa.

"He is the most interesting god of this pantheon. He lived not too long ago and had a sad start to life. He and his mother were placed in a box and thrown into the sea. She held him tightly and prevented the sea from taking him. They were rescued and he grew to be a very successful man. He, like you, was always been challenged because of his good looks and his hand-someness. He was sent on a quest to bring back the head of Medusa. He had great difficulty finding her but received help from both Athena and Hermes. Hermes presented him with the winged sandals and the sickle of Cronus. Athena presented him with her shield. They also showed him the way to the gorgon's lair. He beheaded Medusa and during his journey home he saw a woman chained to a sea rock. She was about to be consumed by a sea monster when he cut her chains and rescued her. Her name was Andromeda. They became one and now spend eternity out among the stars."

Jacob went into an unexpected deep trance, "Mother!" he exclaimed gasping and struggling for breath, "I see them and they're in grave danger. It's The Darkness. It's consuming the stars. Their realm is next, Andromeda is next and Perseus is trying to protect her. They are in trouble. The gods must find a way." He woke and said, "It's all consuming but what I've seen hasn't happened yet, it's in the future."

Maria asked if he wished to leave and continue walking among the gods later. He insisted on finishing the walk. Next to view was Chiron, half-brother of Zeus. He is the most important of the half horse, half man Centaurs. "Do you know that he is the only centaur whose front legs are as a man, the front legs of all other centaurs are as a horse? He is famous for his teachings and his compassion. He was tutor to a very young Achilles as well as the Argonauts, Jason and Peleus."

Jacob replied, "When the Light travels he will answer, he will assist the centaur armies and become protector of all equines."

Lastly to the right is the human image of Pegasus, king of the Horse Lords, he is more known for his image as the winged stallion and he is a son of Poseidon therefore a nephew of Zeus.

"I see him as my saviour," said Jacob. "He's my cousin and will answer to the fifth shard of light. He will lead the horse lords and will be my counsel. When he takes to the sky all horses will bow before him, they will spread around the world and carry the warriors in defence of the Light."

On their final turn to the left is a vacant plinth with the engraved name of Hades. Maria said, "He's the one god whose work never ends and as a result he seldom visits Olympus. He is Lord of the Underworld and guardian of the gates to both Heaven and Hell. You will meet him soon enough."

"Ah, my favourite class, Shane and I loved the classics, especially Greek mythology and the stories about the Underworld. Can you imagine having his power? Imagine ushering the good souls through the gates of Heaven, then having to forcefully push the evil ones through the gates of Hell. Such power."

The last statue to meet is the statue of Eris, daughter of Zeus, best known as the Goddess of Strife, Chaos and Discord.

"Oh my," laughed Jacob. "This is going to be interesting. She's dynamite; she, when she wakes will cause havoc. I see her at a party, pillars fall, tables upturn, glasses break but I see a warrior, he is like me but not me, he will overcome her."

Jacob really enjoyed his walk through the Great Hall and the brief description of each of his kin. He had studied the classics in school and looking at all the gods before him made them all more real. He wondered why there are three empty plinths and was informed by Maria that there are no more gods worthy of a place in the halls of Zeus.

While climbing the steps she said, "I enjoyed sharing the history and especially the prophecies, some of them are quiet vivid but the ones that bother me are the ones showing you involved in all kinds of troubles."

"It seems mother, my destiny involves war and strife, but other visions show me in a happy place, I'm not too worried."

They reached the doors. Jacob turned and marvelled again at the gigantic columns and colossal statues. He was enthralled at the sight of the golden beams of the midday Sun bouncing off the throne of Zeus and illuminating every corner and crevice, "You've now viewed twenty four gods and goddesses," said Maria, "twelve of whom form the Olympus pantheon. There are many more but they live out among the stars. Their part in the story of mankind will unfold as time marches on."

Jacob left his mother and went to sit on the sill of the south facing window. He liked watching the villagers walking by. The temple was floating back and forth through time allowing him to observe small villages along the sea shore turn to towns and then to cities. He was surprised by the speed at which the Roman legions built or repaired the roads to Egypt. He watched ships sail by, even the one carrying the Emperor of Rome. He waited to watch as some time later they'd return, bringing the spoils of war back to the Eternal City. He never felt lonely but was envious when watching young girls and boys swimming, chasing and playing all around the lagoon, he often wanted to join them. He was intrigued they couldn't see him or the temple, yet he observed everything. He occasionally teased some youths by throwing stones through the shield, causing panic as the stones crashed into the water.

He did notice the occasional glimpse of recognition fleetingly appear on the faces of some people as they walked by. He bore witness to a huge crowd gather to listen to one man talk about his God and marvelled at how this man captivated those before him. He got excited when he realized who the man was. He watched, on one particular day, fishermen catch only two fish and bakers bake only five loaves yet that huge crowd left the gathering well fed. He saw the people leave and watched the man gather his friends together to begin planning their next gathering. He watched the man go to sleep then rise to lead his followers passed the entrance of the temple. He stood by the door when the man stopped, faced him as though in recognition. He was in awe of how serene and calm the man was. He knew of this man. They both bowed to each other. It was then when he felt his mother's hand rest on his shoulder and listened to her say,

"You are looking at someone whose destiny

it is to change the world"

Chapter 4

Time slipped by for Jacob without him really noticing all the changes happening around him. He travelled out into the vastness of the Olympus realm where he continued with his training regime, a regime well established since he first joined the schools rugby team.

Olympus was travelling back and forth through time showing him many more changes. He watched villages build, be destroyed, only to get rebuilt again and again. He continued to watch as night followed day, tides ebbed and flowed and storms came and went. All in all he never got bored, each day always brought something new and he, just like his mother, began to really love his time in the temple.

It was a strange feeling to have his every whim looked after by the stewards but he soon got used to it. He missed his normal clothes, his loose t-shirts and shorts were always kind of comfortable. His track suits made him look sporty but the robes and shawls of Olympus were getting on his nerves. It took some time for him to feel comfortable while being almost half naked, especially around his mother.

His greatest pleasure came when he sat by the window to enjoy watching life passing by. He also loved watching and listening to the waves crashing out beyond the sand bars that protected the lagoon.

One particular day he watched four girls from the local village arrive, bath and swim in the warm waters. One of the girls caught his eye, she was fair skinned, fair haired and with the most piercing blue eyes he'd ever seen.

Each day he'd race to the window hoping the girls would again be in the lagoon. When they appeared his day brightened. He watched them for almost two weeks before plucking up the courage to make his move. An overwhelming feeling gripped him, and he left the temple to join them. It was the day of his sixteenth birthday.

He sought his mother and found her reading in a nearby annex. He leaned forward to kiss her on the cheek but this time she sensed a change, she foresaw what was coming and reminded him that if he left the temple he wouldn't be protected.

"Mother," he said, "I love you more than anything but it's time, I've seen it. Today is the day everything changes. Please don't worry."

"Mothers always worry," she responded, "you might be a prophet but so am I. You're going to break my heart."

He left and made his way towards the main door but was alerted to a movement at the back of the temple. He turned and saw Poseidon standing before the statue of Zeus. He attempted to make contact but was too late, Poseidon had faded into invisibility. He shook his head thinking he was seeing things; then saw that Poseidon's plinth was empty. He ran back to his mother, "Remember when you said we were in one of the temples of Olympus? I think we're in the main one. Poseidon has come to life and then disappeared before my very eyes."

"I've always known that we're in the main temple. Where else would you see such a gathering of gods? If Poseidon has risen it means he's preparing the creatures of the deep. Be careful son, don't cross him."

"Why would I cross him," asked a very surprised Jacob. "He doesn't even know me." He backed away and made his way back to the main entrance. After walking through he crossed the garden to where a portal magically opened allowing him to enter the realm of man.

He approached the lagoon full of confidence until he got closer and saw that the girls looked uneasy. He saw them cover their breasts and look across to where their clothes were. He immediately tried to reassure them saying they were in no danger.

The girls had never seen this stranger before but, although uneasy, they were intrigued by his kind face and incredible handsomeness but it was his smile that disarmed them. After a few awkward moments he plucked up the courage to ask if he could join them. They giggled and agreed.

He began to disrobe, hesitated when he realised he would be standing naked in full view of four absolutely stunning girls. He removed his sandals and shawl then untied this skirt but held it tight for a few moments. He thought of Shane 'if only you were here, bud' then dropped his skirt revealing the body of a god. He quickly entered the water and introduced himself. He wondered was he actually in Heaven? Three of the girls surrounded him causing butterflies to fill his stomach. He continued to admire their beauty and remarked to himself how each of them surely surpasses the beauty of his aunt, Aphrodite. He found it difficult to take his eyes from one girl in particular, the very one that caught his eye when he sat on the sill of his favourite window back in the temple.

The girls had been busy earlier. They had each gathered assorted flowers and made garlands in different colours and when they felt comfortable enough they offered to place them around his neck.

He stood in silence as the first girl approached, "I am Oba" she said placing a garland of the rarest red Jasmine over his head. He closed his eyes as her breasts rested on his chest sending tingles through his body. Her beauty made him weak. He eventually opened his eyes and said after tapping into his recently discovered power of prophecy,

"You are a river goddess and will quench the thirst of those in need; you will be my messenger and carry the 'Light' to the far south."

The second girl approached and he hoped that she too would rest her breasts on his chest but she didn't, something stopped her. She stood slightly to his side and placed a garland of white Peony's around his neck, "I'm Panya," she said.

He, as before, closed his eyes but felt nothing. He opened his eyes, "You will be crowned with the Laurels of victory and the north will kneel before you. I see you as a Queen, I see you….." He stopped and looking unsure said, "You are going to be very special to me, yet you are not going to be with me, I don't understand, there is 'Another'." He stepped back and stared then thought of his mother mentioning 'Another'. He wondered what was going on.

The third girl approached, "I am Mulan," she said placing a garland of blue Magnolias around his neck. Like Oba she too rested her breasts on his chest but this time he closed his eyes and had difficulty keeping control. He opened his eyes and said, "You will walk for a thousand years to become the Flowering Tree of the East, you will be my Warrior Queen and the gatherer of the gems of beauty, your journey will be fraught with danger but you will have the wisest and strongest of guardians. I see the gods by your side."

Jacob wondered why the fourth girl hadn't approached and slowly turned to face the water's edge. When he saw her, still sitting on the ledge, his excitement rose and his heart suddenly raced. She looked at him coyly and then stood up. As they watched each other time seemed to stand still, the waters parted allowing them to walk unhindered towards each other. He was in awe of the apparition of great beauty standing before him. He observed her hair first and the way it gently wisped in the light breeze, he loved the way the four plaits hung across her shoulders. Her pale and piercing blue eyes called out to him. As they got closer she raised her arms, and while resting her perfect breasts on his chest she placed her garland of mixed Dianthus around his neck.

"Please don't close your eyes," she said moving even closer to him. "In case you don't remember, I'm Ealasaid and while in the Dream World you called me Eala. There I saw my future and you were in it. Over time I will be known as the protector of the west, but most will know me for my devotion to the Ancient One."

Jacob looked confused; he had no memory of meeting her before. He was mesmerised by her beauty, but also intrigued by how she could see into their future and how they seem to be sharing it, "My hand wants to rest on your shoulder, it's been there before, but I don't remember. My lips want to be with yours, they too have been there before. The softness of your skin to my touch sends shivers of pleasure through my body. Your scent is intoxicating and it's a scent I do remember. He succumbed to her beauty and for the first time in real life kissed a girl. He experienced the beginning of true love.

He went to kiss her for a second time but she placed her finger across his lips, "Our story has been written and it says our paths won't cross for the next two thousand years. Look around at your new friends, you've chosen us and will soon send us on a quest. I see guardians, eight of them."

"Now I remember. It was a happy time in the Dream World, it showed this very day. It also showed the quest you speak of. I remember seeing a future of many paths but you kept saying there was only one, there's not. I can see many paths; we are on all of them and guess what? I will kiss you on many of them. Where I come from it is believed that what is to come is not set in stone. Gods and man have the freedom to change the future by the choices they make. It is only the past that cannot be changed."

He went quiet for a moment sensing that he and the girls were not alone but he didn't feel threatened so decided to just enjoy his time. He encouraged the girls to follow him into deeper waters where he used his powers to invite the abundant and colourful sea life to join them. He brought the girls to the oyster beds and showed them an amazing city of shells. He pointed to a torch light in the distance; it was in much deeper water, and shook his finger indicating they should swim no further. They returned to the surface and continued enjoying the warmth of the shallower waters making this one of the days Jacob felt made his life worth living. He was so happy he felt lost in time. Every now and again, when standing beside Eala, his hand just floated across to rest on her hip, he was thrilled when she moved closer to rest her head on his shoulder.

This moment of tenderness was interrupted when Jacob again felt they were being watched. He looked about, then focused on nearby sand-dunes and identified one with a light shrub covering, "I know you're there, show yourselves," he yelled.

Soon eight teenage boys appeared from behind the shrubs; they had being watching the girl's bathing. All eight slowly emerged, looking embarrassed. Being caught meant they were in for a verbal onslaught and they knew they'd never be allowed to live it down.

"It seems my prophecy has just come to pass," said Eala smiling at Jacob

"How long have you been watching us?" asked an angry Oba.

"Most days," sniggered one of the boys.

"Perverts," said Panya.

"I don't think this is fair," said Mulan trying to suppress a smile. "We should watch you for a while and see how you like it."

The boys, without shame, quickly stripped and dived into the water. Panya dangled her little finger using a well known gesture indicating she wasn't impressed.

Jacob and Eala remained quiet. They had both seen this in their dreams and knew their path was now set. For Jacob the strange thing was, his part in the story was still concealed and it bothered him, but somehow he knew his part would soon become clear.

The boys occasionally glanced across at Jacob wanting to say something but found him intimidating. They had seen muscular youths before but never one so handsome, tall, broad and powerful. They felt a little inadequate in his presence.

Jacob sensed their reticence and moved closer to greet the first boy who said, "I'm Faer, son of a fisherman,"

"You are the traveller," said Jacob, "and you will lead 'my future' into the west. You will be a guardian to a consort. You will be a messenger of the Light, and you too will be of the Light." He paused, thought for a moment and wondered what he meant by 'my future'.

Girish was next greeted and he introduced himself as a son of a farmer.

"You will be known as Lord of the Mountains," said Jacob. "They will open their passes, reveal their caves, quench your thirst and guide you to the east. Your path will change many times; you too will be a messenger of the Light."

Next to Girish was Garuda and when Jacob placed his hand on his shoulder he said, "Ah. The son of a shepherd! You will be my mythical bird, emperor of the skies, and king of all birds. When you fly the mountains will bow before you, your call will bring forth the wrath of bird kind. The Light will cherish your protection. Carry it well, guardian of the Light."

Jomo was standing slightly further back and after Jacob reached out to him, he said, "Ah, a master craftsman, I see you are the son of a stonemason. You will be the carrier of the Flaming Spear. Armies of the south will fall before you. You will be seen as the god you are destined to be. The Light will bring all of the Africa's to bow before you."

Jahiri was next greeted, "Now before me stands a son of a blacksmith. You are the essence of eternal youth. You will bring your strength and a loyalty to the south. The tribes will rise up and follow your lead. When the drum beat sounds, all will know a new God of the Light is present, and the armies will walk by your side in defence of that Light."

Jacob walked over and took the hand of Baldor, "You are a son of the baker, a noble trade; you, my friend, will be the quiet one yet you will be the God who carries a beacon of light in the dark lands of the frozen north. You will be the torch bearer Asgard will follow. A powerful Goddess of the Light will be your burden, protect her well for she will carry the future of Asgard."

He then took the hand of Thanases, placed his other hand on his shoulder and said, "I now hold the hand of a warrior's son. You will change the ways of the North and have the power to grant immortality, use it wisely, stories of your life will stand for all time. Many will fall under your protection and you will be tested. The Goddess of the Light will also be your burden."

He then turned to the last boy and offered his hand. He asked his name and the boy answered, "I am Fafner, I know not my father." To which Jacob replied,

"I see your father, you bear his likeness, he was an Emperor and with his queen he rests in the vast tombs of Elysium. Trust me when I tell you how he has never taken his eyes from you, I see how he still loves you," Jacob struggled with this prophecy and when he composed himself said, "For me, you will be my Mythical Dragon and will be the guardian of my future."

This was the second time he used the term 'my future' and it bothered him. He then said, "Fafner, my friend. I see you coming to my aid, I see you as a guardian to another consort, one who is special to me. I also see many sad trials in your life and what upsets me is my vision shows the tombs of Elysium holding your name."

He held on to Fafner's hand for much longer than the others, he searched and searched, but couldn't find him. He let go, walked over to Eala and quietly said, "We are among those who, for eternity, will be our friends. I searched but can't find him, he's not there; I fear we're going to lose him."

Eala saw Jacob was getting upset; she pulled him closer and held him tightly. He was taken aback but decided to enjoy another fleeting moment of pleasure, he rested his chin on her shoulder and continued to enjoy the warmth of her embrace. She then whispered in his ear, "Earlier you spoke of how the future has many paths; maybe his path takes him elsewhere, away from all of us. I heard you speak of him as 'Your Mythical Dragon' maybe he goes to the dragon realm, hidden from the gaze of the gods." Jacob was comforted by her words and began to relax.

Eala wasn't finished, "Look at them, they're bewildered. You've unnerved them with your prophecies. Take them to the oyster beds; let them see and feel the magic beneath the waves. They will soon relax in your company and then realize their lives have changed." Jacob did what was asked.

After spending another few hours enjoying the warmth of the crystal clear water it was time to begin making their way home.

Just before they left the water things began to change. Some got dizzy, others unsteady. Then, a mild tremor rumbled beneath their feet. All but Jacob and Fafner ran from the water in panic, they quickly dried and dressed. Jacob was slow to move; he was uneasy and couldn't take his eyes from the horizon. He was joined by Fafner who also showed his concern.

"It seems you are becoming my guardian, Dragon Lord," said Jacob.

Fafner continued to stare out at the horizon, "There's something out there and the sea is getting angry." He turned to Jacob, "Why did you call me Dragon Lord? I'm not a dragon,"

Jacob responded, "I'll say no more."

They continued watching the horizon, everything was screaming out to them that something was wrong but they couldn't put their finger on it.

"I know you saw nothing in my future," said a worried Fafner. "You mentioned Elysium. I promise you, if that's my destiny, I'll go there a hero."

Jacob got emotional again, he couldn't look at him, just said, "No doubt you will."

Chapter 5

A second and more violent tremor shook the sands and sent ripples across the sea. It caused Fafner to stumble, lose his balance and fall towards Jacob. As he fell forward his forehead thumped off Jacob's nose causing him to bleed. Jacob held his nose before plunging his head into the healing waters. When his blood reached the waters it dispersed causing the gentle waves to get more violent. He had a very uneasy feeling and ushered Fafner to run back towards the sea shore, while he ran close behind. They dried themselves, grabbed their clothes, and proceeded to dress as quickly as possible. Jacob turned to Eala showing a troubled look. His instinct was telling him something momentous was about to happen, something that would confirm their lives had changed.

He continued looking beyond the protective sand banks out to the open sea, knowing that whatever was about to happen will come from beneath the waves. He felt his spilt blood was the cause of the ripples that turned into raging and violent waves, but he also felt peace would follow allowing the waters to bring forth a mirror-like calmness.

From the beach they continued staring out to sea where soon a dark and sinister head rose from beneath the waves. What first caught their attention was the appearance of a three pronged trident followed by an enormous and crowned head. Jacob recognised this colossus to be his grand uncle,

Poseidon. He was intrigued and wondered how to deal with him, but even though he was looking at one angry god, he didn't feel afraid.

In a loud and thunderous voice Poseidon bellowed, "Who has spilt the blood of a god?" No one answered causing his anger to grow, he then repeated the question, "I ask again. Who has spilt the blood of a god?"

Jacob waded back into the sea, showing no fear, but if the truth was known, he was very uneasy. He stared at Poseidon and said nothing. His nose was aching and there was still a small trickle of blood flowing. He continued showing no fear and then did what he always did in the past, he plunged his head back into the water and this time the wound instantly healed. He continued standing between his friends and his grand uncle, taking up a challenging position. He thought of what his mother showed him and believed at the blink of an eye he could outmanoeuvre Poseidon. What worried him was he didn't know what powers the God of the Seas possessed, or if in the event of an attack, would he be able to save all his friends at the same time.

Maria, who was walking through the garden, sensed Jacob was in trouble and briskly ran towards the sea shore. She reached him and moving him aside took her colossus form, something Jacob had never seen her do before. She stood as a powerful goddess and made it clear no one was going to hurt her son.

At that moment, all across the sea, legions of the Mer-people began rising from beneath the waves. They bobbed in the now mirror-like waters and could be seen out as far as the horizon. They were summoned earlier by Poseidon because of his concerns as to why sea creatures from the depths were being stranded or dying on beaches and rocks across all oceans. It concerned him because they were found with two puncture marks near their heads and were carrying what looked like a poison of fire that was racing through their veins. It troubled him that none of the sea creatures survived the attack. He was angry because some of these creatures were his friends, his escorts through the deepest and darkest canyons within his realm. Others were the cleaners of the sea, some brought light where light shouldn't shine. His grief at their demise was obvious to all who saw him. He also sensed that a battle was coming and wanted the Mer-people to prepare to defend theirs and his domain from an unseen and unknown force he believed would soon be aligning against them.

Jacob's friends stood on the shore in fear but at the same time they marvelled at the sight that was the God of the Seas. They were also mesmerised by the beauty of the colossus goddess now protecting Jacob. While looking out to sea they were also in awe of the wonderful sight of the Mer-people gently bobbing about in the now calm sea but most of all they couldn't believe the bravery of Jacob and admired his stoicism. This wondrous scene was against a backdrop of a most beautiful sunset where in the distance the strange blood red sun met, touched and kissed the ocean.

When Poseidon began asking his question for the third and final time he was interrupted by a further tremor that sent all but the gods tumbling to the ground. This tremor was different and troubled both Poseidon and Maria; it shook with a sinister menace.

The Mer-people turned and faced the distant west. Poseidon also faced the west. He then placed his palm into the tremor induced ripples, "Calm my friends, there's still time," he said hoping to reassure his followers.

He turned back to face Maria and attempted to speak again but was prevented, "Don't ask your question for the third time!" yelled Maria. "The blood of a god was spilt; it's the blood of my son, a grandson of Zeus. He and I have been hidden for many years. I'm a daughter of Zeus, and the goddess Dione."

Poseidon didn't seem shocked, "Olympus is the strangest of places, each time I wake there's more to tell yet in my dreams your face, your beauty. I've seen it." He looked at Jacob, "I wondered how long it would take before you appeared to walk among the gods?" He looked down at Jacob's friends, "Zeus won't be happy," he said while shaking his head. "It's forbidden for the children of Eve to set eyes on the living Gods of Olympus. The lightning bolts will be released this day."

It was after Maria announced Jacob as a grandson of Zeus when a loud rumbling was heard emanating from the temple. Dust fell from the statues of both Zeus and Dione. Zeus opened his eyes and stepped from his throne. Dione woke and stepped from her plinth. Zeus, as expected, showed his anger by launching two lightning bolts that exploded in a bright light across the cosmos.

The pounding footsteps of the King of the Gods racing in anger from the temple, sent shivers and fear through the ranks of the Mer-people causing Jacobs friends to tightly embrace and fall to their knees in terror. The roar of his thunder was so loud they shook to their very core. Jacob tried to reassure them, telling them he wasn't afraid, "I've a plan," he insisted, "I'm a grand nephew of Poseidon and a grandson of Dione; two most powerful gods of the seas. Their powers are my powers and I will use them to protect you."

Jacob was surprised by his new found bravery but felt he was being guided. He placed his two hands into the sea, closed his eyes and asked the waters for assistance. He raised his arms and felt the water climb his legs; he felt it trickle up his back, across his shoulders towards the tips of his outstretched fingers. There it formed two sharp, slender swords. He returned to the water's edge, pointed one sword towards Poseidon and the second he pointed towards the temple in anticipation of the arrival of Zeus.

"Boy, you forget who I am?" said Poseidon, "I felt your request when your hands rested in my waters, and through this I know how special you are. Lower your sword, you or your friends have nothing to fear from me. Look to the temple and await your grandfather. That's your challenge." He then turned to the Mer-people, "Go back to your homes, we'll meet again, prepare your aged and younglings for their journey to the cold seas of the north. Seek the protection of the Ice Nymphs, a battle is coming but it's not this day. Slowly the Mer-army went beneath the waves.

Jacob, as suggested by Poseidon, turned to face the oncoming Zeus. He held both swords ahead of him. He was anxious but determined, prepared to protect his friends. The thunderous arrival of Zeus, who was now in his co-lossus form, caused all close by plants and animals to scurry for cover. Alt-hough the sun was shining there was darkness and menace, an unwelcome ending to what started as a beautiful day. Jacob watched him approach and never took his eyes from the lightning bolt in his hand.

Zeus burst through the shield with Dione running close behind. He trundled towards the water's edge where he acknowledged, with a bow, his beloved brother and then turned to face Maria. He raised his bolt and yelled, "Many years ago my decree was clear, no more gods were to be born. I wake from my slumber and find two new immortals, what do you have to say?" He then saw Jacobs friends and was horrified, "I've also forbidden the chil-dren of Adam to see the Gods of Olympus, now what do I find?" As his anger grew and he prepared to release the lightning, Jacob summoned all his strength. He closed his eyes, called on the winged horse lord and after gar-nering the power of Pegasus, he took to the sky to challenge his grandfather.

He had no idea if his plan would work but he was determined to try. He intended using one of his water swords to sever Zeus's arm. There was no love so he didn't care about the consequences. He flew from side to side in the hope of distracting Zeus enough for his plan to come to fruition.

It was as the sword was about to touch the soft flesh of Zeus when Maria used her power, she blinked and froze time. She crossed to where Zeus and Jacob faced each other. She thought it funny when she saw her son suspended in mid-air as though held by invisible vines. She removed the lightning bolt from Zeus's hand and the water swords from Jacob's hands then blinked causing Jacob, who was now unarmed, to continue towards Zeus's arm to end up wrapped around his grandfather's wrist. It was the full force impact that winded him; he then fell towards the ground only to face the indignity of being rescued by the colossal hand of his mother.

"When did we last see such bravery," asked Poseidon. "Such friendship, loyalty and valour, he is but a boy and yet he challenges the mighty Zeus, he truly is your grandson. Brother, there is no harm here, no danger."

Zeus wasn't impressed and had real difficulty with the disregarding of his decrees. His anger wasn't abating until he looked again at the terrified faces of Jacob's friends. Dione feared he was about to explode, but she was wrong, in the frightened faces he saw something and couldn't quite put his finger upon it.

Dione took Maria by her arm and approached Zeus, "Look on her, my love. See in her the beauty of the cosmos. It's time to accept that today there are two new gods in Olympus and they should be made welcome. One is your daughter, my daughter, and she has done well to conceal her son for all these years. Make them welcome, give them a place on the plinths in your temples. They are our kin, your kin. Feel the love between them and see how the Light shines through them, they are a force for good. They have a new power not seen in the past and..."

Dione was interrupted as a new tremor shook the sands beneath the lagoon; it was much more violent than before. It shook the land and stirred the sea; this one entered the realm of the gods prompting Zeus to summon all other gods from their slumber. Poseidon cupped his hands and placed them in the water. The pooled water created a vision enabling him to look into the depths of the oceans. He followed the vision until it reached the island of Santorini near Greece. He was joined by Zeus and together they were taken beneath the volcano where they saw a gateway to Hell. They looked through the gate and with one voice they said, "It cannot be!" They looked at each other, "Cronus is rising!"

Zeus no longer cared about the disregarding of his decrees; there was something far more urgent to be dealt with. He, Poseidon and Dione were troubled and briskly made their way towards the temple. Maria and Jacob were unsure what to do but were called by Dione to join them. Jacob joined his friends and asked them to follow, and as each god disappeared through the shield Jacob's friends looked on in awe wondering what lay beyond. Jacob crossed over but quickly returned when he realized his friends were prevented from entering. He called to Zeus, "These are my friends, and you must let them through."

Zeus turned and went on one knee, he pointed his finger into Jacob's chest almost upending him, "You're young, and new to Olympus." I can forgive some indiscretions but not the deliberate breaking of our most sacred laws, one of which is 'it is forbidden for mortals to enter the realm of the gods'. Do you understand?"

Jacob wasn't giving up, "Sometimes laws are bad, other times ill thought out and this is one of those times. You need to understand something about me. I will respect laws, at least the ones that make sense, and will challenge bad laws, especially the ones that are absolute. Like my mother,

I'm a Time Lord and can tell you that my friends are special, and allies of the gods even if you can't see it. Their destiny is set and it starts in this very temple. Allow them in for they will be my eyes and ears over the next two thousand years, they will sow the seeds of greatness and will also prepare all those who walk in the Light for the last battle. They will be there for the rising of the next age of man. Let them in, Please."

Zeus was taken aback by Jacob's determination. No other God had ever pleaded for mortals in the past. He felt his passion and sensed his essence and then there was his Light, shining brightly around him. The one thing he definitely saw was a thread of light binding him and Eala together. He still hesitated then saw the Light pulsate around all twelve youths. Remembering Jacob's bravery and his valour, he relented, opened the portal and allowed them enter. He also remembered an ancient prophecy telling of a young god coming to Olympus to be a saviour of the Light, he knew then his grandson would be that god.

Zeus secured the portal and proceeded to the doors of the temple. Poseidon and Dione had already entered and were greeting all the Gods of the Olympus Pantheon who had in the meantime arrived.

When Zeus reached the doors he raised his hand and the doors reacted by shutting with the loudest of bangs. Dione panicked but she need not have feared. All Zeus wanted was to briefly speak with Maria and Jacob before entering the temple. He wondered how they felt about him. He felt Jacob's hatred but felt nothing from Maria, "There'll be a time for explanations but it's not this day. There is a far bigger problem, an evil that gets stronger as each day passes. When the time comes we'll talk and I hope you'll understand my actions, taken all those years ago." He turned to Jacob, "In you I see the future of Olympus. You'll rule in my stead, it seems with my blessing so that must be good, but not just yet. You'll learn to love me but it'll take time. You will one day learn of the burden of what it is to be the King of Kings." He turned back to Maria, "Will you do me the honour of escorting me into the temple?" Maria offered her hand so that they could walk in side by side. He reopened the doors, took her hand, smiled and proceeded to walk into the temple.

All was quiet as they entered, the look of shock on the faces of the gods was priceless, they were amazed at the sight that was before them and waited for Zeus to explain.

Zeus beckoned Jacob to join him and as he held his hand announced, "My brothers and sisters, today is a great day for the Olympus family. Today I bring before you two gods destined to bring joy and new powers to our great pantheon." He raised Maria's arm and said, "This is Maria, my daughter, she is a Time Lord!" and as he raised Jacobs arm he said, "This is Jacob, my grandson. One, it seems, knows no fear. He too is a Time Lord but is much more powerful, he can tap into all our powers. I ask you to accept them as our equals. Befriend them and assist them to learn the ways of the gods."

Hera walked over and hugged Maria, this surprised all the other gods as her reputation for attacking the children of Zeus other than hers is legendary. She brought Maria amongst the gods and one by one they fell under her spell. Jacob watched Zeus proceed through the Great Hall to sit on his throne, and it was obvious to all that he was seriously troubled. Jacob joined him, "I know you must come to terms with our arrival and this may not be the time, but there is something I need to say to you."

Zeus just nodded, his mind was elsewhere. Jacob leaned forward and out of earshot of all others said, "For the first time in my life I learned to hate and I hate you for what you did to my mother. I swore if I ever met you I'd kill you. Have you any idea of the pain you caused her? Have you any idea of her sense of loss? How much she yearned for the love of a family?

She struggled because of the loss of her great love, my father. I don't even know who he is. What gives you the right to destroy families? Who do you think you are? My mother is the most caring, loving and wonderful person in the whole world. She gave up the love of her life for me. She deserved better and you deprived her of that."

Dione was close enough to hear this confrontation and everything Jacob said. She decided to intervene, "Leave your grandfather rest, for all is not what it seems. Hiding your mother was my choice, right or wrong I believed she was in danger but since your arrival I can see how wrong I was. Look at him. He accepted you and your mother almost without question. He even allowed mortals into Olympus. He's changing and like me, he can see that in the future you will stand by his side and the time will come when he will kneel before you."

"Enough, let us say no more, we will talk of this again," said a troubled Zeus.

Jacob was having none of it, "How could you want to kill babies? How could you threaten your family? My mother was always looking over her shoulder. You still haven't answered me!"

Maria was now in earshot and heard everything Jacob said, she was so proud of him, she always knew he was fearless but never did she think he'd take on the King of the Gods. Jacob wasn't finished venting causing Dione to intervene again, she used her power and Jacob soon found that even he couldn't resist the soothing powers of his grandmother. She placed her hand on his shoulder and didn't remove it until he completely calmed down.

Jacob backed away to join his friend when he started moving his head from side to side. It was as though he was trying to decipher something being whispered. There was nobody beside him so he couldn't identify where the voices were coming from. He felt a slight threat but decided it wasn't a real danger.

He looked across at his mother and was certain he'd never seen her so happy. When he glanced back at Zeus he felt compassion. He walked back to him and said, "I don't really hate you. There's not an ounce of hatred in me. I challenged you because of how you've hurt my mother. I need you to understand that I'd do anything to protect her. Please forgive my outburst. I know you don't know us but you'll find we will be very loyal and always by your side. Earlier I sensed your pain and, from a young god to the greatest of them all, you need to share that pain."

"There's nothing to forgive," said Zeus, "I'm in awe, never before have I been challenged in that way, it was impressive. What you did was out of love for your mother, not for yourself and shows you are full of honour. With regards to the pain I feel, you're right, I am troubled and will take counsel. I plan to share my fears with my brothers."

Zeus looked intently at Jacob and thought how this young boy reminded him of someone else; that someone else was himself, thousands of years ago, when he was about to challenge Cronus. He saw the fire in Jacob's belly and could see the power he, one day, would wield. He then ushered Jacob to join his friends and enjoy the hospitality of Olympus.

On the candle, and flower adorned trestle tables was laid the finest of food and drink, and around those tables was shared many stories of great battles and glorious times. Through all the merriment Zeus sat alone with his head resting on his clenched fist. He wondered as to how Cronus could rise. He felt a betrayal but couldn't put his finger on it. He was joined by Poseidon and Chiron who both felt the same thing. Zeus told them he had also summoned their Underworld brother, Hades, as he felt that the explanation lay there.

Another tremor was felt but this time Zeus just sat back, folded his arms and smirked, "Speak of the Devil!" The doors slowly opened and smoke bellowed in. The smell of burning was over-powering. All went quiet and a loud voice called out, "Greetings brothers, I've heard your call and let me say I too have sensed a great restlessness. May I enter the hallowed hall of my brother?" Zeus beckoned him in and what a sight he was.

He stood inside the door with flames shooting from his arms, shoulders and head. Smoke wafted from his legs and feet. He patted himself down and was heard to curse his choice of the Underworld at times like this. As he walked towards his brothers the flames and smoke began to disappear allowing him to take on the image of a true god of Olympus. He acknowledged his kin as he passed and held a special greeting for his sisters Hera, Demeter and Hestia. He paused when he sensed the presence of two new gods, he saw both Maria and Jacob, glanced again at Zeus, saw Jacob's friends, turned, looked at Zeus again and said, "It feels strange that my brother would break his most sacred laws, there must be a great story to be told!" He walked forward and greeted each of his brothers by gripping their arms in turn.

The four brothers left the temple and walked the gardens under a now very bright white moon. When the discussion turned to the Underworld and Cronus, Hades wasn't able to assure them that no soul had escaped Hell. He told them of the countless numbers of souls who have passed through his gates. "I'm glad I've been called to Olympus because lately I felt that some souls entering my domain seemed familiar. Recently souls entering my realm seemed as though they'd passed me before. I ignored it for a while as the safeguards in place shouldn't allow souls to escape. My suspicions grew and I left my domain to walk in the realm of man. I was cloaked, using the Helmet of Invisibility given to me by the Cyclops. My suspicions were confirmed and to my horror, when walking near the ring of fire, I watched souls being escorted out of Hell through the erupting volcanoes."

He paused for a moment then walked close to ornamental pool, "I searched the caverns around other volcanoes and can confirm that vile souls are leaving Hell through a portal beneath the volcano on the island of Santorini. They leave as serpents; seven feet long with prominent fangs and seem to have the ability to introduce a poison of fire into all whom are bitten. The poison is difficult to cure. I captured one near the ice lands of the north and dragged him through the gates of Hell. This serpent held out against all my trials and fought all my efforts to find out as to who is his creator, I'll never know, just before he succumbed, he said, "With the strength of the Archangel, 'Cronus will rise'. The only Archangel I have is the one called Lucifer, placed in the darkest recesses of Hell by the Archangel Michael and the ancient god of the cosmos, I check on him regularly. He's secure but he must have followers who have found a way to release the Serpents of Hell. Cronus hasn't risen; his dismembered parts are so well hidden, no one will find them."

Zeus said, "For thousands of years we have had peace between the immortals, if Cronus rises that peace will be shattered but somehow I feel that there is more to this than meets the eye."

Their meeting ended and they returned to the temple where they joined the gods and shared their fears. Zeus was still surprised he allowed mortals enter his temple but was happy with his decision when he saw the spark of life and felt vindicated. He then looked at Jacob and was happy to see how relaxed and happy he and his friends were, how they were full of fun and had brought a joy to his hallowed halls, something he hadn't witnessed for over ten thousand years. He stood for a while to rejoice in the Light that now shone through Olympus.

He crossed the hall and went to sit with his visitors. He listened and laughed at their stories, loved their songs but most of all he saw again the connection that had developed between Jacob and Eala. He turned to Jacob, "You've brought warmth back into my heart, a feeling I'd long forgotten. I look across at your mother and see a shining light, long missing from these hallowed halls. Look how she smiles as she walks among the gods. See how they've all accepted her into the pantheon of Olympus. It's with my blessing that she and you will hold a plinth in all the temples in my realm." Jacob was about to speak when Zeus excitedly held up his arm, "I sense the arrival of a dear friend, an old friend of Olympus, I can hear the wheels of his chariot, we'll talk again."

Chapter 6

Zeus walked to the back of the Great Hall and took his place on his golden throne. All the gods and goddesses including his brothers stood before their plinths and waited for the temple doors to open. Hades stood alongside Zeus. Maria, Jacob and his friends stood alongside Apollo. With great fanfare the royal heralds announced the arrival of an emissary of Asgard and as the immense doors silently opened gasps of disbelief were heard. Much to the shock of Zeus there stood a very young man, not long since been a boy. He was tall, brown eyed, muscular and very confident. His long wavy flowing fair hair had a slight red tinge and was held in place by a silver band secured on both sides by the golden leaf of the Asgard realm. His breeches were made of calf skin and his cape made from the hide of the great elk lined with the fur of the arctic fox. On his shoulder was a bronze hammer.

"My lord Zeus," he said as he walked through the door, "I carry a message from your old friend. My grandfather, Odin. My name is Odi, May I enter your Realm?"

"How is it that a boy can carry the Hammer of Thor?" said a bewildered Zeus, "But of course you may enter my realm."

"I carry the Hammer," said Odi while walking towards the throne, "because I am a son of the God of Thunder, and as I reach my sixteenth birthday the Hammer has chosen me to be its master, a gift I share with my father."

With these words Maria raised her hand to cover her mouth, her knees buckled and she weakened. Apollo felt her distress and assisted her to sit on his plinth. Jacob rushed to join her and was taken aback to feel her tremble so much. She looked terrified when asking, "Do you remember when I mentioned 'Another'? One who also had to be protected when you were born?"

"I do," replied Jacob.

"Look at him. Does he remind you of anybody?

Jacob looked at Odi and felt a nervous sickness building in him. He looked at the anxiety in his mother's face, backed away and rested against the nearest column. He was shocked as it dawned on him as to whom the 'Another' was.

Odi slowly walked through the Great Hall, bowing reverently to each god as he passed. Through the corner of his eye he caught a glimpse of Jacob and he too felt strange. Feelings that were reminding him of something unknown which he felt was always missing from his life. He continued staring, as an awareness grew, suggesting their lives touched in times past. Maria stood beside Apollo and they both bowed in acknowledgement of Odi. Maria trembled so much that Apollo held her tightly. He furrowed his brow, looked at her knowingly and assured her that everything would be fine.

On reaching the throne, Odi bowed, "My Lord Zeus, Odin senses a change in the cosmos which is not good. He feels the forces of Darkness are once again on the march. He also believes there's another force at work. He and my father will visit within the next three days and asks that preparations be put in place to house the Asgard escorts, and stable the horses. They wish to share with Olympus the words of our oracles. My grandfather also recommends you call a Council of the Gods and feels you must include the Astral Lords."

Odi was about to speak again but stopped, he was now totally distracted. He turned to look across at Jacob. His nerves were getting the better of him. Jacob felt the same, left the column and cautiously walked towards him.

All present knew they were looking at twins. The boys slowly circled each other, confused, staring, and unsure of what was going on. They continuously circled as though no one else was present. Their movement caused 'Time' to slow down and then freeze. Maria, because of her power over Time, wasn't affected allowing her to walk over and join them. Apollo assisted her and because of that he too wasn't affected.

"Wow," said Apollo, "never before have I seen such as this, all gods frozen in time including Zeus, incredible! Such power these boys possess."

"I remember you." said Jacob while continuing to walk.

"We swam together," replied Odi, "I remember now, it was a warm place."

"I remember you holding and protecting me," said Jacob still looking confused. "You guarded and comforted me."

"I remember their voices, kind and gentle," said Odi

"I remember the love between them," said Jacob. "It was infectious."

"It was their love for us I remember the most," replied Odi

Jacob got a bit concerned and looked tense, "I remember you been born and the panic when I was left alone."

"I remember your panic," said Odi, "I tried to wait; you were close behind."

They both said together, "I remember the nymph, Adamanthea; she cradled us both and brought us to the water's edge."

Odi had tears gathering in his eyes, he turned to Maria, "Is it you mother? I remember you raising me towards the stars, you held me tightly, and I felt your tears."

"I too remember being raised towards the stars," said Jacob, "but I don't remember by whom."

"You were raised to the heavens by your father," said Maria, "even though he held you so gently I saw his strength wane as the grief took him. He was broken hearted knowing you were to be left behind."

Hugging Odi, Maria said, "I've never forgotten you. My heart still breaks each time I think of your father cradling you, and taking you away into the mist. I remember him looking back with tears in his eyes. While walking away he bent forward to kiss you. He was trying to reassure me that you would always be safe in his care." She told both of them of the love she and their father shared and the love they had for both of them, "Your father and I stood each side of Adamanthea, we held you tightly waiting for the arrival of Cynosure. We watched her bright light cross the southern sky before taking the form of a Stork and then transform into a most beautiful nymph. Cynosure used her magic to conceal you both, and put in place the plan that sent your father and Odi back to Asgard and me and Jacob to the year 2000."

Time started to move again. "Wonderful," said Apollo, "I'm a music master and the song I compose to tell this story will be sung for all time."

Jacob and Odi continued staring at each other, trying to take in everything before them. They were identical in almost every way, same coloured eyes, same height and the same build. The colour of their hair was the only difference. It was then when Jacob raised his hand to touch Odi's face. Odi reacted but hesitated; he raised his hand and touched Jacob's face. Their foreheads met and they entered each other's minds allowing their powers to become as one.

Zeus by this time was getting impatient. He cleared his throat letting all know he was waiting for the rest of Odin's message. Although impatient, he was prepared to wait, realising what was happening before him was more important. He was looking down on another grandson he knew nothing about and it pleased him. He saw that between them an alliance was being born, an alliance so powerful no force could stand against them. Apollo then said to Maria, "I told you all would be fine."

Dione looked down at her grandsons with tears of happiness trickling down her cheeks. She was happy Zeus had accepted his new family and this filled her with a sense of pride. Never did she imagine she would be grandmother to twin boys, sons of the mighty Thor and her beautiful daughter. Her visions showed her grandsons as true gods of Olympus and of Asgard, young warrior gods who will bring great changes to the cosmos.

There was great rejoicing in Olympus that night. All the gods wanted to sit and talk with Maria, Jacob and Odi, while the stewards ensured Jacob's friends were well looked after. Maria made many efforts to hug her boys but every time she went near them another god got there before her. Eventually Odi, Jacob and Maria managed to make their way to a quiet corner in one of the many annexes around the temple and talked, laughed, hugged and cried. They had many stories to tell.

Odi relished in the attention he was getting from his mother and his brother, a hole in his heart was now filled and he was pleased. He knew his mother wanted to talk about his father but chose not to broach the subject until she was ready. He didn't have to wait too long. "I've never forgotten you or your father?" said Maria as she linked Odi's arm, "I'm living for the day he visits Olympus, and it can't come fast enough." She was also so happy her secret existence was now out in the open and has been well received.

"There were times," said Odi, "when I'd watch my father standing alone on the highest turrets in Asgard. It broke my heart to see him look so lonely. I can, even now, hear his cape fluttering in the solar winds. Sometimes I'd sit with him but I always knew there was no point in bringing up the story of my mother. He'd always shut down the conversation and my instincts told me there was a great love lost and it was breaking his heart."

There intimate moments were interrupted when a steward arrived, summoning Odi back into Zeus's presence. Zeus asked, "You've more news from your grandfather?"

"Yes, my lord," replied Odi. "Rumours have reached Asgard, speaking of two fanged serpents crossing the ice lands. Dead seals, bears, birds and foxes have been found in many places. The bodies of two men have also been found. It's as though their souls were savagely ripped from them. Odin's instincts tell him that a great evil has already entered the realm of man meaning the signs of the End Times are mounting."

Zeus looked troubled and went back into his pensive state. He then suggested Odi return to his mother, spend time and get to know her.

Zeus left the temple to sit in the ornamental gardens and ponder this dilemma; there he sat alone for many hours. His fears continued to grow especially as earth tremors were now entering the realms of the gods. He still struggled with the idea that Cronus may be about to rise again especially with the precautions he and his brothers put in place. He wondered who had the nerve to seek out the darkest reaches of the Underworld where no other God, soul or man would dare to enter. This knowledge made him feel that maybe the serpents are being released by another force as Hades had indicated. The more he worried the greater Odin's recommendation that a council be called made sense. He decided that a council was indeed required.

In the meantime, while Odi was in the temple, Jacob took the opportunity to speak to his mother. "This is very hard to take," he said, "all these years I've had a brother and you kept this from me. I'm trying to understand, but I'm having difficulty."

"Remember son," she replied, "all those years Odi also had a brother. We needed to protect both of you. We believed Zeus was very clear when he said that he'd ensure, after his decree, no new babies, born to the gods would see their first sunrise."

"Mother, I don't blame you but how am I to get to know him; he's led such a different life. He's experienced much more than I have. When we were in each other's heads I saw him lead the armies of Asgard. I saw him having fun with other warriors. He was always falling in and out of love. I've never had any of that." He stood to walk away, "I'm not sure I can deal with this."

"Have you any understanding of how all this affects me," said Maria as she got agitated. "When you and I hug, I feel the eternal love that exists between us. When I hugged Odi I did feel love, a love lost. It was then I realised I actually have lost Odi and its breaking my heart."

Odi was standing just outside the door and before walking in he heard the last part of the conversation, "Mother!" He was taken aback when he said that, Maria's heart nearly missed a beat and Jacob said nothing, "I can't wait to get to know both of you. I know it's not possible for you to feel my love but it will come. Every ounce of my being is telling me my life is soon to be complete and that can only come from being with you."

He turned and said to Jacob, "The stewards tell me my room is ready, it seems we're sharing. I'm tired and need to sleep. Can we meet in the morning? There's so much I want to know." Maria hugged him and walked him to his room, Jacob went and joined his friends and continued to party for most of the night.

The following morning Jacob rose early, looked across at a sleeping Odi before heading out on his daily run. He hadn't travelled too far when he heard the sound of another runner coming up behind him. It was Odi, "We're more alike than I thought, early risers and distance runners, I'm impressed."

Jacob began to run faster only to be caught by Odi again. They ran deep into the meadows and through the woods towards the dense forest. They quickly became comfortable in each other's company and enjoyed the banter. They teased and attempted to outdo each other while racing through the enchanted forest that took them to the passes that led them to the snow-capped mountains. They climbed higher until they reached a ledge allowing them look back across the vastness of Olympus. There they sat and talked for hours, sharing stories and learning about each other, they were becoming the brothers they should always have been. Odi then raised his hand and placed it on Jacob's cheek.

"Up to a few days ago I'd have punched you for doing that."

"Why?" asked a bemused Odi,

"Where I come from men don't touch other men's cheeks. It could cause a problem." replied Jacob.

"Put your hand on my cheek." suggested Odi. Jacob did, and together they began to travel deep into each other's consciousness. They travelled all the way back to before they were born.

"Can you see the light? See how bright it is."

"Yes, I see it, is that what I think it is?" asked Jacob

"I think it's the spark of life, our lives," said Odi, "look how it splits in two."

Jacob crossed his arms while snuggling himself, "It's so warm here, I want to stay. What's that muffled sound?"

"Ah, I recognise that voice," replied Odi, "its father, he never stops talking."

"His voice is strong but sounds kind," said Jacob.

"You don't want to be in the way when he shouts," warned Odi, "he's got an angry side as well, I know. I've been on the receiving end."

"I've never had a man in my life, it's always been mother."

"I think we should stay here for a little longer," suggested Odi.

"Ah, I've just noticed, you're growing! You're a bit fatter than me!" laughed Jacob.

"Cheek, anyway you were always the weakling," said Odi gently punching Jacob on the shoulder, "I think that's why I always held you. I was terrified of losing you. Could it be that the spark of life knew we were going to be separated?"

"Never mind the spark of life," said Jacob. "Weakling, the cheek of you, I'm not the weakling now."

Odi got serious, "No, you're not the weakling now, you are going to be the King of Kings and I, like all in Asgard, will bow before you."

Jacob went quiet. After a moments passed he said, "You're an oracle?"

"One of my powers allows me to see many things that haven't happened as yet," replied Odi, "I've never told anyone. You're the first. I see many things, some I know will never happen, others I fear. The one thing I clearly see is you wearing the crown of Olympus."

"I've seen the crown, it fits my head," said Jacob, "I'm not sure I want it. Oh, I need to ask. Will you find love for our mother? She needs you to tell her, I sensed it when she and I were alone. Please find that love."

"Did you not feel it," asked a surprised and confused Odi, "you and I have just spent hours here in her womb. You showed the love to me, it was always there. I do love her and I promise I'll tell her tomorrow."

The boys loved being back in the womb, they lay back and enjoyed each other's company, they were happy in the one place they always felt safe and comfortable. They then fell asleep.

Jacob yet again was first to awaken. He sat up, and looked out over the Olympus meadows. He enjoyed watching the white mares racing across the grass plains and frolicking in the cool river. Odi stirred and then he too sat up.

"By the way," said Jacob, "I too am an oracle, it's one of my powers, it began showing itself when I was about twelve."

"Today," said Odi, "a big gap has been filled in my life. A vision showed you and me together forever, this one is set in stone." They both rose and began their run back to the temple.

Chapter 7

Zeus spent the night in the gardens waiting on the sun to rise. He also took great pleasure in watching his grandsons returning to the temple. He called them to join him as he prepared to call a council of the gods.

Together they walked into the temple, and Zeus made his way towards the centre of the Great Hall. He summoned Jacob, instructing him to send his friends back to their village; he also advised that he should remind them of how time in Olympus travels slower than time in the realm of man. He suggested they be prepared for a shock, as many months may have passed while they may have only spent a few hours in Olympus.

Jacob did as was instructed and called his friends together. He brought them to the portal and ushered them through, and after wishing them well he said he'd be in touch soon. He chose not to tell them of the task that was being prepared for them, a task he felt might frighten them if spoken about too soon. He asked them to enjoy their time with their families because when they return they may never see them again.

After running through the portal, Jacob's friends rushed to meet up with their families. Fafner was next to go through, he was in no hurry, he had no family. "There are many who will miss you," said Jacob after noticing the sadness on his face, "seek them and say goodbye. It's your destiny, and remember, all is not what it seems."

Last to pass through was Eala; she stopped, looked at Jacob, took his hand and brought it to her lips. He had his other hand to her hip and gently pulled her towards him. She was taken by surprise when he kissed her, but loved every second of it. They hugged and held each other for what seemed like an eternity. She kissed his neck, then his ear before moving back to his lips. He put his hands to her head and kissed her forehead then stopped. "I thought this was not to be?" she said.

"You're probably right but one thing I do know is the future has many paths and I see you on all of them, it shows you and I are meant to be to-gether." He kissed her again then continued, "It hurts me to watch you leave but Zeus has spoken. The great thing is it won't be long until we meet again." He watched her run home, never taking his eyes from her. He was pleased to see the relief on her parent's faces and was happy to see her back in their arms.

He closed the portal, re-entered the temple and joined the other gods who were watching Zeus pace around the centre of the hall. He observed him look up to where the friezes were inserted at roof level. The gods fol-lowed Zeus as he studied the friezes, each depicting the heralds of different pantheons including representatives of the Astrals.

They watched him call forth the heralds from the Dark Continent and were in awe of what they saw. As if by magic, five drummers came to life and alighted from the friezes carrying their Djembe drums.

The drummer's bowed, and then began sending a strong and rhythmic beat creating a sound loud enough to travel over the southern mountains, down the great rivers, across the hottest deserts and through the darkest jun-gles towards the far south. Their loud and rhythmic beat called forth the Gods of the Africa's. The pounding sound, after this night, would not be heard in the realm of man for another eight hundred years.

Zeus looked left and called on the two heralds of Asgard to step forward and blow the golden horns of Gallehus. Two Viking heralds alighted from the friezes. They bowed to Zeus and then faced the North. They raised the horns to their lips and sent out the loudest sound that travelled across the cosmos to summon the Gods of Asgard. Odi was in awe of them. They appeared, wearing his realms royal garments and looked so tall and powerful. He had only ever seen their likes in the great portraits in Odin's palace and he knew of them from the mythical stories of old.

The next frieze to be called upon was the heralds representing the Astral Wizards, the Oracles and the Elves. Three winged elves alighted, bowed to Zeus, faced the West and proceeded to play the harp like Celtic Lyre, the Flute and the Bodhran. Together they produced the most haunting sound imaginable, a sound set to endure the passage of time, music destined to define the Celtic peoples of the mystic west for generations to come. It was a sound that would awaken the wizards of old, and a drumbeat that would break through the shroud protecting the realm of the elves and call them into the presence of Zeus.

He then turned to his right and called upon the herald representing the Far East, one who is a loyal servant of Lord Buddha. His bold and striking orange civara robe set him apart from all other heralds. He bowed to Zeus, raised his mallet and pounded the lotus shaped Bonsho Bell allowing it to resonate its way towards the Far East, as well as break through the barriers of the Underworld. Jacob raised his hands to his head, he was receiving a vision. Odi joined him; he too could see the vision. "The messengers," said Jacob, "will suffer most when that bell tolls." Odi agreed.

Next, Zeus looked at the Indus heralds, summoned them to do their duty and call forth the Gods of the Indus. As they came forth they acknowledged Zeus with a bow, produced the Murali Bamboo Flute, the Tabla

Drums and the Bamboo stringed Vina. Together they composed the sweetest music that was sure to serenade its way to awaken the sleeping Gods of the Indus peoples. Jacob was still receiving visions as was Odi. "I still see these messengers," said Jacob, "and they are suffering the most. It will be the Indus that saves them. She will be most powerful. Adopted daughter, what does it mean?" Odi just shrugged.

Finally Zeus turned and looked high above his throne to where the stone image of three angels was placed. These were heralds of the most ancient god in the cosmos. Zeus called upon them and they answered. They stood together wearing the whitest of white gowns. Their auras emitted a brightness that clearly came from the first source Light. They faced the heavens and began in unison to blow the herald trumpets summoning the seven Archangels, guardians of the gates to Heaven, escorts and messengers of the Ancient One.

Silence then descended on Olympus as the last notes of the angelic heralds faded into the distance.

Zeus requested all the heralds to join him for supper, but before he could finish his invitation Odi interrupted. He pointed to the rafters and said, "Grandfather, what about those warrior heralds still standing as stone?"

"They were called in the past and didn't answer," said a displeased Zeus. "They chose the wrong side and will never be forgiv....." Odi interrupted again,

"But grandfather, my visions show the battle that's coming will be against The Darkness. There's something sinister as well. If we lose, all we hold dear will be gone. Surely they should be given a chance to redeem themselves?"

Zeus approached Odi and placed his hand close to his neck, pulling him closer, "I fear you have forgotten I'm the King of the Gods. I've made my decision. Never question me again or I may forget you are my grandson."

Jacob's eyes widened and he remembered his initial disdain for Zeus. He tried so hard to suppress his feelings but couldn't watch his brother been threatened. "Let my brother go," he yelled. "He speaks as a tactician of war. He's a general of Asgard and knows what he's talking about. Can you not see how all help is required?"

"Neither of you were there," responded Zeus, "I've spoken, my decision is final."

Zeus then ignored them, and joined the heralds insisting they share in the hospitality of Olympus. He showed how good a host he was by providing the best of food and drink, suitable for all tastes. He shared all the news he could remember, knowing each group was hungry for as much information as possible from their homelands. At the same time he was aware of a low rumbling sound coming from the North and knew he had to prepare. He excused himself and called Odi and Jacob back into his presence. "I look on both of you as the future but still I see two very young gods and I worry. You must understand that the pantheon of the Americas almost brought about the destruction of Olympus and that's unforgiveable. I know I must learn to trust you and if, on this issue, you chose to go against me, it's quite likely I will not move against you."

Both Odi and Jacob understood what he meant. They apologised and bowed. Odi left and went to join his mother out in the gardens. He planned to finally tell her how much he loved her. Jacob remained with Zeus.

Chapter 8

As supper progressed, the rumbling sound got much louder. It was the sound of a hundred chariots from the Asgard realm, and they were escorting Odin and his son, Thor. Zeus was delighted to be welcoming them earlier than expected. He immediately arranged for the tables to be cleared and the heralds to be seated next to the side walls. The Olympus gods then took up positions, next to their plinths in anticipation of the arrival, and as a tribute to Odin, a god among equals. Zeus would normally sit on his throne to receive visitors but this time he chose to stand in the centre of the Great Hall.

The doors to the temple opened and a loud voice was heard to say, "May a god from the cold north enter the realm of Zeus."

"No, a God from the cold North may not enter my realm," replied Zeus. "But a long missed friend may."

Odin walked through the doors and made his way to greet Zeus and the warmth of their embrace showed the respect they held for each other. Odin then took on a more serious face and ushered Zeus out to the garden.

"Time," he said. "Time may not be on our side, have you summoned the council as I suggested?"

"I assure you," replied Zeus, "the heralds came and all pantheons have been summoned, I expect them to answer my call within the next two days."

"And, the Gods of the Americas?" Enquired a sheepish looking Odin.

"There's no forgiveness, I still can't forget what they did, but I've planted a seed in your grandson's head."

Odin nodded knowingly, "Somehow I always knew you'd find a way."

Thor, in the meantime, assisted in stabling the horses before heading to the temple. On arrival at the doors he leaned forward and pushed them open to enter the temple as one of the most powerful gods ever to grace the halls of Olympus. He entered to an acknowledgement from the Olympians of his royal status, greeting those he knew from past adventures and introduced himself to those he only ever heard of. His status as a Warrior God was obvious from the way he carried himself. His height, red tunic, flowing elk skin cape and his red tinged fair hair held by a silver band, stood out as he walked the hall.

He saw Odi up near Zeus's throne and looked forward to meeting him. He thought it odd that Odi's hair had changed colour, he didn't realise it was Jacob he was looking at. Jacob backed away wanting to be alongside his mother when he met his father for the first time. He joined Odi and Maria who were still in the quiet corner they found earlier, and broke the news of Thor's arrival. Odi leapt up and ran in to the hall to greet his father. Thor thought he was losing his mind when he saw Odi's hair had returned to its original colour. Thor hugged his son and commented on his changing hair colour. "My hair hasn't changed, come with me, I've someone for you to meet."

Thor followed Odi but wasn't happy to be leaving the gathering as he thought it was very rude. Nothing Odi ever did surprises him, but this time he wasn't prepared for what was before him. He gasped as he rested his eyes on the only women who ever captured his heart. He saw Jacob but couldn't take his eyes from Maria. He had difficulty finding the strength to speak bet he eventually did, "I've longed so much for this day. The last sixteen years have been the loneliest place for any man to be. No one to share my life with, I was without the woman I loved," he got closer and reached out to touch her cheek, "I've longed for your scent just one more time. I've missed the softness of your touch and the passion of our time together." He turned to Jacob, "Each day I'd look on your brother and dream of his twin. I climbed the highest towers in Asgard and pleaded to the brightest star in the southern skies to bring us all together, to be a family. Is it too much to ask that my prayers are now answered?"

"Both your prayers are answered," said Jacob.

He took Maria into his arms and gently caressed her hair before giving her a kiss that, in both their minds, erased the loneliness of the last sixteen years. At that moment Odi and Jacob gestured to each other and proceeded to leave but were stopped by the powerful arm of their father. Thor looked at Jacob and with a tear in his eye said he now felt complete. He held both of them promising never again to allow his family to be split apart. Maria stepped back wanting to take in the sight of the three most important men in her life, finally together. Her boys were slightly taller than their father, and although handsome and muscular, they were no match for their father who was more handsome and much broader.

Thor and Maria discreetly left for the meadows, determined to make up for lost time. Maria shut Jacob out of her mind, wanting no interruptions. When Jacob looked out across the meadows he felt lost, he realized he no longer had to protect his mother. She, at last, had his father. He'd never seen his mother with a man, other than Owen who was an elf posing as a man, and felt this was odd. "That's my dad out there," said Odi, while snapping Jacob from his thoughts.

"That's my mother with him, strange feelings," replied Jacob.

They laughed and then made their way towards the lagoon, on their way they met with Odin and Zeus. Jacob bowed and Odi said, "Grandfather. I finally met my mother; she walks in the meadows with father," he placed his arm across Jacob's shoulder. "What do you think? You thought I was bad. There are two of us now. This is Jacob, he's my twin. Is this where I say, be afraid, be very afraid?"

"Afraid? I whipped you into shape, two of you don't frighten me," snapped Odin.

"Whoops, I think it's time to go," sniggered Odi

Odin acknowledged Jacob as they walked away, and said he will meet with him the following day.

They hadn't reached more that eighty paces when they both felt the impact of sandals hitting their heads. They turned to see Odin stand, sandal-less, with a smirk, "Even at my age I still have it, one throw and I hit two."

Odin then turned to Zeus, "Did you know?"

"No, I'm as surprised as you. Kept in the dark for sixteen years and then I discover I've another daughter and two more grandsons."

"My son and your daughter?" smiled Odin, "Who would have thought?"

Chapter 9

Jacob and Odi continued their walk towards the lagoon and as night fell they quietly lay on a grass covered dune, situated inside the safety of the temple grounds. They lay facing out to sea, but for them it was the most wondrous sight of flickering stars stretching across the Heavens that got their attention. At times they watched shooting stars, almost damaging their neck muscles, as they followed them across the sky. They then smelt the sweet scent, and freshness, blowing in from the pristine waters. They were relaxed and happy.

Jacob turned on his side and faced Odi hoping they'd get to know each other much better. He wondered about all the things that they, as children, missed out on. In particular, all the fun they should have had together.

"There's so much I want to know and so much I want to tell you," said Jacob, "I don't know where to start."

"At the beginning," replied Odi.

"For me, as far back as I can remember, I led a sheltered life, always watched over by mother. It started in England and then we moved to Ireland. My life was brilliant."

"England and Ireland?" asked Odi

"Of course, you'd know them by their Roman names, Britannia and Hibernia," replied Jacob while thinking of how happy he was, "I've had so many friends, the rugby team, the convent girls, then there's Shane, he's brilliant, I love him and really miss him." He hesitated for a few moments thinking of Shane, and then continued, "The awakening of my powers really rattled me and the constant nightmares terrified me. I was so afraid, all because I didn't know what was happening. All my achievements meant nothing because I felt I was just lucky even though I was well trained." He lay back and rested his head on his hands. "The anger ate away at me when I discovered our mother was hiding from her father because she feared for our lives. I couldn't understand how any father would want to kill his child."

He told Odi of the day he found out about his mother's turmoil and how he wanted to travel back in time and challenge Zeus because of the pain and hurt he caused her. In his mind he had planned many ways to make him suffer but when he met him for the first time, and entered his head, he found that he was tough and ruthless on the outside but fair and gentle on the inside. He spoke about how in just a few days he learned to admire and respect him and how he learned to love him as a grandfather. He now considers him a great and powerful leader.

"I know our grandfather has terrible regrets, all because of a misunderstanding sixteen years ago. I saw him look at us and our mother; it was the look of happiness. Now think about it, if this misunderstanding never happened, our mother wouldn't have met our father, we wouldn't be born and wouldn't be sharing this magic moment. My visions tell me that you and I are going to be involved in many epic adventures. We can't have them falling to others. All of this means we are part of some grand design."

"It's my turn!" said Odi. He looked at the stars and thought of how much lighter they were compared to the stars that shine in Asgards darkest nights. He turned back to Jacob, "I've always known there was something missing in my life. I believed it was my mother but as I got older I felt it was something else and that has to be you, brother. Father never spoke about our mother and that bothered me. He was always protective of me, I think that sometimes Magni and Modi resented me as a result, and that's why they relentlessly teased me but I love the two of them and I know that they'll always have my back. They're our older brothers. I can't wait for you to meet them."

"Wow, wow, wow, hold on...older brothers, I've got older brothers?" exclaimed Jacob.

"Stop!" insisted Odi, "It's my turn. We'll talk about them later." He then continued with his story. "I didn't have the easy life you've had. Father put me in school at six, into armed training at ten and then I quickly worked my way through the Asgard ranks to become a general at fifteen. Working, training and fighting is my life now so I've always played hard, especially with Magni and Modi. I've met many girls and always had a good time, but I've never fallen in love with any of them. By the way, one of your friends looks nice. I've got these funny butterfly type feelings since I first saw her in the temple. I've never felt anything like them before. When she returns to the temple will you introduce me?"

Jacob had had enough, "Brothers, older brothers, and you're only telling me this now. This is unbelievable."

Odi went quiet for a few moments, he was getting annoyed, "The least you could have said is 'yes' and regarding our brothers - I don't want to talk about them. Tonight is about us."

"Ok, I'm sorry. Her name is Panya, and yes, I'll introduce you."

Odi continued, "I know I'm a god with many powers. I have the strength of Heracles. I too can heal using the power of the water, which I know comes from Poseidon. I sometimes have the power of prophecy but not all the time. My father's hammer also answers to me. I don't believe I can time travel, but after we entered each other's heads I now know that it's a power soon to develop. We as twins must be equal in all ways." He paused for a moment then said "Just so you know; I too will learn to love Zeus just as much as I love my other grandfather. When you get to know Odin and learn to love him, he will be your greatest ally just as he is for me."

At the rear of the mound is a seating area with a full view of the temple and it was from there that the sound of a tankard falling and rolling along the ground could be heard. The boys looked over the mound and were slightly embarrassed when they saw Zeus sitting on one of the benches, and when he looked up at them they knew he heard everything they said. They watched him smile to himself and could see he was happy. Zeus said nothing, just waved to them, walked away, and entered the temple.

Chapter 10

The boys returned to stargazing, enjoying the continuous twinkling and beauty of what was above them. Occasionally, they'd look across at the village hoping to see their friends. They watched the villagers prepare a festival in celebration of the safe return of their missing children. The music, songs and the dances brought warm feelings to both boys and they wondered if there was a way they could attend. The aromas reaching them brought on a pang of hunger and the thought of the a few sly glasses of wine encouraged them to find a way to break the rules.

Jacob, like all teenagers, had thoughts and needs satisfied only by being with his girlfriend. He also felt that this could be an opportunity for Odi to properly meet Panya. He wondered if the power of Hade's helmet would protect both of them, allowing them to be with the girls without the villagers finding out. He discussed his idea with Odi and they both agreed it would work.

They returned to the temple and sought an audience with Hades which was granted. They explained what they wanted to do and were surprised at how quickly he agreed to assist.

"Who am I to stand in the way of love," laughed Hades who thought their plan was cute. "I see how serious you are so I must caution you about abusing your abilities. Always remember that when gods use their powers, evil is alerted."

He fetched the helmet and encouraged them to touch its crown, request invisibility and go on their way. Within seconds they were invisible allowing them to quickly make their way down to the village, where they immediately sought out Eala and Panya.

Although there was great merriment Jacob was bothered. He saw lots of tears as mothers and fathers listened to their children's stories. He watched those parents hug their children and struggle to accept that their children's return was only temporary. He felt guilty knowing he was the cause of the tears but reassured himself that there was no choice. What was about to happen was all part of a plan set long before his time. He knew the girls were going to be messengers of the gods and the boys their guardians. He consoled himself knowing how important the message was. He worried because the journey was destined to last for two thousand years.

Jacob looked around at those who were singing and dancing and soon put his reservations aside. He joined Odi at the wine casks, "No sign of Panya or Eala?"

"No," replied Odi. "Here, try this, it's amazing. I think I'll stay here for a while."

Odi loved the singing and dancing and continued to enjoy the free-flowing wine. Jacob didn't drink as much; he was more interested in watching out for Eala. Both found the music infectious, they swayed and at times gyrated to the wonderful beats. Most of all they enjoyed watching the stunned faces of the elderly men, those who were guarding the wine. What the men saw were filled glasses miraculously rising up as though held by invisible hands, they watched them tilt before returning, half empty, to the table. Time and time again the old men watched the glasses rise and fall, not knowing there were two young gods drinking themselves into a stupor? There was no stopping Odi, and as the night progressed he kept going back for more. He became unsteady as did Jacob, a few more drinks and both boys fell to the ground unconscious, still invisible to all around them.

Quite a few hours passed when Hades became concerned, he decided to check on his grandnephews. He reached the village and shook his head on finding two unconscious gods close to the wine casks. Placing them over his shoulders, he carried them back to the grass verge inside the temple shield to sleep off the effects of the wine.

Thor and Maria watched from their balcony window and were not impressed. Maria shook her head in disgust, "I'll break his neck, I warned him about drinking, and he just defied me."

"I was sixteen once, it's kind of a rite of passage in Asgard," said a cautious Thor, unsure of how Maria would react, "I think we should let this one go."

Maria was having none of it, "I've already warned Jacob about drinking and I'm very upset. He's ignored me for the last time. The only good thing about tonight is they're back safely and under the protection of the temple, but come the morning? Watch me lose it."

"Should I fear for the safety of my sons?" said Thor reaching in for a hug.

"Keep hugging me like that," she said snuggling closer, "and my concerns might evaporate, maybe tomorrow things will be different."

The next morning the first rays of the rising sun climbed towards the grass verge. The rays touched the boy's feet and began moving up their legs, bringing warmth that disturbed their deep sleep. Jacob woke first. He groaned while putting his hand to his forehead and trying to lift his head. His neck muscles wouldn't work. He managed to turn his head slightly and saw Odi still in a deep slumber. He kicked him causing him to roll down towards the water. The shield surrounding the temple prevented Odi from falling into the realm of man.

"What the F...? Why kick me?" yelled Odi.

"I never met Eala and it's your fault!" screamed Jacob. "Mother is going to kill me, you got me so drunk."

"I got you drunk? You poured your own wine," replied a still angry Odi, "I didn't hold your nose and force you."

Jacob again tried to lift his head but gave up, closed his eyes and dosed off. Odi also fell back asleep, this time with his face firmly pressed against the shield.

Several hours later when the sun was at its highest, Jacob felt a shadow cross his body. He opened his eyes to see the giant stature of his father standing over him. He got partial relief from the shadow caused by his father's cape flapping in the wind, deflecting the sun from him. He looked down at the shield and saw his mother trying to rouse Odi.

Odi woke, looked up at Jacob, and laughing loudly said, "We need to do that again, my first real party. Oh, my head, that was some night!" Thor offered his hand to pull Jacob to his feet, it didn't go well. Jacob struggled and stumbled, fell back to be caught in a tight grip by his father. Odi staggered up the grass verge, assisted by his mother, and he too struggled. Both boys were so drunk they'd no idea where they were. At times they sniggered, and then laughed before singing, all while being briskly pushed towards the temple. Odin and Zeus stood back as Thor escorted his sons through the doors. Dionysus arrived and looked puzzled, knowing wine shouldn't affect a god in this way.

When in the temple the boys continued laughing, singing and dancing before embracing each other. They were in a terrible state and got more obnoxious before getting aggressive. Apollo was watching and like Dionysus, he too felt something was wrong. He observed two puncture marks on both Jacob and Odi's heels and shouted, "Stop". He grew to his colossus form, grabbed the boys and raised them high so that he could examine the marks.

He looked across at Zeus, "These boys have been attacked. There's a poison, it spreads through their veins like fire. It's a poison of fire. The wine they drank is at war with the fire."

Dionysus, who was still close by, heard what was said, and fetched a cask of his finest wine. He brought it to Apollo who administered it to the boys; they didn't need much encouragement to drink as much as they could. The battle between the poison of fire and the wine raged inside the veins of both boys and eventually put them into a deeper sleep.

It was many hours, six maybe eight, before Odi woke. He was shaken and confused but glad to see his mother sitting on his bed. Jacob woke a few moments later and leapt up in terror, holding his hands to his head, "I saw them, red eyes and fangs. Father, I saw them bite into Odi's heel. I tried to warn him but a most fearsome pain shot through my body. It was as though it wanted my soul. I saw two serpents crawl over his body and slither away into darkness before a dark mist covered my eyes. Please tell me my brother is safe. Please tell me Odi hasn't gone to Valhalla." He got more distressed until Thor pointed at the other bed, he calmed when he saw Odi was safe and in the arms of his mother, "Odi, I'm sorry, I tried to warn you but the poison took my voice, my powers failed me. The last thing I saw was life drain from your face. My heart was broken."

Maria brought her sons together and held them tightly. She was devastated that an attack from Hell could happen so close to the temple. Thor called for Apollo who checked them and remarked on how the puncture marks on their heels had now disappeared. He was also able to confirm that the poison was gone from their veins. Both boys were still very tired and accepted the battle inside them took a terrible toll, they fell back asleep.

Out in the gardens while waiting on news of their grandsons, Odin and Zeus talked through all the possibilities as to what was happening in the cosmos. Odin's mind was troubled wondering how the serpents could successfully attack a god. He turned to Zeus and asked, "How can serpents from Hell get so close to this temple?"

"They can't," replied Zeus just as Thor joined them. "The attack must have happened in the village."

"The boys are awake and are shaken but they're healed," said Thor. "The attack did happen in the village. Jacob remembers two red eyed serpents crawl over Odi and slither into darkness."

Zeus was furious, allowing his anger show by producing his rod and releasing continuous lightning bolts across the cosmos. He summoned Ares and Athena and sent them to the village to investigate. "Make yourselves known to the people," he instructed, "tell them to meet in the village square and ensure all are present. Use your powers to cleanse every dwelling, every stable, everywhere a serpent could hide. Bring any serpent you find to the gates of the Underworld where Hades will be waiting to use his skills, no better god to find out what we're dealing with."

Zeus released another lightning bolt, knocking the villagers to the ground as it passed. On recovering, the villagers were met with the image of Athena, walking towards them from the east, and Ares coming at them from the west.

The villagers knew they were in the presence of the Gods of War, and were terrified. Those still in their homes were summoned and told to assemble in the centre of the village. "Be not afraid," said Ares trying to reassure them, "last night two young gods were attacked, the attackers were serpents from Hell. We're here to rid your village of this menace. Today the Goddess of War will use a new weapon, one that gets its power from the source Light created at the beginning of time."

The villagers watched Athena walk to stand among them. She raised her arm towards the heavens and opened her hand to release a crystal orb that hovered just above her palm. The brightest of an ancient light shot out in all directions, penetrating all houses, stables, carts and haystacks. Within seconds the most piercing, elongated scream was heard emanating from one of the haystacks, built at the outskirts of the village. Two stunned serpents slithered from under the haystack and collapsed at the feet of Ares. He secured them using the tightest grip before opening a portal to the Underworld where Hades was waiting to take control.

Back in the temple Thor encouraged Maria to rest, while he kept an eye on his sons, she resisted but he was very persuasive. He paced for many hours before eventually resting against the column at the entrance of the bedroom. He dozed but remained very alert. He heard the restless stirrings and the first words uttered, "Odi, are you awake?"

"Yes," replied Odi. "Strange how after all that's happened, I feel great. I've never been invited to a party and last night when you suggested we go the village I felt as though I was dancing on the clouds. I experienced what I always imagined teenagers should feel. I really enjoyed myself. It wasn't the wine and the dance that made me feel free. It was you, I was with you."

Jacob threw a pillow and shouted, "You were nearly killed last night and all you can think of is a party."

Odi threw the pillow back, "You're not listening, I was with you, I've never been as happy and I was having fun."

Thor listened and felt guilty for forcing Odi, at such a young age, to be trained as a warrior and a leader of Asgard. He regretted not allowing him be a child. He then left the hallway and went to let Maria know the boys were awake again and in good spirits.

Jacob lay back and Odi dozed off. He felt for Odi and believed he deserved to be a proper teenager, not a War God, and began putting together a plan. He left his bed, "Wake up, Odi wake up." Odi sat up.

"I've an idea, when I lived in Ireland I attended many parties, they were brilliant, great fun. We did things our parents used to go mad about. My 'Time Lord' skills are still untested but I know I'll master them. I plan to take you two thousand years into the future. I'm going to take you to some of the best party capitals in the world, to a time in the future where mother and I used to live. There'll be no early peaking; we will be there until the death."

"You're taking me to a party and I'm going to die?" said a worried Odi, "and what's 'early peaking',"

"No! Idiot," exclaimed Jacob. "The death just means, the end of the party. 'No early peaking' just means you can't leave early."

Dionysus and Eros happened to be passing by the entrance to the boy's room when they heard Jacob mention going to party capitals and they decided to visit. Dionysus sat on Odis bed, Eros sat on Jacobs. Jacob saw him approach and pulled his bedclothes up to his neck, "Eros, please put some clothes on, you're bits are making me uncomfortable."

"I'll have you know, young god," said an insulted Eros. "My bits are highly sought after, and everyone needs the God of Love. I must always be ready to spread what I have around the cosmos. My arrows never miss."

Jacob shook his head in disbelief and Odi fired some pillows at Eros. Dionysus then turned to Jacob, "We were walking by your room and heard you speak about 'Party Capitals'. Well I'm the God of Wine and Parties. Eros is the God of Love, you two are sixteen years old and deserve a good night out after last night's experiences, we are family, so we think you should include us, we too are in need of a good time."

Jacob left his bed and walked to the centre of the room. He opened his palm just as his mother showed him and called on the primordial source of ancient Light to come to him just as it did for his mother. The Light came and emitted its energy. Jacob quickly disappeared and found himself in the year 2016 standing on a beach in Thailand as the local 'Full Moon' party was beginning. He again called on the Light and reversed himself back to the temple. He tried again and found himself on the island of St Lucia in the Caribbean. He reversed himself back and tried a third time. This time he was on Bondi beach, among the greatest surfers of all time. He reversed himself again and then prepared to take Odi, Eros and Dionysus on the trip of a life time. He was pleased with himself as, after just a few attempts, he felt he had mastered the art of long distance time travel. The arrogance that worried his mother in Gibraltar was showing itself again.

Jacob called Odi from his bed and when Dionysus and Eros joined them, all four formed a circle with their arms around each other's shoulders. "I'm bringing you to the best party capitals in the year 2016, are you prepared for two weeks of sand, sea and lots of everything Zeus, Odin, father and mother would disapprove of?" It was unanimous, they all said yes.

"Just so you know," said Jacob as they were about to leave. "Two weeks partying in the realm of man means we will be back here before dawn. Eros, no offence, you have to put some clothes on. Where we're going you'll be arrested."

Just as Jacob called on the Light, Maria and Thor entered the room. "You can't do this," screamed a furious Maria. "Where are you taking them?"

"Mother, I've had enough, we're going to party, and we need to. Bad times are coming and we want to have some fun before the battles begin. We're going to party and just want to enjoy ourselves."

Thor said, "I prevented Odi from having real friends, trained him to be leader, and never allowed him to be a child, or a teenager. I regret that, let them go, they need to go."

Jacob and Odi looked pleadingly at their mother and got a hesitant nod of approval. They returned back into the circle and Jacob called for the Light. They disappeared and travelled through time to arrive in Thailand, only this time the 'Full Moon' party was in full swing.

They walked through the crowd and what a sight it was as four, over six foot tall Greek Gods, one naked and three dressed in the robes of their pantheon, walked along the beach. They blended in well as most revellers were wearing togas, bikinis and shorts. Jacob grabbed an abandoned towel and insisted Eros cover himself, but it was too late. He had attracted the attention of four Thai girls who insisted he party with them. Dionysus went to the beach bar and discreetly used his powers to taste the vast selection of wines available from around the world. Odi and Jacob dived into the sea where they made many friends. They drank themselves into a form of oblivion but kept enough energy to dance the night away.

It was sunrise when Eros re-joined them, "That was some strange night, it was wild and I'm confused. Two of the four girls I was with were not quite what they seemed."

Jacob knowingly threw his head back trying to stifle a laugh, "Please tell me you didn't."

Eros with a glint in his eye replied, "Well, I am the God of Love. The pleasure is all mine." Jacob just shook his head.

The following night they went to Bali, then, on night three they were on Bondi Beach in Sydney. Night four was spend at the 'Mardi Gras' parade. The boys never experienced anything like the beat and rhythms permeating the air during the course of their night in New Orleans. After New Orleans came New

Year's Eve party time at the carnival in Rio, Brazil. The day started on Coco Cabana beach and moved on to concerts, parades and finally the fireworks display. Day six and seven was spent in Ibiza where after two days and nights the partying began to take a serious toll. Ayia Napa and Mykonos were next on their agenda and the boys really came into their own. There were mini statues of both Dionysus and Eros in the bars and shops in Mykonos and as the day progressed people were beginning to remark on the resemblance. Both locations were very close to their home, but two thousand years into the future. Dionysus and Eros couldn't believe the changes or the fact that the ancient temples were gone, or in ruin. They were in party mode and intended making the most of their time travelling around the world. Day ten, eleven and twelve was spent at a music festival in Berlin followed by clubbing. Day thirteen and fourteen were spent doing what you do in Amsterdam followed by partying again and then just wild clubbing in Manchester.

Manchester was by far the wildest night. They landed in the middle of one of the biggest night clubs during a Halloween fancy dress event. They were already dressed for the occasion, including Eros. By sunrise they carried each other back to their hotel.

It was around noon when Jacob woke and went to the bathroom. He splashed cold water on his face. He then ran the hot water which formed a mist on the mirror. It was then when he went into a trance, the fogged up mirror created images of future events. He tried to break the trance as the visions were of pure horror, showing an evil never before visited upon mankind. He was terrified. His terror was picked up by Odi who, with Dionysus and Eros, ran to the bathroom to see Jacob frozen on the spot, trembling in fear and shedding tears of blood. They too saw the images, Eros grabbed a towel and wiped away the mist breaking Jacob's trance.

Jacob collapsed into Odi's arms before been carried into the bedroom. All four gods were shocked. "We should return to Olympus and report this vision," suggested Eros.

"Absolutely not," reacted Jacob, "we must continue, I believe something else is about to happen and we'll all have to deal with it." Jacob rejected any protests and arranged for them to move to their final destination. Jacob brought them to Dublin.

Arriving in Dublin was exciting for Jacob, his knowledge of the city was good enough for him to choose the best area in which to materialise. He used his powers to arrive, after closing time, in one of the top clothing stores in the city. This store offered the four partying gods the most modern and with-it clothing labels from which they could choose. Before they worked their way through the racks Jacob ensured he disabled the alarms. They then proceeded to pick what they felt best suited them.

Jacob was first ready; he knew exactly what he wanted. He had expensive tastes and always fancied himself in a black waist length fitted leather jacket from the autumn collection. He wore a pure white cotton short length tee shirt over grey skinny jeans. He completed his image with black, half sized zip and strap boots with a matching belt. Odi, Dionysus and especially Eros had never seen modern clothing let alone worn them.

As the boys were making their choices they were discreetly watching Jacob picking boxers and socks, items of clothing Greek or Asgard Gods would never have worn. Odi decided on an almost identical ensemble to Jacob but chose a navy coloured jacket, boots and belt. Dionysus opted for grey coloured chinos with a fitted pink shirt and a dark navy sports jacket. He also went for navy canvas style boots.

Eros had enough of wearing clothes and showed his annoyance at been pressured into picking more. Odi got impatient and in a joking, but firm manner, held his arms behind his back, insisting Jacob and Dionysus pick clothes and start dressing him. All four walked a pretend catwalk, clapped and cheering in a mocking manner as they passed each other. Eros still wasn't happy; he had difficulty adjusting his boxers. When finally happy with their appearance, Jacob used his magic to conjure up enough money to cover the cost of the clothes before resetting the alarm. He then transported all four of them over to West Essex Street for the start of their walk through Temple Bar.

Just like their arrival in the various party locations around the world, the four Gods walked into crowds of young people having fun. When they entered East Essex Street mouths dropped. Revellers on the streets, especially outside the pubs and restaurants were left speechless. The image of four really handsome, well dressed men took the area by storm. When they passed Temple Lane Jacob saw his best friend and two other lads from his rugby team. It was Shane and he lit up when he saw Jacob. He ran and leapt up on him sending him to the ground. They held each other in the longest embrace.

"What the fuck. Where've you been? You and your mother were reported missing in Spain, there's been a Europe wide search going on. It's been three weeks. Jesus, Jacob, my heart's been broken." They both got up and refused to let each other go. Odi held out his hand and said, "Hi, I'm Odi, Jacob's twin, these are my fellow Go…" He stopped himself from naming Dionysus and Eros.

Jacob interjected and said, "Jim and Jack, our cousins."

Shane got emotional, "I thought you were dead, I've been devastated not knowing what happened to you," he pulled Jacob aside, "I thought they kidnapped you, the ones from your dreams. I thought they killed you, I never betrayed you but they just kept interviewing me. You've no idea how happy I am. Oh, all the worry of the last few weeks, when I woke this morning, the worry was gone. Something told me to come in here today, am I getting like you."

"It seems bud," said Jacob, "the gods work in mysterious ways."

Odi, Dionysus and Eros because of their godly hearing overheard everything Shane said. "Jacob may have said too much to Shane," said a worried Eros, "we need to have a chat with him."

"Somehow I don't think there's anything to worry about," said Odi trying to reassure him, "every time he makes a mistake he comes up smelling of roses, he knows what he's doing." Shane's other two friends introduced themselves as Stevie and Callum.

Jacob turned to the gods, "I arranged to meet my school friends here in Temple Bar to celebrate our Junior Cert' exam results. This was planned long before my mother and I travelled to Spain. I really wanted to meet with them, they mean a lot to me. I missed out on our after exam reunion and was determined not to miss out on this night. I've been looking forward to a wild night especially if the girls from the convent turn up and help with the celebrations." Jacob and Shane walked ahead, arm in arm, prompting Stevie to shout, "Hey. Lover boys, wait up." Jacob and Shane put their free hands behind their backs with their middle finger raised, sending a very clear message to Stevie. Odi looked at Eros suspiciously, "Please tell me you didn't use one of your arrows?" They all laughed.

All seven continued walking towards Temple Bar Square where the rest of Jacob's school year had already gathered. The excitement in the area was palpable as the students had been looking forward to celebrating their exam results for so long. The clubs in the area had opened as alcohol free zones earlier that day to cater for the thousands of junior cert' students that were expected to gather in the city. Throughout Temple Bar music was thumping and throbbing, creating a brilliant evening and a wild night for the students. The buskers were providing a wonderful outdoor atmosphere.

Chapter 11

Dionysus and Eros went into a bar and were taken in by wonderful, spirit raising music, traditional Irish interspersed with popular and well known ballads. They were surprised to be asked for I.D. and had to use their power of mind control to secure some drinks. As two very attractive men they attracted a lot of attention especially from some slightly tipsy ladies who were also enjoying the electrifying atmosphere, dancing, singing and waving their arms about. Outside, Odi drifted away enjoying the wonderful sights, sounds and smells of different cuisines when he was approached by three girls who acted as though they knew him. He was surprised, but when he realised they thought he was Jacob, he saw an advantage in pretending to be him.

The girls admired his new hair colour and loved the clothes he was wearing. One of the girls reminded him of his promise to give them long sensuous kisses after the exam results were announced. This was like manna from Heaven to his ears. He readily agreed and then insisted they all kiss him at the same time. He closed his eyes and took in a deep breath while enjoying the sensations swirling around his body, loving the carefree way in which the girls had their hands everywhere.

A few moments later Jacob arrived, he tapped on the girls shoulders causing much confusion. Odi and Jacob embraced, looked at the girls and together announced, "We're twins." Jacob explained how he didn't know that he had a twin brother until a few weeks ago and it was a long story to be told some other time. He rejoined Shane, leaving Odi to enjoy his flirting.

The real reason Jacob had backed away was Eala. His mind was on her and he longed for the day she would return to the temple. He and Shane joined up with his rugby friends and they spent the next hour reminiscing about how successful they were in last year's junior school's Rugby Cup.

Meanwhile Dionysus and Eros were enjoying the ballad session, and the attention they were getting in the bar; then an uneasy feeling crept over them. They stared at each other feeling all was not quite right. They tapped into their powers only to feel a dark and sinister threat. They stepped from their barstools making their way towards a clear space near where the band was playing. They watched each other knowing something strange was about to happen. Their modern clothes fell away to be replaced by the robes of Olympus gods. They became illuminated, emitting a very bright light. The revellers in the bar quietened and the band ceased playing, all taking in the strange scene manifesting itself before them. Dionysus and Eros had never before seen, let alone experienced, a transformation such as this. They again looked around at the bar staff, bouncers and revellers and were unsure about what to do. When composed they rushed out the door hoping to quickly find Jacob and Odi. Unfortunately Odi, due to his wild flirting, was oblivious to what was going on around him.

Jacob stepped away from his friends becoming very quiet, so much so that Shane asked, "Bud, are they back?"

Stevie looked around, "Are who back?"

Jacob backed further away with Shane close behind, "Something's wrong, I can smell them, can you?" Shane shook his head and became alarmed.

"Trust me, whispered Jacob, "They're here, you must do what I say. Gather our friends and head to a different location as quickly as possible. There's an evil gathering around us. It's a dark menace, one I don't recognise. Jesus, it's overpowering, that smell is getting stronger." Shane looked at him in bewilderment, he couldn't smell anything unusual, but he trusted Jacob and did what was asked. He encouraged his friends to walk towards Dame Street.

Jacob discreetly glanced around the square and observed several individuals staring at Odi. He looked towards the bar and was horrified to see everyone backing away from Dionysus and Eros. He saw their Light and it was illuminating them so brightly it was revealing them to all in the immediate vicinity. He then saw that they too were being observed by strange beings which meant that somewhere in the area he too was also being watched.

He held his nerve watching some of the sinister individual's fade away hoping they wouldn't return. From the corner of his eye he saw a serpent bite into a young girl's neck, and this brought back memories of the attack on him and Odi. It was the bright crimson red eyes oozing evil that sickened him especially as they enlarged while gorging on her blood. Jacob felt her pain as her life-force waned, and was saddened to watch her white mist slowly rise towards the heavens.

Odi, in the meantime, was enjoying kissing the girls, his flirting knew no bounds. The young women were besotted with him, holding him against the wall, each wanting a part of him. One girl kissed his lips; the others kissed him on his neck, one on his left and the other on his right. In his mind he thought that if there was a great way to die, this was it. The ecstasy he experienced was soon negated by a tremor shooting through him, a tremor not of pleasure but of terror. He was becoming aware of something sinister and thought of the first lesson his father taught him, 'Trust your instincts son'. He slowly turned, scanning the ground, glancing across the rooftops, trying to see between those around him. He prepared himself for an unseen and unknown threat. It seemed to be the same one that Zeus and Odin spoke about back in Olympus. He looked for Jacob, and when he saw him, he saw the anguish written across his face and became alarmed. He was aware of Jacob's dreams where he was taught the tactics of battle. He hoped observing all the great wars of mankind, and his martial arts training had prepared him to be a fast thinker and quick decision maker. He saw Jacob intently staring across at Dionysus and Eros and hoped he was aware they had no experience in battle, were not warrior gods and would be easy targets for any assassin. He was pleased to see Jacob call the Light and run towards them, grip them and blink, taking them out of danger and back to the temple.

On arrival in Olympus, Jacob briefly met with his parents, and his anguished face showed them their boys were in trouble. He looked at his father, shook his head as if to say, 'This is bad.' He instantaneously returned to join Odi, landing just in time to witness a most spectacular transformation.

Odi had witnessed a serpent slither up a pole and then return to the ground. That same serpent bit two girls, and he had difficulty watching as their souls departed. He decided to take action. He placed the three girls he was with behind him, and then stepped out with his left hand by his side. He raised his right arm to the heavens and lowered his head. He thought of the hammer, calling it to him. He then sprinted forward with his arm held high and suddenly the hammer arrived with such force that lightening shot in all directions. A long and violent gust of wind blew as Odi's modern clothes faded away to be replaced with the attire and cape of a God of Asgard. He stood on the steps holding a pose that was enhanced by the rushing wind, his cape and long fair hair was fluttering in that wind and blowing almost parallel with the ground. He sought out the killer serpent and while remembering the attack on him and Jacob at the village party he used the full force of the hammer to crush him.

Jacob rushed to join him and while running his modern clothes fell away to be replaced with the robes and armour of an Olympus Warrior God. They took up a tactical position, back to back, trying to assess what was before them. Jacob went to his knees and placed his left hand in a small pool of water left over from the rains earlier that day. As happened back in the lagoon, the water climbed up his arm, crossed his back and flowed along his outstretched right arm to form a lethally sharp water sword, giving him a weapon he hoped would surely bring fear to any adversary.

The remaining students and tourists at first thought what was happening was street theatre. It was when they heard screams coming from all directions they realised they were being attacked by an unseen force that turned out to be a legion of violent serpents. Jacob and Odi scanned the square as the serpents continued to attack. A continuous white mist was rising as more and more of the teenagers passed away, their souls were refusing to succumb to the forces of Hell. Those that did succumb became Zombie-like wasted bodies.

"I don't understand," said Jacob, "this attack is not in the time line set as we build up to the battle of the 'End Times'. This is a major attack by the forces of evil. How did they know we were here?"

"Shut it," yelled Odi, "we'll worry about that when the battle's over. Help me figure out how to prevent the serpents moving out around the city. We need to protect these innocent souls and then figure out how to kill the serpents, so stop talking and use your skills."

Jacob was taken aback but acknowledged that Odi was a warrior god and had huge experience garnered during the Asgard wars.

"The first thing I'll do is call on the water," said Jacob.

"Oh, for Odin's sake, just do it...now!" screamed Odi.

Odi paced back and forth, all the time trying to rescue as many innocents as he could. Jacob devised a plan capable of preventing the serpents from spreading from this part of Temple Bar. He called on the power of Poseidon and raised the waters of the River Liffey. The water rose and then trickled, before turning into a torrent. It flowed from the river near the Halfpenny Bridge and travelled along Wellington Quay before turning, and then flowing up Fownes Street. It turned again and flowed along Dame Street and back towards the river by flowing along Anglesea Street. As the volume of water increased it formed an impregnable wall that grew to eventually reach a height of twenty feet.

There were hundreds of students and revellers, maybe as many as a thousand, inside the water wall. This included Shane and the rest of Jacob's school friends who failed to make it out of Temple Bar. Jacob saw them and successfully secured them back behind Odi.

The onslaught by the serpents on those still in the area was merciless; stealing their souls and wasting their bodies.

Back in the temple Maria's visions showed her boys to be in serious trouble and she devised her plan to help. Jacob and Odi were now very aware they were seriously outnumbered and had difficulty trying to protect the students as well as all the other revellers.

Jacob produced a second water sword giving him a span of ten feet. Odi continued to pace back and forth which meant that between them they were able to protect over eighty people situated behind them. They continued pacing but the serpent army just kept staring. They had already placed the zombie-like bodies before them as though they were to be used as cannon fodder. Every now and again the zombies swayed forward in a movement suggesting they were probing the defensive ring Jacob and Odi had created.

After a while the serpents parted allowing a much larger serpent to rise up and transform into an eight foot tall, terrifying Dark Angel. The angel became more upright and all watched in terror when he raised his arms and the blackest wings spread out behind him. He had the face of a demon, the cloven feet and horns of a devil. His red eyes emitted a glare that carried in its stare a hatred of the Light, and an evil presence that brought panic into the hearts of all before him. He was obviously the commander of the forces that had taken over the square in Temple Bar.

As the Dark Angel rose, Jacob and Odi listened to high pitched screams coming from the passage ways and lanes in the area, this further distressed them. All around them white mists rose showing that many of the students fought for their souls. As the minutes passed the mist thickened, indicating the death toll was now in the hundreds. These were pure souls whom Jacob pained over, because he and Odi had failed to protect them.

Jacob fought to put his distress aside reminding himself of how powerful his brother was so he decided it would be best for him to follow his lead. He hoped his own tactical abilities and fencing prowess would help them both win out this day.

The Dark Angel raised his arms again and gestured for the serpents to begin transforming into a legion of smaller Angels. These ones reached a height of six feet and were equally as horrific. Their serpent fangs, when dislodged, expanded to become the sharpest of demonic swords.

Meanwhile back in the temple, Maria put her plan in place. She used her time travelling skills to mount a rescue, and although Jacob sensed she was nearby, he couldn't see her. What he did see was the students and tourists were disappearing as every second passed. He was pleased when he realised his mother was using her powers to go among the innocents and take them, four at a time, out of danger, placing them outside the water wall on Dame Street. Odi also sensed her presence and was in awe of her. She was moving so fast she successfully rescued all but the few who were still hidden around the alley ways. Her intervention allowed Odi to take the lead and prepare a blistering assault on the zombies, serpents and Dark Angels.

Dame Street by this time was now full of emergency service vehicles. There was total confusion. Nobody understood what was happening. Army rangers arrived and decided to deploy a cherry picker to try and scale the water wall but their efforts failed, they were immediately attacked and subdued as soon as they landed at the other side of the wall. The Gardaí found it bewildering as more and more students kept appearing out of thin air. There was no doubting that the students were terrified and traumatised; most found it difficult to talk. The Gardaí, on realizing, as they listened to the stories, that the death toll was possibly in the hundreds, ordered an evacuation of the greater south side of Dublin's inner city. Army regulars arrived and took up position on the north quays as well as each side of Wellington Quay. News media were now in attendance and the first images of an impregnable wall of water was transmitted around the world.

There was panic across Europe as Temple Bar was well known as a major attraction for young revellers and citizens from all across the world. Images of those appearing out of thin air also travelled around the world. What was happening in Dublin was a phenomenon never seen before and there was nothing comparable in the annals of history. Offers of assistance came from France, Germany, Great Britain, Italy and Spain to name but a few. A fleet of helicopter gunships left Wales after requesting permission to enter Irish airspace. The Garda helicopter was noisily hovering high above the square and gasps of disbelief were heard as the crew witnessed the murder of more innocents, as well as the standoff between what looked like two boys wearing historical clothing, and an army of what seemed like, black clad winged angels. The cameras on the chopper were hacked by news outlets and the zoomed in images of the stand-off in the square were then transmitted around the world.

Back in the square the commander of the Dark Angels gestured his arms forward signalling for the attack on Odi and Jacob to commence. The zombie-like bodies stepped forward just as Odi began swinging the hammer, and as he attacked, it decapitated head after head. Jacob also moved forward but didn't have the skills of Odi. He did manage to decapitate quite a few but couldn't keep up with his brother. Odi was so focused nothing could stop him. Jacob increased his efforts but was pushed back against the wall. Although now in severe danger they successfully slaughtered all the zombie-like bodies, a situation that troubled Jacob because he recognised some of his attackers to be pupils from his school.

Odi became more alarmed when he realized they were dealing with an ever growing legion of Dark Angels. It was too late to call on the armies of Asgard or Olympus and he regretted that. He looked across at Jacob and hoped their combined power was enough but he knew it wasn't going to be. He decided to apply another of his father's important lessons, 'attack when least expected, this is the best form of defence.' He attacked.

The strategy of the Dark Angels was obvious. They were swamping the boys with their greater numbers and as the boys got separated their plan involved forming circles around them. It didn't take long before the swords of Hell began raining down on Jacob in particular. Odi was by far the most successful in defending himself; he had the loyalty of the hammer and this gave him great protection. He glanced across at Jacob and to his horror, he watched him slip and fall to the pavement. Jacob continued using his swords by rotating them rapidly; giving him a small degree of protection but it wasn't enough. He was being sliced on his legs, arms and shoulders weakening him with each blow.

The Dark Angels continued to target Jacob, they considered him to be the weakest link and then, alas, it happened. One blade slipped through and pierced Jacob's heart. He held his chest and turned on his side and as the last vestiges of his life ebbed away he looked across at the skilful movements of his brother. One tear gathered and slowly rolled down his cheek, his thoughts took him to the lost opportunities with his beloved Eala. Just as the mist of death crossed his eyes, he looked up at the building opposite to see a figure standing on the roof. He recognised the figure, it was Fafner.

In the meantime, Odi made every effort to reach Jacob. He backed away from his attackers to assist. He had fought valiantly but was now coming under severe pressure especially as the body count was mounting making movement in the immediate area difficult. There was a pool of water nearby and he kicked it towards Jacob hoping it would, as in the past, help heal some of the wounds, allowing him to recover, but he didn't realise it was too late.

Maria returned to Olympus seeking Thor, intending to bring him to the battle in the event her boys needed him. At that point she wasn't too concerned, her visions still showed them in future events. When she reached Thor everything changed, she suddenly stopped and with tears gathering, her visions showed her the final gasps for breath as the Light left Jacob. Zeus, Odin and all the gods in the temple leapt to their feet as the death of any god sends shockwaves across the cosmos.

Odi finally made it to Jacob who was getting no respite from the relentless onslaught. His rage at the suffering of his brother encouraged him to continue fighting like a god possessed, but as the hammer crushed one Dark

Angel there was always another waiting to take its place. The Dark Angels were now taking control but only because of their superior numbers.

The attack on Odi was intensifying and even though he was focused he momentarily caught a glimpse of a figure wearing golden body armour that glistened under the lights emanating from the premises below. He saw the gilded helmet, holding the feathers of the golden eagle. He knew it to be one that could only be fashioned by the craftsmen of Asgard in the forges of Hephaestus. Each gust of wind caused the figures cape to flutter wildly making him look a powerful sight. He too recognised the figure to be Fafner and wondered why he was just standing there with his hands resting on hips. He then saw Fafner glance back and forth and knew he was taking in the battle and devising a strategy.

Jacob managed one last gasp, "Fafner, my friend, my Mythical Dragon." He closed his eyes for the last time. Odi's spirit was now broken.

Fafner raised his arms, leapt six feet up and out from the building, somersaulted and turned into a fire breathing dragon with wings that spread out to sixteen feet. For those watching this was something only ever spoken about in the great stories of old, written hundreds of years earlier. Fafner flew towards the Central Bank and turned back to the square enabling him to attack the Dark Angels. They didn't see him coming. Swinging his head from side to side he used his fire to incinerate Hells army in one swoop, leaving their leader alone and defenceless. Odi limped forward and screamed after placing the blade of his sword across the neck of the Dark Angel, "Why? Why? What did we do to you?"

Fafner landed, and transformed back into his human form. "The Light came to me, said I was needed."

"Fear not God of Asgard," he said acknowledging a distraught Odi, "I see Jacob in my future so my work is not done."

He transformed back into a dragon and raised himself to a height for his claws to carefully grip Jacob. When secure he lifted Jacob's body towards the top of the water wall. He gently lowered him into the centre of the wall, and then called on the water gods for assistance. Jacob momentarily floated before sinking towards the centre of the wall.

The screams of terror that was heard during the battle had now long ceased but the damage was already done, it had caused such panic that an evacuation of a greater area of the city including the north side was ordered. The Garda chopper hovering above was now joined by the six British gunships, all with their cameras trained on Temple Bar square. The slaughter below, the body count, the stains on the streets shocked even the most hardened of the pilots. The Garda camera was still hacked and broadcasting the horrific images. Parents travelled from all over Dublin searching for their children but were not allowed past St Patrick's cathedral on the south side, Chapelizod on the west side and Dorset Street on the north side.

When Fafner was satisfied Jacob was now safely in the hands of Poseidon he flapped his wings and began his assent. As he rose, the gunships, not knowing what they were dealing with, prepared to fire on him. He flew low, close to the buildings, turned and headed towards the Wicklow Mountains. Three gunships followed but soon lost sight of him; he faded and disappeared before their very eyes.

Odi still held the Dark Angel, trying to control his temper and waiting for help to arrive from Olympus. People watching were enthralled. The events unfolding were still being streamed live around the world. One gunship had its camera focused on the section of the water wall containing Jacob's body, and while transmitting back to base, it, like the Garda camera, was hacked and its images of Jacob's body just floating brought tears to the eyes of millions. Jacob was now considered a hero.

The cameras then captured a bright and blinding flash of light entering Jacob's body. It was as though the primal spark of life was just delivered. Within seconds Jacob's arms and legs stirred and he slowly descended down to the cobble stones. He remained in the water wall for a good number of minutes regaining his strength, totally rejuvenating him. He left the wall and joined Odi whose relief was palpable. They knowingly looked at each other and slowly circling the Dark Angel. As happened in the temple, time slowed down and then stopped, but only in the immediate vicinity, giving them what they needed to put in place a plan to deliver him to Hades.

Back in the temple, Maria was still distraught and found it difficult to recover. She'd guided and protected Jacob since the day he was born and never imagined that bringing him to Olympus would place him in so much danger. The shock of his death, and then his recovery, was an experience she never wanted to suffer again. She sat there almost in a trance sensing her boys were playing for time. She ran to the meadows seeking Ares who was patrolling the shield due to the now continuous invisible probing around the temple. She explained what had happened and asked for his help.

Maria and Ares travelled through time and landed in their colossus form alongside Jacob and Odi. They landed with such force the tremors registered on the Richter scale. All around the world people watched in amazement as two colossi appeared in Temple Bar. Many remarked on the beauty of the women, incorrectly identifying her to be the Goddess Aphrodite. Others recognised, from Greek statuettes, the warrior as Ares, the God of War. After assuming their human forms, Maria ran to Jacob but backed off when she saw the horrific face of the Dark Angel. She decided to wait until Ares dealt with the demon.

Those watching were mesmerised at the stature of Ares. He appeared in the golden armour of Olympus and was fully armed with his lethal weapons of legend. He didn't waste any time, he acted so quickly the Dark Angel had no time to react. He opened a portal allowing him deliver his captive through time and space into the dungeons of Hell, for interrogation by Hades. Again people were amazed after witnessing the portal open and four arms stretch out to forcefully pull the demon through to another dimension.

Maria then ran to Jacob and held him so close it showed the world how much she loved him. She called Odi to her and held him in a way he had never experienced before. "Now I know," he said gently kissing her on the cheek. Maria just nodded.

Ares indicated it was time to go. He was irritated by the sounds of the helicopters above him. Jacob and Odi were relieved the battle was over, but their relief didn't last long. They looked around the square to a vista showing mounds of bodies, remnants of totally innocent people.

"Take Odi and Ares back to Olympus," said Jacob after recovering from the horrendous sight, "I'll follow after I close down the wall and try to explain what's just happened."

The seven helicopters hovering above watched Jacob, who was now alone, walk over to the water wall. They watched him place his hand in the wall and bow his head. "I command you to return to the river," those nearby heard him say, "Flow out to sea. Carry the sad memories of this tragic night into the depths of the ocean." The waters then receded and he made his way towards Dame Street. He knew Shane and his friends wouldn't leave without him, and by the time he reached the Central Bank the water was completely gone.

The army and the rapid response units poured into Temple Bar. Three Gardaí ran towards Jacob attempting to arrest him but they'd no chance. He just flicked his arm, using a right to left motion, and magically pushed them away. A second attempt was made using tasers but he again used his power and redirected the wires causing the users to be tasered instead. The rapid response unit arrived and ordered him to stop but he ignored them. They trained their weapons and threatened to fire on him. He responded again and this time he used his index finger to magically disarm the unit. The Gardaí backed away to discuss the best way forward only to concede that this boy seemed to be untouchable.

A news crew broke through the cordon and managed to approach him. He was asked to confirm is name was Jacob Baker. Jacob momentarily stopped then continued walking; he stopped again, "Once I was known as Jacob Baker but not anymore. Just call me Jacob." He stopped the reporter from asking anymore questions and agreed to make a statement.

"My name is Jacob and, alongside my mother, I spent the first sixteen years of my life in the realm of man. Tonight, here in Dublin, mankind has witnessed the first of many attacks by the forces of Hell. They are the allies of, and the bringers of The Darkness. For the last two thousand years Hell has been planting the seeds of war, destruction, pestilence and famine, using their serpents and Dark Angels. They plan to end this age of man, this I garnered when I read the mind of the Dark Angel before sending him back to Hell. Tonight my youth was lost. Tonight I died. Tonight the Ancient One gave back to me the spark of life. Now let it be known that my power and that of my brother will be used to prevent 'The Darkness'. We know serpents are already slithering among man and we're making every effort to contain them. We know there'll be many failures because the battle they're planning must happen. Before discovering who I was I suffered horrendous night-mares where I witnessed much evil. This evil always starts with a bite lead-ing to a poison being spread through the generations until a descendant

rises up to unleash a living Hell. Here in Dublin I sensed, for the first time, the real evil, the real menace, the real terror that Hell will visit on man and I fear what's coming. The Darkness is coming and I will seek assistance from the Light so as to prevent this evil from destroying all that is good in man. This will be difficult because there's such evil in the hearts of so many men."

By now there were numerous reporters present, each firing questions but getting no response. A senior Garda attempted to persuade Jacob to attend for interview, a request he flatly refused telling him he had no dominion over him. The Garda wasn't giving up, "Temple Bar is a major crime scene," he said, "questions have to be asked and answered. There are three hundred and twenty bodies counted so far with many more being gathered. Parents need answers."

"You call Temple Bar a crime scene?" said Jacob, "We call it a war zone and this is the first of many, I've seen it. I came to Dublin to meet my friends and celebrate our exam results not knowing I'd be involved in a battle that killed so many. Be thankful my brother and I were here otherwise the death toll would have been in the thousands. Tell the parents, and I know it's of little consolation, that most, if not all of their children fought the forces of Hell and have gone into the Light, they'll be happy, resting amongst their ancestors. They will be escorted by Hermes to the gates of Heaven. We know this because during the attack, we saw the white mists."

Jacob got agitated as the Gardaí and the reporters continued asking questions. "Enough," he shouted. "It's time to say goodbye to my friends. Leave me in peace." He walked along Dame Street towards Trinity College where his friends were waiting. On reaching them he was greeted, hugged and thanked for saving them. He healed those he saw to be suffering minor cuts and bruises by using water from the previous night's rains. Miraculously all were healed. He spent over an hour with them trying to calm and reassure them but he was now becoming aware that the pantheons, summoned by Zeus, were due in Olympus later that day. He began to say his farewells holding his final goodbye for Shane. He placed his hands on Shane's shoulders and whispered, "You more than any other have always been there for me, and I'll be forever grateful. Thanks to you I know who I am and who they were. I know why my dreams seemed like nightmares, everything has fallen into place. I see you in my future which means I'll be back for you, I don't know when, but watch out for the signs. Always remember, as my closest friend you are everything to me!"

Jacob slowly walked towards the gates of Trinity College but on his way he was stopped in his tracks by a question from a young girl who was the only one who plucked up the courage to ask the one question everyone was thinking but afraid to ask. "Jacob, are you God?" Time seemed to freeze, there wasn't a sound, you could hear a pin drop, reporters nearby raised their microphones, "No, I'm not God," replied Jacob with a smile, "I'm Jacob.......grandson of Zeus." He continued his walk and reached the gates. He turned and waved to his friends, bowed, then requested the ancient source Light. He disappeared and returned to the safety of Olympus.

Chapter 12

Jacob arrived back into the Olympus meadows at the rear of the temple. He was numb. The battle had taken a terrible toll on him and he was already missing his friends. His mind was never far from Shane, Stevie, Al, Callum and Davie and he worried about what was to become of them when The Darkness attacks. He could still smell the stench of decay, and the rotten congealed blood that was caked into his clothes and on his skin sickened him. The horrific images of the battle cluttered his mind and the distorted faces of the poor souls who were taken by Hell haunted him. He felt dejected and didn't want to go to the temple for the moment. He decided to spend as much time in the meadows hoping the sweet scent of the wild flowers would bring him peace. He walked through the long grasses to where the white mares were grazing, patting each one as they greeted him. He smiled while watching the nymphs shaking flowers to release their scent just to cheer him up. He acknowledged, and thanked them for their efforts, but his pain was too deep. In the distance he watched Pegasus race across the sky, then land and cantor towards him.

Pegasus took his human form and greeted Jacob by embraced him and just holding him knowing how he was grieving. It was the overwhelming sense of guilt that made him feel useless. He regretted how his powers failed to protect the students and tourists especially when he thought of the speed, bravery, and power of Odi. He then thought of how he compromised his brother when he allowed Hell's sword through his defences to take his life. The feelings of despair continued to rise when he remembered how his failure brought on the rage in Odi that could have also brought about his demise except for the intervention of Fafner. A small amount of pride entered his mind when he remembered why Fafner was chosen by him and how he had grown into a mighty immortal warrior with the powers of a dragon. He was pleased that same dragon was protecting Eala, his one and only true love.

He held Pegasus tightly as his tears welled up before uncontrollably flowing. He fell to his knees, holding his chest as the grief took him. Pegasus never said a word, just allowed him grieve until the last tear fell. "Even gods are allowed to grieve," said Pegasus, "I've watched you for sixteen years knowing your destiny. Continue to grieve for a short while, young king, and then find your inner strength. You have been chosen to be King of Kings and you were placed in the realm of man to learn their ways so that you would be a good king. It was I who called you into your trance that day in Gibraltar, the trance where you saw your future. It was I who gave you the image of you wearing a crown. I know you said you thought it was only wishful thinking. Trust me, it's not. You will lead the armies of the Light. Your three brothers will be alongside you and will bow before you. The creatures of myth and legend will swear allegiance to you so go now to the temple and command the doors to open. Let all those who are present see that you are King in waiting." Pegasus then returned to his equine form and cantered away before taking to the sky.

Jacob momentarily forgot he was yet to meet his older brothers, Magni and Modi, and wondered what they were like. He thought it odd that Odi hadn't said much about them.

When Pegasus went out of sight Jacob turned back and looked towards the temple, he decided to take his time.

Occasionally he went to his knees to take in, and enjoy, the scent of the abundant flowers. He remained on his knees absorbing their aromas until he felt his strength had fully returned. He enjoyed trying to decipher the constant high pitched gibbering of the flower nymphs especially the ones who chastised him for sitting on their homes.

He stood to look towards the mountains and was enthralled by the mosaic of colour that was before him. It was the eye-watering beauty of the meadows that for him, made these moments his most magical time so far in Olympus, especially when he felt his confidence return and his strength build.

While he grieved in the meadows, Odi was in the temple giving a full report on the battle in Dublin to the senior gods. He was fully aware of Jacob's torment but his duty meant he had to remain in the temple. He was still in the stained attire worn during the battle and was giving off an ungodly stench caused by the blood and guts of the Dark Angels. His sword was heavily blunted by the constant force of the impacts but his hammer still looked as pristine as the first day it was forged. Odi wasn't normally prone to exaggeration but he just had to embellish a few of his stories.

Even when giving his report, Odi was conscious of Jacob's descent into grief and wanted to go to him but was stopped by Apollo who suggested he let him grieve. Being very sensitive to Jacob's feelings he had difficulty following Apollo's suggestion, especially when he felt Jacob's tears flow.

Ares then gave a report on the transfer of the Dark Angel through the portal into the hands of Hades. He told the gathering that he felt the malevolence of the demon and sensed his hatred of the Light. He also believed that this particular demon was one of the inner circle demons who are privy to the plans of Lucifer. He told the gathering that he made his feelings known to Hades before the portal closed.

Maria spoke of her efforts in moving so many people from danger. She expressed her regrets at her failure to save all those other innocents who had fallen to the forces of Hell. She reported on what she saw as an army of serpents with the power to grow in stature to become Dark Angels. She also reported on how their numbers were constantly being replenished and how their fangs became such lethal weapons. In her opinion, after the serpents bit into a human, those humans would either, turn to The Darkness and become empty mindless walking bodies or they would fight the attack. They did this by succumbing to death thereby protecting and releasing their souls into the Light through the white mist when they passed away.

Maria then spoke as a Time Lord, "This attack will happen in the year 2016 as Jacob, Odi, Fafner, Ares and I have witnessed. I believe the type of demons who fought in Dublin don't exist as yet. I believe they will evolve as each incident with a messenger occurs. I believe Jacob and Odi were deliberately led to Dublin for this very battle. They have been shown by the Ancient One what is to come. We now have an advantage and we should use it."

Back in the meadows, Jacob finally pulled himself together. He thanked the flower nymphs for their compassion and support. He told them that they had cheered him up and he now felt ready to face the gods. He walked to the front of the temple and thought of what Pegasus said, 'Command the doors to open.' He walked up the steps and with a slow but assertive flick of his hands he sent out the command and the doors opened. He was impressed that a new power had just awoken and he looked forward to using that same power many times in the future.

He walked through the Great Hall to where Zeus and Odin were sitting and bowed to all the gathered gods. He lit up when he saw Odi and was shocked at his dishevelled condition. He held his nose as he passed and received a kick of affection. He greeted his father, mother and then his grandfathers. He wanted to express his feeling just as they were expressed out in the meadows but knew he had to control himself. Although he felt his strength had returned he still had a terrible feeling of loss making him want to explode.

As he was about to speak he was stopped by Odin, "Jacob, grandson, I'm so proud of what you and Odi achieved this day, together you held back a legion of deadly serpents, they seem to be followers of the Archangel. Your mother has assessed they are a force never before met on the battlefield, and between you, Odi and Fafner, you vanquished them. It was wise of you to read the mind of the Dark Angel. That's a valuable resource you have, a resource that now allows us to plan." He gestured for Jacob to step forward. Zeus and Odin placed their right hand on Jacob's head. Thor, Hades, Poseidon and Chiron joined them. Together they summoned up the memories Jacob garnered from reading the mind of the Dark Angel, they also sought out memories of the dark vision he received in Manchester.

All the senior gods then left for the gardens. They were seriously perturbed by what they saw. The image of the council of Hell with Lucifer presiding confirmed he was behind the serpent attacks. In the background of both visions Odin and Zeus observed a sinister orange glow that shed no light. It bothered them because the last time they saw something similar was at the creation when The Darkness was defeated. They both felt The Darkness was closer than at first thought, "I wonder does Lucifer know how The Darkness takes no prisoners?" pondered Zeus, "He thinks he is the great deceiver, does he not know that The Darkness is even greater?"

"It's not right that one so young should carry such a burden," said Odin. "The images of the slaughter and pestilence that's coming shouldn't have been imposed on him. I'm worried for him."

"Worry not father," said Thor, "I trained Odi as I did Magni and Modi. I'd place my life in their hands. Jacob is my fourth son and twin of Odi, identical in almost all ways. Any skills Odi has will also be Jacobs and any powers Jacob has will be Odi's. You needn't worry for he is a powerful god and it's his duty to carry this burden. We're here to advise and support him. He has my hammer." Odin placed his hand on Thor's shoulder and just nodded in agreement.

Jacob remained in the Great Hall and was being comforted by his mother. He didn't say much, putting on a brave face, she knew he was hurting and hoped her support would ease his pain. Odi left to wash and change as the gods were complaining of the gruesome odour wafting from him. When washed and changed he rejoined the gods in the Great Hall. A short while later Jacob made his excuses and left for his bedroom. He washed and cleaned himself then lay on his bed and thought of all that had happened, things he should or could have done differently. These were the times when he preferred to be alone especially when he felt so low. No matter how hard he tried to forget he still felt responsible, dejected, demoralised, worn out and tired. He dozed off.

Several hours later Odi came to their room. There was one torch still burning and Odi could see Jacob was weeping in his sleep. He felt for his brother and sat on the bed beside him hoping to comfort him, praying he could take away some of his pain.

As the night progressed, Jacob's inner turmoil abated. His dreams brought him back to happier times, his last rugby match and holding the schools trophy high above the heads of his classmates. He dreamt of his time in England when he played along Hadrian's Wall with his friends from the village. He could smell the sweet flowers of the meadows and he was getting excited as the beautiful scents were leading him to the one person he wanted to be with. He looked around and saw her walking near a small ridge. In his dreams he remembered her in the lagoon and felt her body rest against his. He felt her breath on his neck and was again happy.

He woke and was surprised to find Odi sleeping beside him and was glad he was there knowing he could always depend on him. He placed his hands behind his head and enjoyed the butterfly sensations that were growing in intensity in his stomach, feelings that only ever appeared when he thought of Eala. He was also counting down the days to when Eala would be brought back to the temple and those thoughts increased the intensity of the butterflies. He wished for the council to be concluded so that he could put in place his plans. He occasionally got upset when thinking of how his plans included Eala going on a long walk that would take up to two thousand years to complete, but also knew that for her to prepare for her long walk she would have to be granted immortality and this excited him. He wanted this to happen as soon as possible as he planned to spend eternity with her. He accepted they would be separated for two millennia but eternity was forever and he could live with that.

Odi soon woke, "You actually want to spend eternity with her?" he said turning to face Jacob.

"Prick, you were in my head again," yelled Jacob belting him with a pillow. "The next time I'll embarrass you so badly that you will think twice about messing with my mind."

They threw a few friendly punches at each other showing how they were becoming inseparable. They agreed boundaries needed to be set regarding them entering each other's heads and settled for only entering each other's head when invited.

Chapter 13

The first dawn since Zeus summoned the pantheons was now approaching and the stewards were busily preparing for the arrival of the gods for breakfast. Zeus was as usual, first to arrive and take his seat in the Great Hall. He sat alone at one of the banquet tables and after a few moments passed he was joined by Dione, and they dined together in silence. Neither could bring themselves to speak of her deception at the time of Maria's birth. Zeus eventually looked at his wife and after stretching across to take her hand said, "I've loved many times but never loved anyone as I've loved you, and I'll always love you. I never intended my decree to be used against the birth of the children to true gods. It was intended as a decree against the births of demigods. I was growing more impatient with the amount of children born to humans and fathered by gods because I felt we were losing control of the cosmos and control of the various powers that these demigods possessed. At that time, after the census was presented to me I was satisfied because there was nothing to be worried about."

"I was vulnerable then," said Dione, "I hadn't the strength to take you on, I had this overwhelming desire to leave and somehow felt my destiny and Maria's, was being set elsewhere."

Zeus said, "You mean the Ancient One?" Dione nodded in agreement.

"After all that has happened and all that's about to happen," she said. "There's no other explanation."

"You brought a beautiful daughter into this world," said Zeus. "She's brought two handsome, powerful and talented sons into the cosmos. I haven't been this happy in such a long time. Even though I'm happy, I'm also very tired and think I need to leave. After this battle with The Darkness, I'm going to hand over my realm to the council. I hope they'll see what I can see."

Dione cupped his hands and asked, "Tell me my love, what is it you see?"

"I see them, the twins; I see them leading the combined realms of Asgard and Olympus. I see them as great leaders and protectors; I see them as loyal, strong, caring gods. I see them as fathers and founders of two new immortal houses." He was about to continue when he sensed the impending arrival of more Asgard gods.

A steward arrived and whispered, "Two imperial chariots have been spotted near the pine forests of the north. They're travelling with one hundred escorts."

Odin, Thor and Odi also sensed how close they were and ran from their rooms, headed to a small hill to await the arrival of their kin. They watched the chariots reach the temple escorted by Pegasus and thirty of his finest white mares and stallions. The two leading chariots were carrying the eldest sons of Thor; they were considered two of the finest young generals in the Asgard army. They wore the imperial red tunic and the skin cape of the Asgard realm. As princes, they both wore the silver crown with the gold leaf clasps of their royal house. When they arrived, they dismounted and bowed to their grandfather, then their father and finally they embraced Odi.

Back in the temple the Olympus gods took up their positions and again this was an amazing sight. Olympus always knew how to put on a show for state occasions. Zeus sat on his throne flanked by Hera, Hades and Dione and waited for the arrival of their renowned visitors. The pure whiteness of the imperial dress of the Olympus Pantheon, accentuated by the bright light entering the temple and bouncing off the golden throne created the most majestic atmosphere of grandeur not seen, almost since the beginning of time. It was agreed between Zeus and Odin that Maria and Jacob should wait outside for the arrival of the Asgard gods and enter the temple alongside them. Maria wanted to enter linked to Thor and Jacob wished to be alongside Odi.

As the Asgard gods marched towards the temple, Thor walked ahead of them. He wanted to be with Maria when Magni and Modi reached the steps. He introduced Maria as the mother of Odi and then introduced Jacob as another of his sons and a twin of Odi. They were both shocked; it never crossed their minds that their father was with a woman they never knew about. They'd never seen their father so nervous yet, at the same time, happy and contented. They bowed to Maria and then turned their attention to Jacob. Magni was first to speak.

"Jacob, a royal name, did your man ever tell you about us?" he said winking at Modi, "Did he tell you how we always tease our little brother?"

"No," replied Jacob, "he just said that he was an only child." Magni affectionately clattered Odi across the back of the neck and all laughed, then proceeded to walk up the steps towards the main door of the temple.

Modi whispered to Jacob, "You do realise we now have two little brothers to tease!"

"Well then, let the battle begin." responded Jacob.

"Just for the record, where are your weapons?" asked Odi.

Both Magni and Modi went to extract their swords not realizing Jacob had used his powers to disarm both of them before walking up the steps. Modi said, "Nice one, so it's a war you want."

Thor threw his eyes to the heavens. Odin turned to his grandsons and reminded them that this is a formal event and they are to act with dignity and respect.

Jacob was slightly ahead, raised his hand, and used his new found powers to command the doors to magically open. When they opened the heralds announced the arrival of the Asgard gods. Maria linked Thor and walked through the entrance, Jacob walked through alongside Odi. They were followed by Odin, Magni and Modi. Maria, Odi and Jacob then parted and took their places alongside the Olympus gods.

The gods of the Asgard pantheon proceeded to walk through the Great Hall. Odin stepped back and watched his two grandsons march towards the throne. They bowed to Zeus who promptly stood and formally welcomed the Asgardians into his realm. With the formalities over, Zeus gestured to Athena and Aphrodite to introduce Magni and Modi to the assembly among whom they were treated as old friends.

Magni was intrigued by Maria and eventually made his way to be with her. His curiosity was getting the better of him. "I've always known that my father was lonely, and knew it had to be because of a love that was lost. I always wondered where Odi came from and my questions were never answered." He looked across at Odi, "look at him, the apple of father's eye. Now he has competition, I hope they get along." He paused for a moment then continued, "I promise to always be there for Jacob just as I would give my life for Odi."

Maria reached up and touched his cheek, "I've always been aware of you, War God of Asgard, and it warmed my heart to know my son was safe under your watchful eye. Thank you for being there for him."

"We watched the battle in Dublin through our oracles and it broke our hearts not to be able to assist." said Magni, "We watched Odi's efforts and wondered about the other god but couldn't identify who that god was. We now know Jacob was the other god." He cringed thinking of Jacob's demise. "Jacob needs training in the ways of battle and I'll make it my mission to ensure it happens because our oracles have identified him as a target of Lucifer and possibly even The Darkness. They believe the forces of evil are working to find his weakness and are sure they will find it, they believe it to be 'His Future'."

Jacob passed as Magni said, 'his future'. And in his mind he remarked how it was the third time those words were used, twice in the lagoon and now in the temple. It bothered him that this part of his future was still hidden.

"You're scaring me, Magni," said Maria standing to leave, "I didn't raise and protect my son for him to end up in a battle. I never envisioned my second son been trained as a War God. I, like your oracles, receive visions and the most recent has shown my sons fighting for their lives and it terrifies me. I pray your training will be a success."

❧❦

Soon a messenger arrived and announced to both Odin and Zeus that the gods from the South have been sighted. The messenger said that a vast and colourful caravan had crossed the Mountains of the Moon and entered the realm of Poseidon. They will soon be in the Sinai Desert. He said each god is believed to be travelling with an entourage of five hundred servants and guards.

Poseidon was aware of their sighting; he had already left the temple and made his way to the water's edge. He placed his trident into the waves and sent a message to the army of the Mer-People, instructing them to form a guard of honour for the gods of the southern realm as they crossed the Red

Sea. At the same time Zeus requested silence, "Word has reached me regarding the impending arrival of their southern guests. In their pantheon there are over seventeen hundred gods, and from among them, five have been chosen to represent the south. When they arrive I expect them to be held in high esteem and treated with the utmost respect." He then instructed the stewards to prepare.

The first of the Southern Pantheon to arrive was the Goddess Isis, known as the Mother Goddess whose beauty is reputed to surpass that of Queen Cleopatra. She is known for her kindness and her love of children as well as her desire to help those who are lost and in need. She also assists the souls of the recently deceased to find their way into the Underworld.

She arrived standing on the golden chariot once used by the Pharaoh Ra. She wore a tripartite wig held in place by her trademark throne-seat crown and she was draped in cream and golden robes held together by a gem encrusted belt. Her son, Horus, escorted her along with two hundred soldiers picked from the imperial guards of Egypt. Three hundred servants were also in her entourage.

The next god to arrive was Shango, one of the most powerful deities of the Orisha. He is the God of Thunder and Lightning, and royal ancestor to the Yoruba peoples of Western Africa. He stood on his chariot wearing the red and white clothing of his pantheon and the golden crown of a warrior king. He also wore the magical necklace of red and white beads. His procession was led by one hundred rams, followed by fifty Batu drummers and three hundred and fifty Yoruba warriors dressed in his favourite red colour. The haunting and guttural beat of the Batu drummers helped to announce his arrival at the gates of Olympus.

The next to arrive was the Goddess Mujatis. She is known as the Goddess of Fertility and Cleansing. She commands obedience from the ancient

Lovedu peoples. She arrived with five hundred ladies of the Lovedu nation, many who are her 'Rain Queens' responsible for the gentle rain that falls on the crops of her loyal followers. She is a protector of her subjects from all kinds of oppression; her power shows itself by removing the life-giving waters from any of her lands taken by force. She was dressed in a most decorative, deep forest green gown with a winged scarf draped across her shoulders depicting all the colours of the rainbow. Her headdress was made from the ferns of the forest, cultivated near Table Mountain. Her escorts include her loyal pets, two white mane lions, who are guardians of the desert prides.

Behind Mujatis came the god of the bush men tribes, protector of the Herero and Himbo peoples. His name is Mukuru, a benevolent deity, known for granting only positive energy. He functions by using the ancestors of the tribes to maintain peace. He also brings the rains when needed. He is a healing god and a carer for the sick. He's prayed to for help during turbulent times and always answers. His greatest gift to his followers is the Otjize paste, used as a protection against insects and the incessant heat of the sun in the deserts they inhabit. The very same paste used to solidify the plaits and braids in his hair, giving himself and his followers their identity. He walks at the head of his followers with his entourage, women and men, wearing nothing but a calf-skin skirt.

The final deity to arrive is Oya. She is considered a most powerful Goddess of Spirituality and is a sister of Shango. She was the one who gifted Shango the power to create storms. She is the guardian of the line between the living and the dead and has a great knowledge of the dark arts but she prefers to assist the white witches. She is merciless when provoked and can only speak the truth. She can change from a caring mother figure to a ruthless warrior without much thought. She is known to be a most loyal friend and powerful ally. She arrived in Olympus at the head of five hundred white witches, her most loyal followers. She is one of the most beautiful of the southern goddesses. Her vivid gown made from orange and black woven silk and a high brightly coloured Geles head wrap crown makes her stand out from her entourage who by her decree wear low head wraps.

The gods and goddesses of both Olympus and Asgard stood on the patio surrounding the temple as the Southern Pantheon procession made their way towards the meadows. As each group passed their god was greeted and brought to the steps. When all five reached the steps Zeus summoned the Olympus Pantheon to take their places in the temple. The stewards ensured all escorts were looked after and their animals fed and corralled.

When the heralds announced the arrival of the five Southern Gods, the doors opened and there were gasps of admiration as the most colourful and majestic of deities walked through the Great Hall. Zeus left his throne and was joined by Odin. Together they greeted their African visitors as equals. Zeus had worked with Isis and Oya in the past; it was during the fall of the Pharaohs. He had fought alongside Shango during the cosmic wars when they both needed to use their Thunder and Lightning powers to bring down a rogue demigod. He'd never met Mujatis or Mukuru. The Olympus gods made their latest visitors very welcome while waiting for the next arrivals.

It wasn't long before word reached Zeus that a herd of over one hundred elephants, had crossed the mountains of the east, carrying the gods of the Indus. He was pleased when told they are being assisted by the Yeti nation who is ensuring they safely cross the white lands. They were close to entering the meadows.

In the meantime the entourage from the Far East entered the meadows close to where Pegasus and the white horses were grazing. They were a group of one hundred priests and priestesses from temples located throughout Lord Buddha's realm. They were sharing the burden of carrying the golden image of their deity on a colourful and gilded palanquin. The load bearers alternated every hour ensuring the burden was shared. The priests and priestesses were shaven headed and dressed identically wearing the orange civara robes of the Buddhist clergy.

The procession reached the steps of the temple and the bearers placed the palanquin on the ground before uncovered the image of Lord Buddha. They prayed for a few moments before the gold leafs started falling from the statue. The wind increased and gently lifted the remaining gold leaves allowing the image of Buddha to soften and begin coming to life. He sat for a moment and then began to rise. As he rose his followers strained to get a glimpse of their god. They were mesmerised by how beautiful he was, how handsome he was, how tall he was. None of them have ever seen him in real life as he had moved into enlightenment over four hundred years earlier.

Lord Buddha walked up the steps of the temple and waited for the heralds to announce his arrival. When the doors opened and the heralds began their announcement, he walked towards Zeus. Again Zeus left his throne and greeted Lord Buddha as an equal. They had met before and were comfortable to be in each other's company. Lord Buddha enquired as to why he was called considering he never included himself among the gods. Zeus replied that he was needed for his calmness, his insights, his knowledge, his awareness but most importantly his wisdom.

The trumpeting of the elephants carrying the gods of the Indus could be heard and were getting louder. They entered the meadows close to where the white horses were grazing. The three gods representing the Indus pantheon decided to leave the elephants corralled near the temple and walk the remainder of the journey. On their way they were greeted by Thor and the Asgard pantheon. These two pantheons worked and fought together in the cosmic wars and had become great friends. Thor was particularly excited to meet his old friend, Lord Shiva, known as Shiva the Destroyer, also known as a creator, a protector, and a transformer within the universe. Thor was surprised he was there because he is known to rarely leave his home on Mount Kailash, but the call of Zeus was too strong. Thor then greeted Lord Krishna, also known as a reincarnation of the supreme god Vishnu, the Preserver God. Lastly Thor greeted Lord Brahma, the Indus Creator God of the Universe. All three gods prepared themselves for their entrance into the temple.

Zeus was quite excited and eagerly waiting for the arrival of the Gods of Indus. He'd never met them but was aware of their exploits. The stories of the vivid clothing they wore and the strings of precious jewels that adorn them were legendary.

The temple doors opened and the heralds of Olympus announced the arrival of the Indus gods. Lords Shiva, Krishna and Brahma proceeded to walk the length of the Great Hall acknowledging all those present as they passed. Zeus again left his throne and greeted them as equals. Odin joined Zeus and a brief but very serious conversation ensued.

Lord Shiva became distracted when he saw Jacob and Odi standing close to the plinth of Apollo. He excused himself and approached them. He placed his hand on Odi's shoulder, complimenting him on his powerful defence of the innocents during the battle of Dublin. He took Jacob's hand, closed his eyes, and watched as the future began to unfold. He then looked deeply into Jacobs eyes, "I can't see all of your future, that's strange. I do sense it; it's your future, or possibly you, Lucifer's after." He took the boys aside, "I've a confession, I was there during the attack. I was being prayed to in a small Indian restaurant to the side of Temple Bar square and had decided to answer those prayers. It was just as the forces of Hell unleashed their might. I tried to come to your aid but I was in a different dimension and I couldn't find a way to cross over to assist you. I'm so sorry. It was as though Hell's power was holding me back." Jacob and Odi bowed to him and acknowledged his regrets.

Zeus then asked all present to enjoy the hospitality of Olympus while awaiting the arrival of the next pantheon.

Three loud knocks were heard and the temple doors burst open. Without fanfare, two of the greatest wizards entered. One was Apollonius the Wanderer, Guardian of the Middle East and the second was Merlin the Great of the Mystical West. Behind them were three supreme elves, Ariella, Thalia and Kalen, representing all of Elf-kind. Zeus remarked on the beauty of the elves, admiring their long slender frames, their perfect faces and glistening hair. He wondered at the antiquity of the wizards with their ragged grey hair, pointed hats, long grey robes and staffs that had seen better days.

The Elves and Wizards proceeded through the temple as though gliding, drifting on a cloud. They greeted the gods as they made their way towards Zeus. "Always an honour to attend a gathering of the gods" said Apollonius as he embraced Zeus, "Like the elves we have come to represent all creatures of myth and legend."

"Your presence, wise wizard, is most welcome," replied Zeus. "All is threatened, and all should be represented." He then arranged for them to be introduced to the gathering in what was now a very crowded temple.

Zeus excused himself and walked towards his throne, he stood before the gathering and raised his hand in a gesture all understood to mean silence, "This is the greatest gathering of gods and astrals since the beginning of time. Enjoy this evening, tomorrow we discuss a most pressing and troubling issue. When the sun rises a difficult day awaits us. By your leave I ask your support in bestowing the gift of immortality on twelve youths from the local village. I believe their destiny has been set by the Ancient One. They will be the first to rise up against the power of Lucifer. When first I saw them I was angry, then in them I saw the spark of life, the primal Light, the first Light, I knew then they had been chosen."

All pantheons expressed their trust in Zeus's judgement and consented to immortality being granted. He then retired to his chambers and, after much more discussion; the stewards assisted all others to theirs. It became quiet as the Great Hall emptied except for Jacob, whose heart was racing. He was ecstatic knowing Eala was to be granted immortality the following day. He didn't hide his excitement as he anticipated himself and Eala being together for eternity.

Jacob's happiness meant that he couldn't sleep, he just wanted to celebrate. He was aware Odi had, earlier that morning, hijacked and hidden three casks of Dionysus's finest wine and he was determined to have a good time. It didn't take much to persuade Odi to party but they both forgot that due to the huge gathering, and shortage of rooms, they were sharing with Magni and Modi. They needn't have worried; Magni and Modi had also secured two small barrels of ale and had already emptied one.

On seeing Jacob, Magni said, "Tell me young god, will you be able for to keep up with us? Your mother said she kept you safe and protected."

"Fear not old man," said Jacob uncorking a cask, "Shane and I had a hiding place behind our school gym and on many a night we drank and smoked, things mother wouldn't approve of. I'll drink you under the table."

"You challenge the Asgard God of War?" said Magni moving to upend Jacob.

Odi quickly lined up four glasses and filled them, "Jacob is my twin and for the first time I'm confident you're going to be beaten. Drink up and shut up."

The four sons of Thor partied until early the next morning, emptying all casks. The drinking games played that night became legendary and the talk of the temple. They joked, sang, laughed and wrestled, then one by one fell asleep.

The following morning their absence didn't go unnoticed. It was unacceptable for princes of Asgard or Olympus not to be present at breakfast to greet guests of Zeus or Odin. Thor reached their room to find a state of devastation obviously caused by a wild and drunken party. All four of his sons were comatose. Magni was on his back with his head and shoulders hanging from the side of the bed and one of his legs dangling over the bedpost. Modi was at the top of the bed with one leg hanging over the headboard and his other leg touching the floor. Jacob and Odi were both lying across their beds one face down and the other on his back with both their feet resting on the floor. Thor's temper rose so high he used his hammer to hit the floor causing a tremor that shook the boys out of their sleep.

Odi was first to waken, he didn't care when he saw his father standing over him, "Hi father, still proud of me, now go away." He then fell back asleep.

Magni was half awake and heard what Odi said, he covered his face in horror "Oh Odi, Idiot, have you learned nothing? You don't talk to the mighty Thor like that. Thanks for that, we'll all pay."

Thor's anger continued to grow. He gripped Odi and Jacob by their ankle and threw them over his shoulders. He carried them across to the cold water bath and dropped them into the icy waters. This time Jacob was first to waken, he gasped as the cold waters, at first shocked him, and then began to resuscitate him. Odi woke while under water and struggled to expel the water from his lungs. His head was pounding and he started retching. He saw Jacob was recovered and begged him for help. Jacob stretched across and placed his hand on Odi's head. After a few moments Odi recovered. They left the water and with their heads down they did the walk of shame passing their father. Odi had difficulty containing himself, knowing what was about to happen to his two older brothers.

Jacob and Odi sat on the edge of their beds watching their father's temper grow. Odi got particular pleasure watching Magni being grabbed by both ankles and thrown across the room. It was a perfect throw as Magni landed directly into the ice cold water. He groaned as he flew across the room and yelled loud enough to awaken the dead as he hit the water. Modi by now was fully awake and decided to hide at the side of his bed but he should have known better. Thor used one hand to lift the bed out of his way leaving Modi very vulnerable. Modi knew what was coming and decided it was best not to resist. He stood, walked over to the bath, and threw himself in.

Thor looked again at his four sons and shook his head in disappointment. He insisted they be in the Great Hall, dressed in their ceremonial robes, and ready for the council in fifteen minutes. Magni pleaded to be excused as his head really hurt but one look from his father said it all.

Thor left the room, slamming the door. Odi, being Odi just couldn't let it go, he began teasing but Jacob stopped him, knowing this council was just too important. He decided to sort everything. He helped his brothers to recover. He then used his time-travel powers and went back by two hours to the kitchens, to when the cooks were preparing the first breakfasts. After returning to his room they fed and quickly dressed, then briskly made their way towards the Great Hall.

They stood at a side door of the hall, took a deep breath and walked in, in single file. They looked really impressive in the full ceremonial robes of the Asgard pantheon. The relief on Thor's face was tangible and, although he was still angry, he looked at his sons and was proud, they might have embarrassed themselves last night but they knew when to play, most importantly they knew when to present themselves as future leaders. The great bell of the temple then tolled, summoning the gods out to the amphitheatre, situated to the left of the walled garden just next to the wildflower meadow.

Chapter 14

Zeus exited the temple from behind his throne and walked by the ornamental pond next to the wildflower meadows. He made his way towards the walled garden to take his place in the amphitheatre. In the distance, the sight of the snow covered mountains leading to the enchanted realm of the northern nymph lords was breath taking. He stopped to take in the view, a view which up until now he never really appreciated. He remarked to those close by how the view across his domain was awe inspiring. It was then he summoned Jacob, "I've a task for you. Go to the village and bring your friends back to the temple. I intend granting them the gift of Immortality before the council commences. It'll be good for them to witness the greatest gathering of immortals since the beginning of time."

Jacob had difficulty containing his excitement and just as he was about to leave, Zeus warned him, "Tell your friend their fears and apprehensions will pass, their grief for their families will lessen. The gift of immortality will bring them many of the strengths required for the success of their journey. Help them understand that as the years pass, their abilities will become more powerful."

Jacob used his powers to transport himself to the village where he materialised out of view, and immediately gathered his friends together. Their families also gathered and there were a lot of tears as they realised the time had come for them to say goodbye, and they were fully aware that this goodbye was forever. Jacob felt guilty when he saw the distress he caused but he put that distress aside, remembering the importance of what was about to happen. He tried to comfort the families.

After a short time, he, his friends and most of the villagers walked to the outskirts of the village. On reaching the portal he said, "Today will be the last day you will see your families, you have been chosen by the Ancient One for a grave task. If you feel you cannot move forward you must decide now. There will be no going back. You'll face great dangers and may even face death but you will be trained to deal with each challenge. Are you still prepared to enter Olympus?"

Eala's father took her into his arms and said trying to hold back his tears, "My beautiful daughter, you will always be treasured in our hearts. It pleases us that you have found favour with the gods so go with our blessing." The other parents also encouraged their sons or daughters to go.

Fafner had nobody to send him on his way. Jacob felt his sadness. He stood next to him and quietly said, "Always remember you've been chosen by the Ancient One. The moment you walk through the portal you become part of my family, I'll always be there for you.....and yours."

Fafner remained silent looking at the grief around him, and then asked, "You called me your mythical dragon, why did you say that?"

"I said it because I know who you are," replied Jacob while guiding him to a nearby stream. "Look into the water and tell me what you see."

"For a moment, a fleeting moment, I saw a dragon," said a startled Fafner. "What does it mean?"

"Look to the hills and tell me what you see," replied Jacob.

"There's two, are they watching me?" asked Fafner.

"Yes," said Jacob while guiding him back to the portal. "They've always been watching over you, they're the spirits of your parents. You were never alone. They're of the dragon realm and are waiting for you to return there to become who you were born to be." Jacob backed away and then bowed, "Hail Fafner, Emperor of the Dragons." Fafner wanted to say more but Jacob gestured for him to say nothing.

The time arrived for the portal to be opened and it was also a time for heart wrenching scenes of grief. There were many hugs, kisses and lots of tears as each one walked through the shield.

Jacob opened the portal so wide the villagers were able to look through and view a most magnificent amphitheatre and behind that a vast temple. This comforted them when they saw their children were being welcomed among the gods.

Zeus was present when they entered and he was surprised Jacob had allowed the temple and some of the gods to be seen but trusted his judgement and felt his actions had served a good purpose. When all were through, the portal closed and everyone went towards their seats.

Zeus and the three most senior Gods of the Olympus pantheon - Poseidon, Hades and Chiron took their seats at the northern end of the amphitheatre. The next Gods to take their seats were the three gods of the Indus pantheon, followed by Lord Buddha and they sat to the right of Zeus. The three elves and two wizards representing the Astrals took their seats to the left of Zeus followed by the Asgard gods consisting of Odin, Thor, Magni and Modi. The five southern gods then arrived and sat alongside the Asgard gods. There were seven seats remaining, they were set aside in the hope of the arrival of the Archangels. Zeus hoped they'd appear especially since the first sightings of an Archangel in such a long time happened only thirty years earlier when Gabriel entered the realm of man carrying a message of hope.

After the gods took their seats Jacob's friends were brought to the amphitheatre and were seated facing the council. They sat alongside the remaining gods of Olympus, senior advisers and all the heralds that summoned their respective pantheons only two days earlier.

Zeus, Odin, Shango and Shiva then left their seats and walked to the centre of the arena and were joined by Merlin. Shango stepped forward and called each of Jacob's friends one by one to stand before them. Merlin said in a loud and thunderous voice, "Ancient One, send your Light, allow it touch the souls of those who stand before us."

Within seconds the crystal stone at the head of his staff illuminated sending beams of light out to enter the heads of all twelve causing a brilliant iridescent light to completely surround them. The girls were first to step forward and when they settled the gods placed their hands on each of their heads bestowing on them the gift of immortality. The eight boys then stepped forward and when the gods placed their hands upon them, they too were granted the same gift. Through all this, all twelve kept their eyes closed allowing their senses absorb all of what was happening to them. What they didn't realise was their senses were taking them out across the cosmos where they were being shown the ways of the universe. They were being shown the planets and the stars, comets, pulsars and quasars. They were being subsumed into the very essence of the universe. They were now immortals.

It was a moving and emotional ceremony with each of them receiving different powers but the most important one they all received was the power to call on the Light. When the ceremony ended they opened their eyes, were a little confused but felt very different. They bowed to the gods and returned to their seats.

Zeus summoned Maria, "Today is a momentous occasion and it should be recorded. Once I knew a man, it was over eight hundred years ago. He amused me, was entertaining but most importantly he was a scribe, poet and chronicler. His name was Homer. Use your Time Lord power and bring him to the council with a request for him to record all that happens here today."

Maria immediately left and within minutes returned with Homer. The poor man was terrified but he was also excited when he recognised he was recording and witnessing a most wondrous event. He sat before Zeus and without question laid out rolls of papyrus and prepared to start writing.

Zeus stood and marvelled at all those in attendance. It was the gathering of pantheons full of colour, variety, complexity and a wide assortment of powers. It was a magnificent sight to behold. He composed himself and then began -

"My sisters and brothers," he said while composing himself. "Never before has there been such a gathering. I called you together at the behest of Odin, my great friend, because we are facing a terrible and sinister threat. The oracles within our pantheons have been alarmed for some time now. They have foreseen the End Times for this age of man. As you are aware, over the last number of months serpents have been appearing in our realms, probing the defences of both man and gods. They first appeared in the northern ice lands of Asgard, they also appeared in the oceans attacking the realm of Poseidon. Then, outside these very walls, they attacked two gods of Olympus and almost succeeded in killing them. In the distant future, while travelling through time those same gods will be attacked in the city of Dublin. This attack will cause the death of one of those gods and, but for the intervention of Poseidon we would be mourning him. What these attacks show us is the evolving power of these serpents. They have the power to shape shift, they have the power to transform into Dark Angels."

Zeus paused for a moment before continuing, "Let me remind you of the beginning! All that there was, was The Darkness. The Ancient One said, 'let there be light', this infuriated The Darkness but the Light prevailed. He then created the first man, Adam and after him came Eve, the first woman. Even then The Darkness was planning their downfall. For millennia Adam and Eve lived in harmony. Their home was the Garden of Eden and they were happy with all that was natural. The Darkness didn't give up. It sent a serpent, similar to the ones who are appearing now. That serpent deceived Eve and was responsible for bringing about the end of the first age of man."

Zeus paused again, looked around before continuing, "The second age of man began with the expulsion of Adam and Eve from Eden. They had four sons and two daughters. It wasn't long before a serpent appeared again. This serpent was cunning and different, he broke his allegiance with The Darkness and set up his own domain, he too was a shape shifter who in fact was an Archangel. Lucifer was his name and he alone was responsible for the fall of the angels. He created discord, disharmony and jealously leading to the first killing. The eldest son of Adam, Cain was his name, murdered Abel, one of his brothers. The descendants of Adam then came from Cain and two of the younger brothers, Seth and Enoch. There were also descendants from the two daughters but it was too late as again the serpent had corrupted the line of Adam. For generations those who bore the mark of Cain prevailed. They slaughtered their cousins, they brought famine and corruption. They abused their wives, daughters, sisters and mothers. They ignored the wishes and righteous laws of the gods. They poisoned their lands and then took their neighbours lands. They destroyed the forests. They used the animal kingdom for sport. They angered me."

There was absolute silence, not a sound, Zeus continued, "Ten thousand years ago, I, without your consent, decided to end the line of Cain. I brought forth the storm; I used the thunder and unleashed the rains that flooded the land of Cain. It was the great flood. This was my plan but again the serpent was watching and waiting. He punctured the walls of the highest mountains and opened the natural dams in the valleys. He caused the flooding of the lands of Seth, Enoch and the daughters of Adam. Mankind was all but wiped out but for the survival of two men. I looked in their faces and a great guilt entered my heart. I reached out to them and decided man deserved another chance to repopulate the Earth. I asked them to follow the laws of the Ancient One. To go forth, multiply and be happy and free as it was always intended. I showed those two men a way, told them to walk along a lonely road, each to pick up a pebble and throw it over their shoulder. I assured them that from each pebble will grow a man or a woman therefore taking away their loneliness. They were to do this every few paces until they reached the end of the road. They followed my guidance and from this was born the third age of man."

Zeus again looked around at the gathering and saw they were all enthralled with his story, especially the younger gods, he continued, "Today, yet again we watch as man goes down the path of folly. Man has forgotten the Ancient One; he has allowed the serpent back amongst him. I ask you all. Do we together save this age of man? Do we allow the Dark one to destroy everything that is good, everything that has come from the Light or do we fight?"

Just as he was about to continue Hades stood up as though a bolt of lightning had struck him, he was in pain. He looked confused and slowly walked towards Zeus. He stopped many times before reaching him; it was as though some terrible images were flooding his mind. He placed his hand on Zeus's arm and whispered, "Something's wrong, I've weakened. The Underworld is slipping from my grasp. I must go and go now." He excused himself and weakly walked towards an exit.

Jacob left his seat to assist and as soon as he placed his hand on Hades' shoulder he saw the images of Hell and sensed all that was going on in the

Underworld. He stopped Hades, "You're being deceived and you're walking into a trap. Bring Ares and Athena with you. They will be your protectors." Hades was getting weaker and his judgement clouded. He knew Zeus absolutely trusted Jacob so agreed for Ares and Athena to join him. Together they opened, and then entered a portal, allowing them access to the Underworld. Jacob watched them cautiously travel towards the gates of Hell. He saw that the Gates of Heaven were shut tightly and were being guarded by armed Angels. The portal closed and he returned back to his seat.

Zeus, although unsettled by the interruption resumed his speech, "We know the serpents have entered the realms of Poseidon, Asgard and Olympus, and now it seems the Underworld. It's time to make a choice, fight to protect what is good in mankind or choose to end this third age of man before their souls are destroyed, taken to the domain of The Darkness or the dungeons of Hell. Yesterday we saw through Jacob's vision what an onslaught from Hell is likely to be. Do we allow this to happen?" He sat and waited for a reaction.

The Indus gods, Lord Buddha and the southern pantheons all disagreed with the ending of the third age of man. They wanted to fight and insisted Olympus and Asgard should do the same. Shango spoke, "For centuries our peoples have adoringly revered the Orisha and we in turn brought forth the harvests. Our peoples deserve our protection."

"I agree," said Lord Shiva. "Look how they have evolved, their art, their writings the architecture. Don't punish them all for the sins of the few. The serpents haven't slithered into our lands as yet, we can prepare."

The elves agreed. The wizards intervened and suggested it was not the place of the War Gods to undo the plans of the Ancient One.

The Asgard and Olympus pantheons, being War Gods, were more ruthless and were prepared to end the third age. They didn't expect to stand alone especially as all the senior gods were leaning towards an ending, they had expected their allies to support them, a support they didn't get.

Jacob saw the confusion in the faces of both of his grandfathers. He also saw the confusion and turmoil in the faces of his friends who were getting more concerned for their families. As he and his mother were the only gods to have lived among men he sought permission to address the gathering which was granted. He left his seat, joined Zeus and after a brief conversation turned and faced the gathering. He prepared to speak.

Just as he was about to speak, a vibrant white light appeared above the amphitheatre. The light split into seven shards and travelled down to land at the seats set aside for the Archangels. Jacob's jaw dropped, he'd only ever read about three Archangels and now he was about to meet seven. The Archangels took their places, remained quiet and waited for Zeus to greet them. Zeus welcomed them each by name, Michael, Gabriel, Raphael, Uriel, Selaphiel, Raguel and Barachile. Jacob thought it was strange that they didn't bow to Zeus.

Michael stood and was first to speak. He stood as the most powerful of them all. His regal purple robes braided in gold touched the ground and his pure white wings spread out behind him. His golden hair and piercing blue eyes showed all before him that he was touched by the hand of the Ancient One. His legendary sword, the very one he used to lead Lucifer to his incarceration, hung to his left and in his right hand he held a scroll. He appeared as the supreme commander of the legions of Heaven. He walked to the centre of the arena telling those gathered that he carried a message from the Ancient One. He unfurled the scroll, and announced that it was written by that same god. The message it carried was clear!

"Back in the mists of time I decreed that Man, my creation, was to be left to find his own way. Time and time again he's been a disappointment, but even so, I believe he will evolve. I still care. I watched him use his ingenuity to nurture ideas, to share, to create, to make his life and the lives of others better, and that makes me happy. I've also witnessed his failings; his penchant for deceit, his violence, the pain he inflicts seems to know no bounds, and that hurts me. I think of you, Gods of the Cosmos, and am pleased by how your guidance and power have maintained peace, and nurtured the growth, even against the continuous meddling by Lucifer. Your battle against his forces will intensify, leading to what he believes will be the End Times battle. Worse still, he has awoken The Darkness, and it's already spreading it's terror across the Universe. I know some of you want to end this third age of Man, that's unwise, you will need them, so their demise must not happen. Let me remind you that you are my guardians of the souls worth saving; those souls have much to do and achieve. Continue to support and nurture them, they are the ones that will grow and bring great joy. They will be the carriers of a message and will assist in protecting the Light. At the beginning of time I blew a speck of dust out into the universe, a seed destined to germinate in Jacob's mind. That seed has now germinated and he will have begun to put in place a plan to usher in a natural transition into the fourth age of man. There will be many impediments to his journey, many trials, losses and setbacks. There will be times of calmness, golden ages that for some will last for hundreds of years but even they will not last. The one thing common to all your oracles is the End Times Battle. Although the future isn't set in stone, this one is. There are many paths in the future but in this case all lead to the same thing, a battle, a storm; a terrible storm. It's coming. Your challenge is not only to protect man, it's to unite and fight the power of Hell before sending The Darkness back to the Nothingness. If my Archangels have reached you it means there's no doubt Lucifer has risen.

His plan is to destroy me and claim dominion over man; he failed once and will fail again."

Gabriel then stood to join Michael. He was clothed in a sky blue robe, emblazoned with images of the white lily and he too had the purest of white wings. In his right hand he held a shining lantern, the beacon that calls all true souls to Heaven. In his left he held his trumpet, the very one that brings fear to all those who hear its tune. To all those he visited his compassion showed when he said, 'Be not afraid.'

Gabriel began, "Some days ago my brother Michael succeeded in capturing a serpent travelling towards the Indus nations. This serpent was resilient and survived all his efforts to retrieve Lucifer's plans. We knew they were evolving when he transformed into a Dark Angel similar to those that attacked Jacob and Odi in Dublin. He was powerful, well trained in the dark arts and had the skills of a warrior angel but he couldn't withstand my power. He succumbed to my trumpet, its sound blown by the messenger carrying the voice of God. Between screams he told us Lucifer is targeting Jacob and Odi, two new and very powerful gods. They are aware Jacob has developed many of his powers but has not mastered them. They sneer at Odi, knowing he has the same powers and will not master them for many years. In Jacob's future there is something Lucifer wants but the Dark Angel Michael captured didn't know what it was. The Oracles, the angels or the wizards cannot see that part of Jacob's future so therefore we cannot plan his protection."

Raphael joined them and he too stood as most powerful. His emerald green robe was held by a golden belt and his cream wings fanned out proudly behind him. He was dark haired and had the deepest of brown eyes. He is the guardian of travellers and a healing angel. He turned to Jacob,

"It has been decided that my brother's will return to lead the armies of the heavens and I will remain behind to watch over the journey of your messengers and will, on rare occasions, step in to assist and steer them to their destination. I will also be preparing the way for the legions of Heaven to assist mankind if the End Times battle goes wrong. The armies of the Light may one day need us and we will be ready, waiting to answer that call."

The remaining Archangels didn't speak. Jacob knew there was now nothing for him to say, all he wanted to say was said by Michael. He returned to join Eala.

After returning to his seat a portal opened revealing a distressing sight. Hades, Athena and Ares came through, scarred, bleeding and charred. Ares announced the fall of the Underworld and that between the three of them they managed to secure the gates of Hell, successfully stopping the escape of any more demonic serpents. Athena said, "It's unknown how many serpents have escaped, there could be thousands slithering and biting their way through the realm of man, there's no way of knowing."

Hades now presented as a broken god, ashamed his powers failed to see this coming. He looked at his brothers and sisters fearing they'd disown him. He shook his head in disbelief, wondering how he could be so deceived by Lucifer. The Archangels sensed his distress and tried to reassure him, "You do understand?" said Gabriel taking him aside, "You were up against the most cunning of them all and its likely Lucifer put in place his plan to take over the Underworld thousands of years ago, possibly even before the fall of the angels." They then assured him his return to the Underworld would happen; bringing it back into balance but not for many years to come.

Zeus, because of the intervention of the Archangels ended the council. Although concerned, he would never go against a request from the Ancient One. He decided to assist Jacob to ensure the plans he was working on would succeed. He invited all present to enjoy the hospitality of Olympus and asked the Archangels to join him for supper, an invitation they readily accepted. There was great wonderment and jostling among the younger gods, none of them had ever met an angel, let alone seven Archangels.

Jacob remained with Eala, all the time hoping for an opportunity to whisk her to somewhere quiet so they could spend as much time alone and away from the hustle and bustle of the temple. They decided that wouldn't be appropriate. They climbed higher up the steps to seats slightly hidden by a pillar. They sat in a loving embrace, enjoying their time kissing and cuddling. Jacob made himself more comfortable by moving his legs across the next two seats so he could lay his head on her lap. She stretched slightly back, leaning against the step behind, allowing both of them to watch the puffed up clouds scurry by. They had fun trying to identify all kinds of shapes in those same clouds.

It was now mid afternoon and Eala continued to gently caress Jacobs head, neck and face. He was so happy he closed his eyes and slowly drifted away into bliss, he didn't want these moments to pass but as the clouds thickened, shadows grew. One shadow arrived and completely blocked the sun causing him to open his eyes. For a moment all he saw was a purple haze and as his eyes focused he realized it was Michael standing before him. He leapt to his feet and composed himself, apologising for ignoring him. "Walk with me, young god," said Michael gesturing him towards a nearby exit. Eala out of respect backed away and went to walk among the gods.

"You trouble us," said Michael. "We see your future and its many paths. We see Eala all the way to the End Times and you are there, we can't see how you got there as some of your future is hidden from us. We see your brother, his children and grandchildren, we see his royal status. Why can't we see yours? Is it because Lucifer knows more than we do? At times we see something, something so small. Then we see him and his determination.

You have something he wants. Why do oracles say it's Your Future? What is your future and that is the question?"

Michael and Jacob walked through the meadows where they discussed strategies and tactics. It was then when Michael confirmed that the battle for Earth will not happen for two millennia. "Zeus told us of your vision; he believes you have witnessed the plans of Lucifer. He said you travelled through the bowels of Hell and experienced the terror and torment of the fallen angels, and the lost souls. Will you allow me travel into the furthest reaches of your mind and let me see if anything has been missed?" Jacob agreed, he sat on a nearby boulder and lowered his head. Michael placed his hand upon Jacob's head and within seconds began to see and experience the rise of Lucifer.

The other six Archangels arrived and they too saw the rise of Hell, they sensed and felt all Jacob was sharing with Michael. Together all seven travelled through his mind opening every door. They were unflinching and determined while searching every memory until they reached Hell. There they watched and studied Lucifer's followers laying out their plans to deceive Hades. While there they shared in the pain of the lost souls and witnessed the constant state of terror, especially when the hunger grew in Lucifer. They watched him and his generals tease and torment the lost souls, how they used their spears and fires to skewer and roast them. They saw that his reign of terror was unending but they quickly saw that this horror was hiding his true intentions.

Jacob's vision showed Hades departing for the council of Olympus and leaving his trusted guards protecting the gates of the Underworld. It showed how Lucifer gathered his forces and destroyed the guards, pulling them apart and devouring their souls. The visions showed him standing at the entrance to Hell, triumphantly, with his wings spread and the most devious smile upon his face as the dark light of Hell's flames glowed orange behind him. It also showed Lucifer was also being deceived as unknown to him The Darkness was presenting as relentless and all powerful. Planning not to cease until all light was gone including the dim light of the fires of Hell.

Chapter 15

Jacob's vision showed the Archangels how, way back in time, a sequence of events unfolded in hidden corners of Hell. One vision showed the location of a sinister and ominous cell. The Archangels saw it was in a cavern so deep and isolated that no soul would dare seek, let alone enter it. The sense of malice showed it to be the foreboding and dire abode of Lucifer, leader of the fallen angels. It seemed unchanged since he was placed there, hidden and unseen, as he was considered to be the darkest Archangel of them all. Through Jacob's vision Michael recognised the cell and was happy he and Hades had it well secured.

Hades had promised to visit every week to check and ensure nothing had changed. He maintained that practice for thousands of years and never failed in his duty. Jacob's vision showed him regularly visiting the cell including his last visit. It confirmed the cocoon encasing Lucifer, was as always, intact and resting at the centre of the cell. The cocoon presented as a black crystalline marble rock glistening and shimmering through the bars of the cell, reflecting Hells fires. In this part of Jacob's vision Lucifer couldn't be seen. His image was obliterated as part of his punishment for leading the rebellion against the Ancient One.

"It was before the first war," said Michael, "the war between the Light and The Darkness, when Lucifer began to resent the Ancient One. This resentment turned to hatred and led to the rebellion of the fallen angels. After much destruction Lucifer was captured; he was then escorted to Hell under my watchful eye. I've always wondered why he never looked concerned, now I know! It seems some of his most loyal followers, who had escaped the wrath of the Ancient One, schemed and put in place plans which have now come to fruition."

While continuing to watch Jacob's vision, Michael expressed his surprise at how many followers had escaped. He watched them scheme while hiding behind ancient magic and couldn't believe how quickly they worked on a plan to release their master. He saw the geneses of their plot to organise his escape, firstly by seeking from among humanity, men nurtured as warlocks, leading to them becoming masters in the dark arts. Secondly the warlocks, having learned the ways of The Darkness, would become practiced in long forgotten incantations of old. Their whole purpose was to seek out, and then assist in the release of Lucifer. Michael could see that as the warlocks searched, the escaped followers of Lucifer slept.

The Archangels saw that the lair of the followers was deep beneath an old abandoned temple in the ancient lands of Persia and could see that their sleep lasted for millennia. He believed that when the first signs of The Darkness appeared Lucifer's followers would rise.

Michael looked towards the heavens as twilight approached and saw the stars were beginning to shine. "I fear the subtle dimming in the far distant galaxies once seen on a bright and clear evening like this evening. It will be the signal that alerts Lucifer's followers to the spread of The Darkness. They will rejoice in the relentless march and endless appetite for the most translucent and brightest stars as it feeds its hunger. They've awoken and know its coming. They believe it to be an ally and will seek out the warlocks to begin their preparations for the assault on the Underworld."

The Archangels continued to probe Jacob's mind where he showed them how the warlocks had formed numerous covens consisting of twelve warlocks each and how they had spread out throughout the realm of man. They listened to the continuous incantations as the warlocks practiced their magic and used long forgotten spells. Jacob showed Michael how the warlocks stood motionless, chanting endlessly around a bright fiercely burning fire. It was the only light in an otherwise dank and dimly lit chamber. He was showing how they were using these chants to assist them in locating their master. He then showed them how eventually a black mist rose from within several of the fires and took the shape of powerful Dark Angels who proceeded to walk among the warlocks. They could see that these angels were messengers of The Darkness and loyal to Lucifer. They all watched as the Dark Angels gave the warlocks the location and the pathway, to the cell that held Lucifer. With their assistance they had now found a way, they were given the Black Mist.

Jacob's vision continued and showed how a miniscule crack in the cavern wall became its weakest point. It was through this crack that a dark energy, the sinister black mist, entered the cell and began the process of resurrecting Lucifer. The Archangels watched as each visit used more and more of that same dark energy and as time passed the black mist visited more frequently. What troubled them was how the dark mist was protected by what seemed to be a magic known only to those who practiced the dark arts.

Jacob showed how their efforts were meticulous. How their plan began by making contact with condemned souls and forcing them to act as spies, monitoring everywhere he went. These spies reported, checked and re-checked the times when Hades visited. They watched his every movement especially when he called on Lucifer's cell and soon established there were roughly six days between each visit.

It was after his latest visit when the plan was activated. The dark mist used the miniscule crack in the wall of the cell laying a pathway for the Dark Angels to follow. It took many attempts but again, with the assistance of the warlocks, the Dark Angels melded into the black mist and found themselves able to make their way through the crack. When through, they materialised around the cocoon and with the help of an incantation given to them by those same warlocks, they were able to break the binding spell.

They stood back and watched in awe as Lucifer was freed from his incarceration and were amazed at how quickly he broke free. They couldn't take their eyes from him as he rose from a squatting position to spread his dark jet black wings out across the cell, those same wings that had surrounded and protected him for thousands of years. It was a breath- taking sight as they watched their master begin to take control. His chiselled good looks showed he was once a favourite of the Ancient One. His vanity wouldn't allow his followers share his image so he was pleased when he looked on the faces of the Dark Angels and saw that they all bore the face of soulless demons.

To help with his escape more wisps of the black mist arrived. These particular mists swirled, at first softly and then violently, eventually forming into four more Dark Angels, generals who sided with Lucifer during the first war. They stood before their master and confirmed their allegiance. Lucifer immediately seized one of the minor Dark Angels and encased him into the vacant cocoon. He ensured that the cocoon was placed back into the exact spot on which it had stood for thousands of years. He then set in motion his plan for the four generals and the remaining Dark Angels to lead the legions of serpents against Jacob's messengers in the north, south, east and west.

Michael turned to his brother angels and expressed his surprise that Lucifer knew of Jacob's plans but couldn't figure out how he knew of Jacob considering he had been encased in the cocoon for thousands of years, long before Olympus was founded. He wondered as to what else was at play.

Jacob wasn't finished. He then showed Michael how Lucifer located a suitable hiding place and used this place to prepare his plan to deceive and then expel Hades from the Underworld, working under the premise that the longer he went unnoticed; the stronger his position would be to continue preparing his plan for dominion over man.

For Michael it seemed more than a coincidence that this deception commenced near the time when Jacob and Odi were born. Or was it? Michael wondered did Lucifer's power of prophecy foretell the births at the time of his fall from grace, allowing him to know who his enemies were long before they were born. He wondered was he really that powerful.

Michael continued to rest his hand on Jacob's forehead. He established Lucifer had regained many of his powers and after being released from the cocoon, began using them again. He saw that the two powers treasured the most were his powers of prophecy and possession. He then watched Lucifer observe the births of Jacob and Odi and was pleased to see a degree of fear; he assumed Lucifer was aware of Jacob's power and how it was a threat to his dominion over man. He also watched him observe Dione enact her deception of Zeus. The one thing that unsettled Michael the most was the fact that Lucifer was aware of the plans Jacob was preparing for his friends to save mankind.

The most upsetting thing for the Archangels was the part of Jacob's vision showing them how Lucifer turned the Underworld, most especially, Hell, into a place of permanent torment for the fallen angels and the lost souls. How each turn within the caves will bring those same souls to a more sinister place full of unimaginable horrors, starting with the volcanic seas. How the continuous flow of lava would gush like a raging river, in some places forming shallow pools to be used by the demons to dip the distraught souls just for fun. How the foul smell of sulphur and the rancid odour of decay will be their permanent companion. For the poor souls all they will see, beyond the dim light of the lava flows, will be the unending darkness from which the piercing and harrowing screams of other tortured souls will be heard. Within the dim light there is no glimmer of hope as there is no rest only never ending pain, burnings, blisters, whippings then impalement. The worst time for them will be when the hunger takes Lucifer and his generals. How they'd ride out through the vast caverns and spear soul after soul before tearing them limb from limb, chewing them and then discarding them only for the same agony to start all over again.

Jacob also showed the Archangels how Lucifer and his generals will sit within a circle of fire, putting in motion their plans to use the serpents throughout the next two thousand years. How the serpents will be escorted from Hell and given the power to transform into Dark Angels and how throughout history they will target certain individuals. How they will bite them, slightly poisoning them, allowing the poison to turn them towards The Darkness. In time these people will become warrior kings, generals, popes, tyrants, instigators of war and will be responsible for the mass murder of countless innocents throughout the ages. They will send many into the arms of Lucifer feeding his hunger for souls. They will create weapons of mass destruction and be responsible for famine and pestilence, because of them genocide will be a word used many times. These evil people will poison the land, kill the forests, pollute the seas and destroy the skies.

Jacob requested a rest, the constant horror images were weighing heavily on him and he needed to breathe. The Archangels stepped away and he took a few moments. He looked up at the snow-capped mountains and allowed himself to absorb their beauty. He waved back at Eala who was always close by and ready to come to his assistance. He felt her love and warmth reach him and began to relax, he then prepared again for the Archangels to re-enter his head.

They placed their hands back on his head and this time Jacob showed them how Lucifer was building his allies. He showed them how he, once freed, began his takeover of Hell. How he methodically worked his way through the caverns, securing cave after cave and placing his converted demons in charge. His cunning knew no bounds. His strategy was working with the help of the terrorised souls. His efforts were hidden from Hades by the complicity of those same tormented lost souls. His demons and turned souls hid in the shadows as day after day Hades walked through the caverns. Their plans worked as he failed to notice how everything had changed. Their deception of Hades was complete.

The Archangels observed Hades leave for Olympus and then watched in horror as in his absence; Lucifer and his demons rode out from Hell to take control of the Underworld. They heard him threatening and beating his demons into continuing a relentless and vengeful onslaught against the guards as well as the new souls who had arrived for their journey towards either Heaven or Hell.

The biggest prize of all for him is capturing the gates of Heaven, but he knew that this was doomed to failure; even so he never gave up hope. He was also heard pleading for his ally, The Darkness, to come to his aid. They all watched the most violent attack ever to afflict the Underworld continue as Lucifer's army wiped out the remaining guards and loyal soldiers of Hades. They saw that the Underworld had fallen and Lucifer now had his realm but not the prize of the gates of Heaven which steadfastly continued to elude him.

The Archangels continued to probe Jacob's visions. They were concerned for the safety of Heaven. They knew the gates in the ocean and in the sky were secure, with legions of angel's constantly on guard, but they were concerned for the main gate, the very one situated in the Underworld. Jacob's vision showed the gatekeepers successfully closing it, and the guardian angels taking up defensive positions. They watched as the forces of evil attacked, throwing everything they had at it before withdrawing.

Jacob had difficulty watching the onslaught of evil working its way through the Underworld. He was distraught watching Lucifer and his generals particularly target souls of the Light, to be torn asunder in the most horrendous and torturous ways imaginable. The Archangels had the same difficulty; they sent an urgent message to all soul escorts, instructing them to only use either the gates in the ocean, or the one in the sky.

Chapter 16

Jacob struggled; he gasped while receiving a new vision. This one showing a demon carrying what looked like the head of a Titan. It showed three more arriving, carrying between them a torso. Both parts pocked marked not unlike the bark of the great oak tree. "Lucifer is intrigued," said Jacob trying to stand. "It won't be long before he realises who the parts belong to."

"Keep watching and listening," said Michael. "Strange how, with all his powers, he hasn't detected us observing?"

The demons placed the two parts on the ground before Lucifer, and watched as the two parts magically came together. As soon as they joined, the eyes and mouth opened and an unmerciful groan of rage was heard. Lucifer moved closer, it was dawning on him who he was looking at. He circled twice saying nothing, his mind was racing and a plan was coming together. He stood and stared down at the gruesome face looking back at him. Jacob heard Lucifer say, "We meet again. Lord of the Titans."

"You are not one I know," replied the face

"Ah, forgive me, your dismembered parts must have affected your memory," said Lucifer. "Our paths crossed many times. Who was it whispered in your ear when your children were eaten? And who was it who assisted when you attacked Olympus?"

"I...am...Cronus, lord of the Titans, King of Kings. I know not who you are. Set me free."

"They call me many things, Satan, Beelzebub, Devil, but right now I'm Lord of the Underworld and soon I'll have the earth, sea and the sky. They'll all be mine; I...will...have...dominion over all of them. The Darkness is coming, the one thing the gods and man fear the most."

Jacob and the Archangels watched Lucifer pace again, and then watched as he came up with a plan. "Will you join me? Seek revenge?"

"When free, I'll reclaim my throne. Never will I share it," bellowed Cronus.

"Look around, fool," said Lucifer, "right now I'm in control and have the means to dismember you further. I will, if pushed, put you back where you were found and this time, trust me, you'll never be found. I ask again, will you assist?"

"All I want is to reclaim my throne," said a chastened Cronus, "and punish my sons."

"Good," said a happy Lucifer. "We want the same thing. You take on the gods, distract them, bring them down and I will return your realm to you."

Cronus thought for a moment and then answered, "Will those who are loyal to me be left to me?"

"You will have your realm returned to you," said Lucifer, "you will have those loyal to you. All I need is for you to say that you will use your might to destroy the gods."

"I will," Cronus without hesitation said, "I will destroy the gods."

Jacob saw that Lucifer was ecstatic and became alarmed. He knew from his studies that Cronus when free would be unbeatable. He worried about Zeus, who was now so much older and wondered about his abilities to achieve what he achieved when he first fought his father. He thought of the

Titans, who assisted Zeus, and were now long gone, not seen since the war of the Giants.

Jacob continued to watch as Lucifer called his demons into his presence before sending them into the deepest caverns with a clear instruction not to return without the rest of the body parts.

Jacob took his visions several weeks into the future and witnessed the finding of the hands and arms. He watched them attach back to the torso. The anger, hatred and rage, the hallmarks of Cronus had not abated and were felt by all those around him. The rage encouraged Lucifer even more to intensify the search for the legs and feet.

It was several days before the legs and feet were found and brought to Lucifer, who decided to be cautious for fear Cronus would renege on their agreement. He made his way to the chamber and was surprised to see that Cronus had manoeuvred himself over to a wall and was now sitting up.

"Three more parts and you'll have my wrath, three more and I will destroy the usurper. Then you will have your greatest ally."

"There's one more thing," said Lucifer, "one more condition, it's a simple one but it's important to me, will you agree?"

"What is it?"

"In a few moments you will have all what you desire," replied Lucifer, "you will have the power to wreck havoc, I'm asking you to hold your wrath until the armies of Hell are ready to be unleashed. Will you do that for me?"

Cronus agreed and Lucifer was beside himself with excitement knowing the resurrection of Cronus, when unleashed, will cause all before him to fall.

Jacob and the Archangels continued watching as the legs and feet rejoined the torso. They were horrified. In the temple, Zeus, Shango, Shiva and Odin almost in unison stood from their seats, and together exclaimed,

"Cronus has risen!" They tapped into their powers and joined the Archangels watching, through Jacob, what was happening in Hell.

Cronus did rise, at first as a pocked-marked, crusty skinned man before growing to stand over twenty feet tall. His cruel golden eyes unnerved the nearby demons; those who were too close were incinerated. He was again, the most feared of the Titans. He released a most thunderous roar swearing revenge on his sons and daughters.

"Release your anger, express your rage," said Lucifer. "But remember, you've agreed to wait until my plans are in place."

Cronus agreed but his frustration and anger was palpable. He stopped and stared into a nearby passage way. Lucifer also stopped, gesturing for quietness. He paced around the chamber, twitching and straining as though he sensing they were not alone. He closed his eyes and joined his hands as a smile crossed his face. "Aah. The boy who thinks he will be king. Welcome to my domain. See now what awaits you."

Jacob held his nerve but was slightly unsettled; he watched Cronus leave the chamber and followed him as he trundled through the tunnels and caves of Hell. He felt the tremors resonate after each step.

The Archangels had seen enough and moved away from Jacob. Seeing Cronus meant a new strategy needed to be prepared for the defence of the third age of man. They were so caught up in their concerns about Lucifer and the rise of Cronus that they left Jacob alone, failing to notice how numb he was. His brain was fried. He had witnessed so much of Hell, much more than he remembered from his original visions. He listlessly just walked off deeper into the meadows, wanting to be alone.

In the temple, the Archangels and the gods discussed the events of the day and after much debate everyone agreed the Asgard gods would lead the armies of the Light.

Chapter 17

Later that evening the gods gathered for the final dinner before the departure of the pantheons, which was due to begin the following morning. Jacob skipped his dinner; he was exhausted and still suffering from the trauma of his visions. He was troubled after his walk through Hell and what bothered him the most was a feeling he got of a connection to Lucifer.

He arrived back to the temple and had no choice but to walk through the Great Hall. He looked across at Zeus and bowed then slowly shook his head, showing how much he was suffering. Zeus responded with a nod and all watching understood it to mean there was no need for him to stay, he had the approval of his grandfather to leave.

After dinner, when all retired to their rooms, Zeus and Odin left for the ornamental gardens to continue discussing the day's events, especially the rise of Cronus. They smiled watching Odi and the boys trying to be discreet after stealing a cask of Dionysus's finest wine and carrying it towards the far side of the lagoon.

"I don't know whether to break his neck or just give up," said Odin. "But that youngster needs a good talking to."

"Odi is a grandson I never knew I had," said Zeus, "he reminds me of someone sitting not too far away from me."

"Yes," responded Odin, "I suppose, we did have fun."

Later that night Jacob's restlessness got the better of him, every attempt at drifting into a peaceful slumber failed, tossing, turning, the heat, the sweat. His few dreams quickly turning to horror filled nightmares.

He left his room and walked alone through the empty halls of the temple. He was looking for Eala but she and the girls had retired earlier. He then went looking for Odi and the boys only to find them hiding, in the distance, at the far side of the lagoon. He was pleased to see Odi having the time of his life with the boys.

Odi saw him and gestured for him to join them but Jacob declined. Odi wasn't giving up, he ran to him, hoping to persuade him but there was no persuading him.

"You know I was with you all the time," said Odi, "I was there but Lucifer didn't detect me, he didn't know I was there. How come he could only detect you? What could that mean?"

Jacob was still feeling numb and ready to explode. He stared with contempt at Odi, "What is it you don't understand? We had a deal, never enter each-others head without an invitation, you broke our deal. I can't trust you."

"In my defence," said Odi, "I saw you and I saw the Archangels enter your head. I wasn't going to allow you go where they were taking you without my protection."

"I didn't need your protection," responded Jacob getting more irate. "They're angels of the Light, I was safe."

"It wasn't the angels I was worried about," responded a now angry Odi. "It was Lucifer, his powers are unknown and my decision was vindicated when he announced he knew you were there, it was the same image I saw in the mirror in Manchester."

Jacob turned his back on Odi and said while walking away, "You still broke our deal. I can't have you in my head without an invitation especially when I'm with Eala."

"Oh, yeah," said Odi without thinking. "About that, you need a few lessons."

"Piss off, prick," said a mortified Jacob. He didn't realise Odi was so often in his head especially those times when he was thinking of, or with Eala. He continued to walk off, ignoring his brother.

Zeus and Odin were still sitting behind a mound and heard the argument develop. They listened and decided not to intervene as yet. Odi in the meantime had exploded and went after Jacob. He grabbed his shoulder and swung him around, "Don't ever call me a prick again. I'm a War God, a warrior King of Asgard; you will not turn your back on me."

"Take your hand from me," demanded Jacob.

"No," said Odi, "we need to sort this out, I meant no harm. I was really concerned for you."

"Take your hand from me," repeated Jacob.

"No, we finish this now," demanded Odi, "I don't know why you're acting so high and mighty, you're always in my head."

"Your head, that cesspit," said Jacob. "It's been a while. The last time I had to jump out, your mind is so screwed up. Pervert."

Odi reacted by planting an unbelievably powerful punch on Jacob sending him ten feet back against a nearby mound. Jacob was winded but when he recovered he jumped up and ran at Odi, grabbing him around the waist and sending him to the ground. He pinned him down by wedging his knee just below Odi's ribcage causing his breathing to struggle. He clenched his fists and released a torrent of punches to both sides of Odi's face and didn't relent. The rage had taken him. Odi was suffering but managed to raise one of his knees high enough to knock Jacob forward and over his head. Odi leapt up to kick Jacob's groin, side and head. He then straddled Jacob and raised his fist in readiness to launch his barrage of punches. His attack never happened; his wrist was grabbed from behind. It was Odin, he held him so tightly he couldn't move. Zeus placed his foot on Jacob's chest holding him down. "We'll let you go when you both calm down,"

"He was in my head," said Jacob struggling to breathe. "We had a deal."

"You're identical twins," said Zeus. "Is it possible that this is something you cannot control? Is it possible your thoughts belong to each other?"

"Are you ready to be released?" asked Odin. They both nodded.

Jacob was bruised all down the left side of his face. He was bleeding from his left nostril and was holding his left ribs, damaged by the impact of hitting the ground after Odi's powerful punch.

Odi face was black and blue, a tear above his left eye, blood pouring from his ear and a loose tooth in his upper jaw. He also had injured ribs from the pressure of Jacob's powerful knee resting on his chest. At that moment they hated each other and their contempt was palpable. Jacob walked off towards the water, saying nothing. He got no more than five meters away when Odi said, "Great, at last, he's no longer in my head."

"Stop," demanded Zeus, "Jacob, stop!"

Jacob continued to walk away totally defying his grandfather. Zeus called again but this time he used his thunderous voice sending shivers through all who heard him, "Stop!" he repeated.

Jacob froze, realizing his insolence; he turned and faced Zeus who said, "Slowly walk back towards us."

Jacob did as was asked, "He's back in my head," said Odi.

"Walk slowly backwards," said Zeus.

"He's gone again," said Odi

"Can I go now?" asked a fed-up Jacob. Zeus raised his arm and ushered him away.

"It seems you are in each other's heads only when you are close to each other," said Odin, loud enough for Jacob to hear, "all other times is as per your agreement, by invitation only, you must learn to live with this."

Jacob reached the shallows, stripped and waded into deeper water. He submerged and found a boulder in a deep pool where he sat two meters below the surface. He extended his arms and legs to allow the toothless skin nibbling carp heal him. He felt the power of Poseidon reach into him and mend his injured ribs. He was pleased when the moon sent its strongest beams to penetrate the pool and highlight his bruises. He then watched the beams use their power to bring back his clear unblemished tanned skin. He closed his eyes and went into a deep trance, waiting for the pain to leave his body. He remained on the rock hoping the numbness he felt after the visions would also leave, but there was no relief, even when he thought of happy times.

He tried to meditate only to be interrupted by Odi entering his head and when he opened his eyes, Odi was sitting on a rock opposite. Jacob couldn't believe the damage he'd done to his brother and was really upset that he could hurt so cruelly someone he loved.

He summoned the carp and gestured for them to again work their magic; he then called on Poseidon to assist in the healing process on Odi's ribs and face. The moonbeams returned and as Odi's bruises faded, his skin returned to its perfect tanned tone.

Jacob reached across to touch his brother's cheek hoping he was forgiven. He was. He placed his hand on Odi's shoulder, encouraging him to follow. They dived deeper and reached the oyster beds. They continued to dive and reached the reefs. They swam among the reefs exploring and greeting the creatures of the deep. In the distance Odi saw a line of torches and gestured to Jacob, they went to investigate.

The moon light still penetrated towards the sea bed so their journey was well lit up. They reached the first torches and were greeted by the guardians of Mer-City. They were escorted through a colonnade of coral built pillars, each one holding more brightly lit torches, to reach the throne room of the Emperor Toyesh, Lord of the Waters and leader of the Mer-People.

"So like my great friend, Poseidon. You bear the likeness of the gods," said Toyesh crossing to greet them, "I longed for this day. To meet the grandsons of Odin and Zeus is an honour; you've brought hope to our realm."

"Why so many guards? Why such tension?" asked Odi.

"The attacks at first were random, now they're continuous," said Santos, son of Toyesh. "We see them in the distance and with our speed we should be able to catch them but they defy us and disappear. They bring fear to the creatures of the deep."

"We're losing this battle and will need the assistance of the gods," said Toyesh

"Our grandmother is a Goddess of the Seas," responded Jacob, "and alongside Poseidon, she will assist. I will alert them to your concerns."

"We can't help at this time," said Odi. "Our armies are ill prepared. Jacob has a plan as yet untested. It'll take time to be effective."

"Today," said Jacob, "I walked through Hell and witnessed the savagery of Lucifer. Odi and the Archangels were with me. I saw what awaits the realm of man and it's not good. We know he plans to attack the realms of the gods using the Cronus. We know Cronus, if allowed, will destroy the

Astral plains killing off the Mer-People, the Centaurs, the Wizards and the realm of the Elves but most of all his plan is to destroy the gods."

"Because we can't assist at this time you must use your own strengths, you have many. Did you follow the instruction of Poseidon and send your elderly and younglings to the north?"

"Yes," confirmed Toyesh, "we followed his instructions to the letter."

"My Lord, we promise to come to your aid when the need is at its greatest," said Odi while looking at Jacob for approval, "I've looked at your young warriors, they are strong and are surrounded by the Light. Trust them, allow them lead, it's from among them you will find your triumph, let them lead."

Jacob and Odi then bade their farewells and swam back through the coral colonnades. They reached the lagoon shore and walked towards a nearby sand dune. They lay back and stared at the stars. "I can't believe we travelled to Mer-City," said Odi, "I always wondered did it really exist. I also can't believe my powers are advancing so quickly. I'd no problem breathing under water. I'll soon become a Time Lord just like you."

"I'm sorry," said a remorseful Jacob, "I love you brother and would never intentionally hurt you. I'm really so sorry for beating the living daylights out of you."

"Excuse me," said Odi, "I let you beat me. It would take more than a few punches from a minor Greek god to bring me down."

Jacob said, "Yeah, right," and they both laughed.

After a few moments passed Odi stood, held out his hand to pull Jacob to stand before him. He stepped back, "I comforted you when you were frightened. In our mother's womb I held and protected you, I know my place is by your side, my King of Kings." He then bowed to his brother.

"Our grandfather," reacted Jacob, "is King of Kings and we both owe him our allegiance. Please don't ever bow to me again."

"We've both learned to love him," said Odi, "but even he knows you are to be King of Kings. He has appointed a steward who will, near the End Times, place the crown of Olympus upon your head, I've seen it."

They were then both distracted by the shouting and boisterous singing coming from the far side of the lagoon. Odi laughed and decided to rejoin the party, he asked Jacob to join him which he willingly agreed to. By the time they arrived they found three of the boys comatose and the other five almost asleep. Baldor was still capable of standing; he attempted to pour drinks for Jacob and Odi but failed. "I think you boys have had enough," said Jacob taking the glasses away. They doused the fire and covered the boys with their capes, leaving them to sleep.

Chapter 18

Jacob and Odi left the boys sleeping off the effects of their hard nights drinking. They were aware of the importance of them being on top form for the departure of the pantheons, and didn't want to miss the excitement and pageantry. They headed to their room and fell asleep.

Jacob woke early the next morning and then woke Odi. They quickly washed and dressed before running to the kitchens. They scoffed whatever was available and went to join Magni and Modi where they took up their positions on a hill just south of the temple. Together they marvelled at the sight and vastness of the southern pantheon assembling before them. Jomo and Jahiri arrived and staggered up the hill to join them. They looked a bit worse for wear but Jacob quickly relieved them of their pain. He used a pool of nearby water and the power of Poseidon. When recovered, they took their place to see off the gods, who would, in some cases, be their guardians during their journey south. The departure of the southern gods was as spectacular leaving as it was arriving. Jomo and Jahiri showed a great respect to their ancestral deities and saw they were getting special attention as each god passed, they acknowledged each one in turn.

The southern departure was followed by the Indus pantheon and then the caravan of Lord Buddha. Jacob saw that Garuda and Girish were also a bit under the weather and needed his help, which he willingly gave. They were suffering so much they couldn't even walk. Jacob brought with him a jug of water and just like with Jomo and Jahiri he used it to heal their hangovers. When recovered they joined Magni, Modi and Odi, who were standing on an east facing hill. The sound of the elephants trumpeting was deafening, and wasn't helping the remnants of their hangovers. Lord Shiva stopped his caravan to speak with Garuda and Girish, "I see your future," he said after placing his hands on their arms, "one of you will join my family, I look forward to the day when a messenger walks into my domain, to bring to me the greatest gift of all, and trust me, I live for that day." The boys bowed as he departed.

Lord Buddha and his entourage were next to pass. He too stopped and walked over to talk to the boys. "Your passage will be a difficult one, many times 'He' will attack, 'His' armies are waiting but you will, with great difficulty, prevail, there is also happiness for you, especially near the End Times. Your gift to Lord Shiva will be treasured for all time, but you won't know of the gift until the end." Lord Buddha then joined his servants. He returned to his palanquin to become the sitting statue of the Golden Buddha.

The Archangels had departed during the night but Raphael remained as promised. He was waiting for Jacob to set in motion the quest to save mankind. The Astrals also remained, their instincts told them Jacob's future was about to be revealed and their magic would play a major part in protecting it.

Homer sat at a table near the steps furiously writing and trying to describe the scenes unfolding around him. He had earlier asked permission to stay longer as he had completed two works and wanted to check the accuracy before he publishes them. Permission was granted for four more days.

The Asgardians indicated their desire to remain; they planned to assist in training the guardians. They also had difficulty accepting that everything in Asgard was about to change, especially since Thor decided his place was to stay in Olympus with Maria. In the meantime all heralds returned to their positions within the friezes at the base of the temple roof.

Jacob was still unsettled by the events of the previous day and, as usual, when trying to deal with his feelings, he went to one of his favourite places where he sat by the water's edge to just stare out across the lagoon. He loved the way the lagoon and the temple were superimposed over the eastern Mediterranean Sea and how it never suffers adverse weather while the Mediterranean Sea did, and last night one of the wildest storms passed through. He saw the devastation left in its wake and watched the villagers rebuild their lives, he marvelled at their resilience. He watched out for Eala's parents and neighbours and saw they had all survived.

He then prepared for his fitness regime, a routine he continued since he finished playing rugby back in Dublin. He ran a six mile circuit designed when he first arrived in the temple, a route that took him beyond the meadows and back towards the lagoon. Lately he'd been training with some of the War Gods and always looked forward to the next challenge they would, with glee, set for him.

This day he'd asked Ares and Athena to train him in the art of tactical warfare to which they readily obliged. The regime lasted almost two hours and Jacob found it very beneficial. He learned the art of extreme weaponry from the mistress of war and improved his tactical abilities by watching and listening to Ares. He also worked out what kind of training was required for the boys before they set out on their long walk. He ensured their training didn't include anything he wouldn't do himself.

Eala watched the processions leave from one of the balconies surrounding the temple. She also watched Jacob leave for his run and then train with the War Gods. She found it difficult to avert her eyes when he lunged, his black, tight skirt left little to her imagination, increasing her desire to be with him. She turned to Mulan, "Look at him; even from that distance I hear every breath, see every muscle and every bead of sweat. He sends tingles to places tingles shouldn't go. Help me look my best today, something special is about to happen, will you help me?"

Mulan called on Panya and Oba and they helped her look like a goddess. Make-up wasn't really required as her beauty didn't need to be enhanced, but they did apply lipstick, eyeliner and then a light blusher to her cheeks. They partially plaited her hair and strategically placed sprigs of flowers throughout her long and fair locks. Mulan met with Aphrodite seeking one of her spectacular robes. Aphrodite obliged and arrived with one of her imperial gowns, and when Eala was dressed she remarked, "It seems my nephew has stolen the heart of the most beautiful woman in the world."

"You, my lady, are still the most beautiful woman in the world," replied Mulan.

Jacob, when finished his training returned to the temple to wash and dress. He was to meet his mother, Odi and their grandmother for lunch. When ready he left his room, and while on his way to the Great Hall he caught a glimpse of Aphrodite. He waved and continued on his way, then hesitated, a little confused. He stepped backwards to where he thought he saw his aunt and when he looked again, his heart nearly missed a beat. The butterflies that visited him every time he thought of Eala came at him with a vengeance. He stumbled on feeling his excitement grow. It wasn't his aunt, it was Eala and she stood before him as a goddess. He looked for, and found a hideaway, hidden from prying eyes. Their time spent alone was magical but couldn't last; he knew his mother, grandmother, and his brother were waiting. He asked Eala to join him for lunch, after which, they agreed to spend the afternoon together somewhere out in the vastness of the Olympus realm.

On reaching the doors to the Great Hall they paused to steal another kiss. Eala linked Jacob's arm, snuggled into him and took a deep breath. They entered, and their arrival was met with gasps from all around the hall. Jacob stood tall, wearing the white robes of a god of Greece. Eala stood out; her golden robes picking up the light and shimmered as she walked. Together they presented as a young couple madly in love. Zeus even reacted and received a gentle slap from Dione, Odin smirked in envy. Thor nodded his approval, he was so proud that it was one of his sons who found the most beautiful woman in the world.

"We are witnessing the consort to the Boy King," said Odin whispering across to Zeus who replied, "No! I'm afraid you're wrong. We're witnessing a Queen to the King of Kings."

Eala was nervous sitting with Jacob's family but was made very welcome. Maria helped her be at ease, she even did what most mothers do. She embarrassed Jacob by telling stories about his childhood.

When lunch ended Jacob and Eala made their excuses and left to change into something more comfortable. When ready they made their way out into the gardens where they stood for a moment taking in the amazing vista that was before them and just as Zeus had commented, they too were mesmerised at how vast and extensive the temple grounds actually were. They walked by the ornamental pond into the wild flower meadows and then made their way towards a stone folly. From there they looked back at the temple, its white marble resplendent under the early afternoon sun. From there the view of the Olympus realm was breath-taking. They had a clear view to the distant horizon, a clear view of the waterfalls cascading from the snow-capped mountains. Even the ancient trees, standing like sentinels, along the southern shore of the lagoon were in full leaf, creating a picture-perfect image in their minds.

The mountains to the north attracted their attention and with the help of two white stallions they made their way to the foothills. They climbed and soon reached the snow line. Jacob was fascinated watching Eala's reaction when she had felt, for the first time, the crispness of the snow beneath her feet. He'd already felt crunching when living in the north of England and always loved its sound.

They climbed higher and felt the real calmness that came with the extreme cold. They were now both immortals so the coldness and difficult challenges didn't faze them. The sharpness and the pure whiteness of the snow-capped summits invited them into its domain and as they climbed, each ledge they reached gave them a new challenge but Jacob just blinked passed any obstacle.

Nearing the summit they saw a flickering orange light, and on reaching the light they were met by what looked like, eight foot tall snow apes. "In the future," he said, "they will be known as the Abominable Snowmen. Their realm will be the highest mountains and they will become the stories of legend. They will be hunted but never found," he lowered his head in despair, "it saddens me to know that what will be known as 'global warming' will melt the ancient glaciers and their realm will cease to exist. They will be invited to join the Astrals and their memories will live on in the everlasting stories of the gods. They are the Yeti nation, guardians of the high mountains. They are aware of the threat and are preparing to leave."

Jacob bowed as he approached the village elder. "His name is Yaz," he whispered to Eala, "and is God of the Yeti, a great friend of my grandfather."

"Join me," said Yaz inviting them to enjoy the heat of his fire. "Word has reached us, telling us of the appearance of young gods in Olympus, grandsons of Zeus and Dione. I can see you in your grandfather, you bear his likeness. Descendants of my friend will always be welcome at the fires of the Yeti." Jacob formally introduced himself and bowed again.

Eala looked around at all the snow huts circling the village fire. The huts were stacked towards the summit, four or five deep as one looked up the mountain. Eala smiled in a motherly way at the little faces and tiny eyes staring back at her. They were the Yeti children looking nervously out from the huts.

After the pleasantries and small talk was over Jacob related the events of the last few days, as well as the gathering of the pantheons, he then asked, "Tell me, lord Yaz. Is it true, is the Yeti leaving?"

"Yes, it's true," replied Yaz. "Too much is happening and we feel unsafe. We are aware of the gathering of the gods and were pleased the Astrals represented us. We hope your efforts will give us many more years but it's not looking good. Our oracles speak of serpents and Dark Angels, forces of Hell with the power to penetrate our shields. The Yeti has no defences against such evil."

"Hells forces are strong but the gods are stronger, we've defeated them on several occasions, most recently, when I travelled through time, to Dublin," said Jacob.

"Our oracles also spoke of Dublin. They described the viciousness of the attack, the deaths and your resurrection. They also spoke of your plans, twelve youths who will travel the realm of man." Yaz continued, "Our oracles told us to prepare for a journey into a new dimension, a place where we will live in peace for eternity. They believe that several of our kin should remain to ensure our kind stay in the mind of man. Those who remain will be seen by a few, once a generation, and will be heard during the great blizzards as they bellow their sadness and loneliness for all to hear. They will never be captured by man."

Yaz, Jacob and Ella enjoyed listening to the stories and exploits of the Yeti armies. "I promise to tell Zeus of this meeting," said Jacob, "I'll tell him how you made us welcome and how your hospitality helped us to enjoy our time among the snow people. But like everything in life, all good things must come to an end. We must go, for tomorrow the training of the guardians begins."

Jacob and Eala left and made their way slowly down the mountain, they walked through the snow covered valleys towards the tree line before entering a forest of ancient pine trees. They met up with the elk, reindeer, foxes, owls and wolves who called this land their home. All bowed before Jacob, recognising him as a god and they accepted his acknowledgement while passing. They entered the frozen lands, similar to the Siberian tundra. They continued walking, watching the white hares chasing, fighting and boxing each other, as though madness had taken them. They rested while watching the spectacular sight of the Barnacle and Arctic Geese, in their millions, migrate south for the winter, stopping off to water, feed and rest.

Jacob and Eala were happy to be totally alone, no one to interrupt them, no one to take away these magic moments. Their feelings for each other overpowered them each time their arms touched or their hands joined. When he placed his arm across her shoulders she felt her heart race, she felt comfort, warmth, love. She felt as though she was walking on clouds.

They continued walking and soon reached the grasslands where the scent of the wild flowers was intoxicating and became forever imprinted in their memory.

Jacob slowed down as they approached the temple, he didn't want this magic time to end. He stopped walking and held her even closer, "Forget dinner, let's go to the lagoon," he said gently guiding her away.

They made their way to the dunes and found a secluded spot out of sight of prying eyes. He removed his shawl and laid it on the ground before encouraging her to join him. As time passed and the heat of the setting sun waned, he asked her to join him in the lagoon, its warm waters now very inviting.

They stripped and ran to the water's edge, dived in and swam towards the deeper pools. Jacob dived deeper and reached where the white oysters dwelled, he collected two and commanded them to open, showing their treasure. They did, and revealed the most perfectly formed pearls. He asked their permission for the pearls to be presented to Eala and they agreed before returning to their resting place to begin developing their next pearl.

Jacob wasn't finished yet, he located a vein of gold and using the strength of Heracles and the skills of Hephaestus he fashioned the gold to hold the pearls before presenting them to adorn the Eala's ears.

They swam and frolicked for many hours before leaving the water just as night was beginning to fall. A bright moon was rising and its strong light created the most romantic beams that bounced across the lagoon.

They lay back on the shawl and waited for the curtain of white starlight to gain its full strength by opening up across the Heavens. He sneakily lowered his eyes to glance down at Eala's naked body not realising she was doing the same thing, except she had a better view of his nakedness. He moved his hand to gently caress her arms and shoulders hoping for a reaction. He did get a reaction; she turned on her side, rested her breasts on his arm, and softly kissed him on the cheek. He thought of Odi's comment, 'You need lessons' and became uneasy. His confidence was shaken and he said to himself, 'I'm going to kill him'

Eala felt how uneasy he became and asked, "What's changed? Is there something wrong?"

"Yes," he said, "Odi and I had a fight. He teased me by saying I need lessons. He entered my head and read my mind; he learned how much I wanted to make love to you. He mocked me."

"Do you think I know what to do?" she said moving her hand around his chest. "I've never been with a man and looking at you body, so perfect, so untouched, makes me wonder why? You're causing me to tremble," she placed her leg across his, "Don't mind Odi. Just because he's a Lord of Asgard and has lots of experience, it doesn't mean he knows real love." The more Eala spoke, the more Jacob wanted her.

氞氞

In the temple Odi joined his parents, brothers and grandparents for dinner. There was much banter, but it didn't take long for the seriousness of the advancing Darkness to become the main topic of discussion. Plans of attack, methods of defence, weapons, and allies, were all discussed ensuring the gods were prepared.

Although still tense, the gods that night enjoyed the best of food and wine, served from the renowned Olympus kitchens. They listened to the old stories, but the one story they really wanted to hear more about was Odi's exploits during the battle of Dublin. Odi loved telling the story and revelled in the continuous tributes being paid to him. All the tributes spoke about the prowess of a certain young Asgard warrior causing him to feel quite embarrassed by all the compliments and attention.

Soon after, Jacob's absence was noted. Odi, under much pressure from his brothers, reluctantly attempted to use his powers to find him. He entered Jacob's head knowing he risked a promised retaliation.

"Odi has entered my head again," gasped Jacob while enjoying Eala massaging her body against his.

"In your head," said Eala while rolling off him. "His timing is terrible. Does he do that often?"

"We automatically enter each-others head when we stand close to each other but he also has a habit of doing it at awkward moments,"

"If I was to kiss you," said Eala puckering her lips and developing a devious smile. "Would he feel it? Would he feel everything?"

"I think so," said Jacob getting very interested.

"Everything?" asked Eala with a glint in her eye.

She reached across and nibbled on Jacob's ear. He nearly fainted as the most exciting sensations rolled through his body. Odi felt the very same feelings. He rubbed his ear as the sensations travelled through his body.

"Odi can't get out of my head," said a sniggering Jacob, "I've blocked him from leaving. My revenge will be so sweet."

"Hold on a minute!" said an alarmed Eala. "When I kiss you, will I also be kissing Odi?"

"I've no idea and I don't care. If he experiences everything I'm experiencing, can you imagine his reaction if he is sitting at dinner in the Great Hall. I'd give anything to be a fly on that wall."

"But!" said an even more alarmed Eala. "He'll be sitting with his family, his mother, grandparents, his lunatic brothers."

"Oh, this gets better," said Jacob punching his fists into the air, "I'm going to have so much fun."

"Hold on for another minute, making love with you is one thing, making love to you and your brother at the same time, NEVER."

"No. no, no...It doesn't work like that," said Jacob trying to reassure her. "He won't feel your touch, he won't feel your kisses, he will only feel the sensations going through my body and won't be able to control himself."

"I think I might enjoy this little bit of power over him," said Eala.

"Trust me, you will." replied Jacob.

Eala slowly brought her fingernail across Jacob's bare chest sending even stronger sensations around his body. She moved her finger towards his belly button and then a little lower, taking his breath. She then kissed her way up his body to nibble on his ear.

Odi was startled; finding the sensations tickling his left ear strange and a bit disconcerting, especially when they travelled to his right ear. He then placed both arms across his chest, the sensations travelling through his body were starting to do things to him and he was doing everything in his power to stop himself from being noticed. It didn't take long for him to realize what was happening; he regretted saying what he said to Jacob before their fight. He looked at Magni praying he wouldn't notice his discomfort. Beads of sweat were gathering on his forehead, under his arms and across his back. Wearing his imperial Asgard robes right now was a mistake; they were too heavy for the heated discomfort he was feeling. Eala stopped her teasing and enquired as to how Odi was doing.

"You're thinking of my brother while making love to me!" exclaimed Jacob. "Never mind him; just keep doing what you're doing to me."

Eala blew gently and slowly across Jacob's ear causing goose pimples to rise, including on poor Odi who was now seriously compromised. He couldn't leave the table as to do so before his grandparents finished eating would be considered inappropriate. The beads of sweat continued to gather and then the worst thing to happen, happened. Magni looked across and saw how uncomfortable he was, and how he was pressing himself closer to the table.

Magni was aware of the bond between Jacob and Odi and it didn't take long for him to work out what Jacob was up to, especially as he and Eala were missing and alone somewhere in the realm since earlier that day. He gestured to Modi and between them they prepared to have fun.

Meanwhile Eala passionately kissed Jacob causing Odi's lips to involuntarily move. Odi continued holding his belly but had no choice but to free up one hand to cover his mouth. Eala's and Jacob's passionate kissing was now being manifested through Odi and he couldn't hide it.

Magni planned to show no mercy, he slid back on his chair, discreetly removed his sandal and stretched his bare foot under the table to rub up and down against Odi's leg. At the same time Modi placed his left arm behind Odi's back and continued the teasing by gently massaging him. Odi was by now mortified beyond belief. He had three brothers teasing him in the worst possible way, one in his head, one opposite him and the other beside him.

Jacob and Eala were now in the most loving of embraces, so passionate they lost control to become one. As their breathlessness increased their passion grew, causing cascading sensations to roll through their bodies, and that of Odi. The sensations were so intense Odi lost composure, kicking Magni's leg away, and flopping back into the chair, gasping, trying to regain control. He crossed his legs and grabbed a cushion to cover his embarrassment. In his mind he pleaded with Jacob to stop, but that wasn't going to happen. A fire was burning and nothing could extinguish it. Odi deteriorated.

Magni and Modi were so happy they had great difficulty containing themselves. Zeus, Odin and Thor were too engrossed in their conversation to notice Odi's predicament and then it happened, an explosion of epic proportions sending a subliminal light shooting across the cosmos.

Zeus looked up knowingly, looked over at Eros who shrugged as if to say 'nothing to do with me'. Zeus and Eros are the only gods who understood the light; they both recognised it to be the 'spark of life', they knew a new god had just been conceived. In the dunes, Jacob momentarily opened his eyes and saw the light, he wondered what it was.

At the very time that the light shot across the universe Odi got weak kneed and slouched deeper into the chair, his heart was racing and his breathing rapid. His arm dangled by his side and the beads of sweat flowed from his forehead down his cheeks. His legs shot apart and he fell back, flopped to the floor, damaging the chair on his way. Modi jumped to his aid, trying desperately to contain himself. Thor wasn't amused; he was always protective of Odi especially against the pranks played by Magni and Modi.

There was no going back for Odi. His embarrassment was set to become a story of legend. While still on his back he pleaded to be excused, jumped up and ran to his room, holding the chair cushion before him. Magni and Modi were in hot pursuit and it didn't take long for them to catch up. They were each side of him and in hysterics, tears flowing from their eyes.

"Why so flustered?" asked Magni after placing his arm across Odi's shoulder. "You must have enjoyed it, was it as good for you as it was for us?"

Odi stopped, ground his teeth and grabbed both of his brothers by the scruff of their necks, "This is war. I'm going to kill him. I swear I'll kill him. He did that deliberately, wouldn't let me out of his head."

"It's your own fault," laughed Modi trying to get him to walk again. "There are times you shouldn't be in other people's heads, especially when a god is making love."

"You're both pricks, you made me," said Odi. "You pushed me into finding him for dinner."

While Odi was declaring war, Jacob and Eala remained in the dunes, their bodies stuck together unable to part.

"I think we should return to the temple," said Jacob showing a little bit of nervousness, "I'll have to face the music. Odi's on fire, he's going to kill me."

They dressed and made their way towards the temple, not realising they were over two hours late for dinner. When walking through the Great Hall they glowed showing those watching how much they were in love. They were beaming as though sprinkled with star dust, they looked so happy.

Maria was pleased. Thor impressed. To see his son so happy lessened the pain he felt after been separated from the one he loved for so long. Eala excused herself and went to her room; Jacob also went to his room. Zeus instructed Eros not to tell Jacob about the subliminal light.

When Jacob reached his room he was met with an exhausted and furious Odi, who met him with a torrent of strong and blasphemous words that turned the air blue. Magni and Modi couldn't stop themselves, and their teasing of poor Odi was relentless. Jacob cringed when he realised Odi's embarrassment actually did happen in the Great Hall during dinner, and in the presence of their grandparents, but it didn't prevent him from joining in on the continuous teasing and humiliation.

Thor arrived and expressed his anger at the behaviour of three of his sons. He demanded an explanation. When Magni tried, Thor knew where the story was going, "Stop!" he shouted while raising his arms to the heavens, "I don't want to know." He looked at Odi, who was still very embarrassed, said nothing more, and walked out of the room with a smirk on his face.

The four brothers again shared the bedroom that night and after a few punches, which landed every now and again on Jacob, things calmed down.

Modi and Odi drifted into sleep but Magni lay awake, the warrior in him was mulling over the plans being considered for the protection of Earth. Jacob couldn't sleep either; he was still on a high after his time with Eala.

Magni looked across at Jacob who was lying awake with his hands resting behind his head; he also had what looked like a permanent grin on his face. Magni was happy for him. "I wish I'd known you before now. Modi and I always loved Odi and would die for him, we were so proud of how you and he fought in Dublin. We can sense the bond between you and will miss him because we know he won't be returning to Asgard for some time. He'll never leave your side because he's the most loyal, most generous, most friendly and the cheekiest brother anyone could have."

Jacob showed some remorse, "I love him to bits and shouldn't have embarrassed him the way I did, I planned to release him earlier but the passion was stronger and I kind of forgot he was there. Do you think he'll ever forgive me? I respect him. When he took on the Dark Angels; I saw the strength of father come through. When I fell I felt his grief. When, by the power of Poseidon I was restored, I sensed his relief."

"Odi is used to us teasing him but what you did beats all our efforts and just as a warning, beware his revenge," laughed Magni thinking of all the times he and Modi set him up. "His revenge will be best served cold and I pray I'll be there to witness it, I've never laughed so much." They were unaware Odi heard everything.

Jacob then got serious and asked Magni if he had come up with any plans. Magni thought out loud, knowing Jacob also had a reputation for tactics and was hoping for a second opinion. "The Asgard warriors will be split into four armies, each one led by one of the four sons of Thor. Odi will lead the armies of the north and will call on the Huns, and the Goths. Modi will lead the armies of the south and will have the assistance of the Zulus, the

Yoruba, and the kingdom of Kush. I will lead the armies of the east. The Mongols, the Manchu and the Han will fight by my side. And you, my brother, will lead the armies of the west. You will have the assistance of the Celts, the Francs and the Saxons. The gods of Olympus will support us with weapons and tactics. I fear you are the weak link, so I will ask Ares and Athena to continue with your training. My instincts, just like the instincts of the other gods, tell me that for some reason, you are a target of the Dark Angels. I can't quite put my finger on it, but the way they distracted Odi just so they could target you worries me. Their assault on you was so relentless." Magni went quiet for a few moments.

"Go on," insisted Jacob.

"Your grandmother," continued Magni, "is a Goddess of the Sea and by her power I know you will have the support of the Mer-People. They've gathered close to the northern ice lands and have strengthened their defences in the Mediterranean. They've secured access to the western seas. You will also have the support of the oracles, the wizards and the elves. Did you see the way they stood and then before you they bowed? There's something special about you that the Dark Angels fear, or worse still, there's something you have that they really want. Then there's Cronus, in my dreams I saw him rise, and wondered. We now know this has come to pass."

"I too had dreams," said Jacob. "They began four years ago and showed me the badness coming to man. They also showed me the achievements. The Ancient One has given us time, I believe there will be many skirmishes over the centuries but no major battle for about two thousand years, it will definitely happen. Their campaign will start immediately by probing, and there will be more murderous skirmishes just like the one in Dublin. They'll find ways to turn people towards The Darkness, and that is by starting wars throughout the ages and we'll have to be there each time, on our guard at all times."

"My plan," continued Jacob while getting emotional, "is to send my friends in four different directions, a journey that'll take them to all corners of earth. It'll break my heart to send Eala away, I love her so much. I don't want her to go but my head tells me she's needed in the west. The four messengers will all be needed, they will sow the seeds of greatness and that greatness will be passed to descendants of those chosen, leading to the greatest army ever created. They will come back together before the battle of the End Times. Magni, would you let her go if you loved her as much as I do?"

"I'm a warrior not a lover," lamented Magni, "I've never loved the way you do. You said her part in this story starts tomorrow, she has to go. You are a God of the Light, you must let her go." Jacob hoped Magni would find another way but it wasn't to be.

Although upset Jacob felt he was bonding with his oldest brother. There was no more to be said about the battle plans so his curiosity about Magni's personal life grew,

"Are you happy?" asked Jacob. "All I hear is the stories about your tactics and your prowess on the battle field and I love listening to them but I want to know my brother. I want to know who you are. I never knew I had a brother let alone three. I feel you will become my greatest ally and I know you will always be there for me. I'm worried about you. Earlier I sensed in you a desire for love especially when you see me and Eala together. I want to hear about you as the lover. Has there ever been one who stole your heart?
"

"Once, in the distant past, there was someone I loved," said Magni after been quiet for a few moments. "We parted many thousands of years ago."

He reached across to grip Jacob's hand and when Jacob entered his mind all he said was, "Oh, I understand." They fell asleep.

Chapter 19

Jacob was first to arrive in the gardens the following morning and, as usual, he began his daily fitness regime, warming up by the ornamental pool. When ready he ran down the left side of the temple, across the front door and back along the right side. This was a pattern he religiously followed before beginning his more arduous run out into the vastness of the Olympus realm.

On returning to the front steps, he saw Baldor and Jomo. They were suffering after another night of wild drinking with Dionysus and Eros. They joined him but found themselves very queasy and soon realised they couldn't keep up. He had no sympathy and teased them about their fitness. He decided to show no mercy. He sent them back to the temple with an instruction, "Tell the boys to meet me in the ornamental gardens at noon. There we'll begin your training for the great adventure that awaits you. Tell them not to be late."

After watching them stagger back to the temple, he turned and jogged out into the meadows where, since he arrived in Olympus, he had created many structures and obstacles as tools to assist in his training regime. He caught Baldor and Jomo watching him from the steps, so decided to show off. He made this way towards a two hundred foot long wooden pergola that led towards the woodlands. He managed to leap and on reaching the first beam he swung back and forth, before building up a momentum allowing him to swing one arm after another from beam to beam until he reached the end. He then did an amazing double summersault ending with a perfect landing. The boys were in awe of his strength, skill and speed and worried they'd never reach his standard. They felt sick watching him run up hill after hill and on reaching each low summit he'd summersault twice before continuing his run towards the woods and out of view.

It was near mid-morning when he arrived back to the Great Hall looking as though he hadn't even broken a sweat. To all watching he seemed fresh and ready to go again. Baldor and Jomo had already told the other boys of what to expect, and they weren't happy.

Jacob saw they were subdued and enquired as to what ailed them. Faer was first to speak, "Jomo watched you sprint like a gazelle, swing like a monkey and then climb like a leopard. You expect us to achieve all that in three days? There's no way. We spoke earlier and feel you may have picked the wrong boys."

"I don't expect you to be able to complete my regime," laughed Jacob, "you're not fit enough. After today's training I expect you to be able to do most of it tomorrow." He said no more, left the table and headed to his room to wash and change, leaving the boys with their mouths open and very worried. Before he went out of view he said, "Find the girls and ask them to join us at mid-day."

After resting, washing and changing Jacob returned to the Great Hall. He was happy to see all were present except for Eala which surprised him. He excused himself and went to go seek her out. He was upset to find her weeping while sitting alone out in the gardens. He sat with her, held her gently and asked as to what was upsetting her.

"Since our time together out in the meadows and especially in the dunes I feel different, everything in me has changed," she said resting her head on his shoulders, "I've feelings that are now overwhelming and I don't under-stand. In four days I'll be leaving and may never see you again. At times I can see my future and occasionally I see you there but there's always another presence, it's 'Him'. He seems to know everything, he terrifies me."

Jacob continued holding her, trying to reassure her, "In my dreams I too can see you and we will be together. I feared our parting was too long to be separated but think about it, we're immortals; destined to be together for eternity, and guess what? Eternity is forever. I can wait, can you?" She nod-ded, felt his warmth and then felt happy again. They made their way to the Great Hall.

All was quiet and somewhat sombre in the temple when Jacob and Eala arrived. There was a lot of tension. The boys had been talking and felt that what was ahead was beyond them. Some had already developing their pow-ers of prophesy and could see nothing but turmoil and carnage in their future.

Jacob was having none of it because he had every confidence in them, "Pull yourselves together," he said. "The time has come to prepare for your journey and it...will...start...four...days...from...now. Do I have your sup-port? Show me you can fulfil your destinies."

He was disappointed to get a half hearted answer until Thanases said, "Jacob, we're just frightened, we might be immortals but inside we're still human, we look at you and Odi and we see all powerful gods, we don't have your powers or your confidence. Give us time."

Jacob felt for them but knew he had made the right choice. "I need you all by my side. I've seen how powerful each of you will become. I except you're scared and I understand that, but you haven't even tried yet. Come with me, train for a few hours and then judge, a lot depends on you, really, there's no going back."

Merlin arrived and brought with him a calmness that spread to all the boys, he sensed their reluctance and tried to encourage them. He advised them that all was not what it seems and said that the acrobatic display that Jacob put on earlier was meant to happen. "I've seen how you too will have the skills, strength and endurance to achieve the very same abilities, all within three days." He could see they weren't convinced, then continued, "By the time of the fourth dawn you will have concluded three days of intense training, you will have become masters in tactics and weapons, skills you never thought you would or could possess. Go, follow Jacob and be the warrior messengers of the gods. Go fulfil the prophecy given to us by the oracles."

Jacob backed away and began his warm up, encouraging the boys to copy everything he did. He started with a slow walk in a large circle, then a quickening of the pace. He continued by raising his knees while standing on the spot, and then showed them how to extend their neck and shoulder muscles without straining, before teaching them to stretch their groin and calf muscles. The boys copied everything he did and then as he began to jog, they were enthused enough to begin enjoying what they were doing.

In the meantime Merlin took the girls to meet with Apollonius, who would become their mentor in the ways of the Astrals. He showed them the power of the Light and how to control it, especially when called on by the gods. He showed them the ancient ways of the Earth Mothers and how they brought balance to all lands. He introduced them to the song of the seas and how that song would be used to bring peace and calmness when the great storms had passed. He waited until the end to bring forth his magic and showed them how magic must only be used for good.

Back in the meadows the boys had travelled no more than four hundred metres when Jacob saw they were lagging a good distance behind. It was the beauty of Olympus that held their attention. Every direction they looked in held their gaze. To them the grasslands just seemed to travel on forever. The northern snow-capped mountains shimmered under the midday sun reminded them of the great fables. The forest line, with its many shades of green, created a mosaic of colour along the horizon that enthralled them. Most of all they were in awe of the beauty and swiftness of the galloping herds of white horses. Their concentration was gone while taking in the stunning majesty and beauty that surrounded them.

Jacob had trouble getting their attention and let his feelings be known. He was a hard task master knowing his toughness will ensure their skills could handle any dangerous situation that may arise. He finally got them running again, and this time, he refused to allow them rest until at least two hours of difficult training had passed. He made the next few hours into a real endurance test. The strange thing was, the boys managed to complete the course, they were already fit young men; working with their fathers, uncles and neighbours, in the fields, on the boats, in the workshops and in the forges, since their early childhood.

He finally allowed them a short break when they arrived beside the lagoon. They stripped off and submerged themselves into the cool, refreshing and invigorating waters where they really appreciated and enjoyed the short time they had in the sea just floating, swimming and relaxing before leaving the water when some light refreshments arrived from the kitchens. After lunch they were taken over to join up with Athena and Ares where they commenced their weapons and tactics training.

This at first seemed to be very difficult as they were sons of farmers and fishermen and most definitely not warriors. What surprised them was how easily they took to their new training regime causing them to wonder if they were indeed gifted by the Ancient One. They wondered if it was their fear of letting Jacob down that encouraged them to try harder, or if the truth was really known, was it their fear of the legendary wrath of Ares and Athena?

The regime was arduous and what troubled them the most, it was destined to continue for another two days. They were very conscious that on the fourth day they had to be ready for their journeys to begin.

Ares in particular was tough, he forced them to repeat and then repeat over and over, every tactical movement in fencing, shield use, and spear throwing accuracy; until he was satisfied they could hold their own in any conflict situation. He tutored them in the posture and decorum required to intimidate any opponent. He was a master tactician and was wise enough to know how praise was the greatest motivator. He let it be known how impressed he was at how quickly they were picking up the art of warfare and self-defence, especially after only a few hours training.

Athena watched the training session and was delighted with their performance and their ability to learn quickly. She then stepped in and went through the weapons and tactics available to them. She also showed them the mystical weapons she was working on and hoped to have them ready before they left on their quest.

By the end of their training session the boys were sore all over and exhausted. They were sticky and smelly and needed to clean themselves but found that they had great difficulty walking as every muscle in their body was now aching. Jacob noticed they were struggling and their walking laboured, he felt sorry for them and suggested they get into a large water trough that was at the side of the temple. He sniggered while assisting each of them as they struggled to climb into the trough. When settled he placed his hands into the running water, closed his eyes and using his powers, brought on the healing. The water rippled then created small and regular waves. In each wave could be seen hands created from water and as each wave passed, the hands massaging each boy. After a short while the hands successfully relieved their aches and pains. For the boys they had only ever imagined what a massage would be like, never in their wildest dreams did they think that they would feel so at peace and so relaxed. They had trouble finding the strength to leave but the chiming of the dinner bell soon brought them back to reality. They leapt from the trough and rushed to their rooms to wash, change and prepare for the grand dinner that was being held that night in honour of Zeus and Odin.

At dinner Jacob and the boys enjoyed the banter and teasing, their laughter and boisterousness was quite loud and all listening could hear and see the changes happening to them. Eventually Jacob said, "Your training went well today, I already see differences in you." The boys looked at each other, confused, they couldn't see a difference. "Tomorrow," continued Jacob, "just before breakfast, more intensive training will commence and then it will continue in the afternoon and again in the evening. You will continue to be pupils of Ares and Athena. I hope you realise that they are the greatest warrior gods known to man, from them you'll learn the ways of the gods, especially how to be guardians and protectors. Under their guidance you'll be taught about weapons, tactics and planning. You will also be trained by Chiron on how to master the power of negotiation; he will teach you how sometimes the pen can be mightier than the sword. By Apollo you will be taught the skills of medicine, the beauty of music and dance. The magic of Hade's helmet will be yours and you will learn to harness its power of invisibility which will allow you be concealed from the gaze of Lucifer and his generals." He then instructed them to meet up with Hephaestus before the light fades any further.

The boys left the Great Hall and went to meet Hephaestus in his workshop. When they arrived he placed them in a single line, stood back and was surprised how all eight were exactly the same height; just under six feet tall. They were, more or less, the same muscular build, making his job all the more easier. He looked closely at Faer and then chose him because he was slightly broader than the others; he measured him for the template of their new tunics, capes, belts and golden breastplates. He then stood back again, massaged his chin trying to figure out whose head to measure for the protective helmets. This time he choose Baldor because he reckoned his was just slightly wider than the rest. When he established the boys were all right-handed he instructed each of them to take a soft claylike substance into their hand and squeeze gently which left an imprint of their hands and fingers allowing him to create the perfect bespoke sword handle for each of them. He had to measure them individually for their boots and sandals after establishing they had different sized feet. His work was then done and he ushered them away, asking them to return, after breakfast, in two days for a fitting.

When the boys left, Hephaestus went to work. He called on the fire nymphs of Santorini whose skills for forging the greatest weapons were legendary. They were the Blade-Smiths of the gods. He then called forth his apprentice cobblers, the very ones that created the winged sandals worn by Hermes. That call was followed by an urgent request to the famous shield and helmet shapers of the Asgard realm, master craftsmen who specialise in perfectly moulding steel, gold and bronze. His next call went out to the elves from the ancient and mystical realm of the west, they were considered to be the greatest tailors to the gods.

It took several hours before Hephaestus' call was answered and by the use of magic all arrived into his workshop. They worked with a sense of urgency, all day and all night, bringing to fruition the majestic designs created for the long walk of the Messengers of the Light.

The boys returned to the Great Hall and joined in with the gods as they continued to enjoy the excellent and finest of Dionysus's wines. They listened to the stories of myth and legend that were being recalled, embellished and enhanced, all for the benefit of Homer who was busily recording every last word. Apollo gave a rendition of his latest song, written in recognition of the prowess of two young gods and the friendly dragon that fought during the battle of Dublin. He also sang a second composition in honour of the Time Lords who froze Olympus. Time Lords, he believed, were destined to become the greatest War Gods of all time.

Jacob joined his mother and the Asgard Gods who were discussing plans for the future, especially as to whether Maria would travel to Asgard with Thor or whether Thor would stay in Olympus. Odi expressed a desire to stay by Jacob's side and sought permission from his grandfather. This permission was slow in coming as Odi had been earmarked by Odin as a chief Warrior God of the Asgard pantheon.

Apart from the serious side to the discussions there was also a little trick-acting going on. Magni and Modi had stepped aside and were trying to distract Odi. They were up to something which could only mean they planned to embarrass him again. Modi got Odi's attention by discretely holding back the lapel of his tunic revealing a small cask of what could only be fire water, brewed in the highlands of the far west. He gestured for him to join them and Odi just nodded succumbing to the temptation. He had learned to play hard because he had always worked hard, he joined them and reached across to take a mouthful when Jacob intervened, stretched over, held his arm and said, "You stupid prick. Haven't you learned anything, father's watching and I don't want to be at the receiving end of his wrath again tonight."

Thor heard everything and was pleased at least one son was listening to him. Odi didn't like been called a prick again but accepted Jacob's intervention and whispered, "You owe me one and I think I know what I want."

Jacob cringed wondering what was coming. "Talk later," said Odi with a smile from ear to ear and his middle fingers raised high. He quickly walked away to prepare for the banquet.

Chapter 20

Earlier that day Jacob had arranged with the kitchens for a large round table to be placed in an annex room next to the Great Hall. His intention was for his friends, himself and Odi to move in there after the banquet. He wanted them to be able to talk in a way that everybody could comfortably see each other as well as understand his strategy. He was nervous because he still hadn't worked out all the issues that might arise on their journey. He wondered should he use his 'Time Lord' abilities and travel into the future and see what lay ahead for each of the messengers but decided against this idea, he knew the future had many paths and even his abilities would have difficulty choosing the correct one.

The banquet was a sumptuous affair, the finest of foods and wines, all set under a magical ambiance created by the many candles and lanterns set throughout the hall. Jacob didn't enjoy the dinner and was anxious for it to end. Zeus sensed his anxiety and, knowing how important the meeting was, called a conclusion to dinner and requested the gods and astrals leave the Great Hall and make their way to the gardens. Jacob then called Odi and his friends over to the annex leaving the stewards to clean up and prepare for breakfast the next morning.

Jacob was first to sit and while waiting for all others to join him, the doors opened and Magni and Modi entered. They insisted on attending believing they too should understand the plan. The door opened a second time and Homer rushed through requesting permission to record the meeting. This was denied because Jacob couldn't understand how his movements, as well as Odi's, were being shadowed throughout time. He felt that if the meeting was recorded it would make it easier for Lucifer to upset his plans. Homer respectfully left and joined the gods in the garden.

Odi sat beside Panya, and because space was tight, due to Magni and Modi being there, his knee kept accidently glancing off her leg. At times their eyes met causing his heart to miss a beat. For the first time ever, when with a girl, he was stuck for words, he had developed a shyness which took him by surprise. He'd been dreaming about her since seeing her that first time when he arrived in the temple. She coyly looked away for she too had secretly liked him but was afraid to let it be known.

Jacob stood and all went quiet. He shifted from his left foot to his right and was taken aback at how his nerves were affecting him; he was used to public speaking. As captain of the schools rugby team he was used to taking control and making things happen. He then realised that in the past his leadership was just 'sport' but today, it was about life and death and he feared making a mistake. He sought reassurance from Magni who shrugged his shoulders as if to say, 'Get the finger out, you can do this.'

He again looked around the table trying to control his nerves and every time he looked at Eala he became distracted. He loved her very much and was trying to think of ways to hold on to her but deep down he knew her path was well and truly set, and that path didn't include him. He looked at Magni again and saw he was getting impatient; he took a deep breath and began.

"My friends, for four years I've been having troubled dreams showing me terrible things. Those dreams were horrible; in fact they were mainly nightmares. I wept in my sleep because all I ever saw was violence, famine, death, war and real hatred. I sensed it, saw it and heard it. I smelt it, touched it and felt it. I didn't know I was a god and I certainly never imagined I was being guided; it seems by the Ancient One, to set in motion a plan to end all this evil and bring peace back to the realm of man. My night terrors showed me how widespread evil was to become and how, it could be responsible for ending this third age of man." He stood to walk around the table,

"At times pleasant dreams showed me a lagoon where I swam with twelve friends, it came to pass and you are those friends. My dreams showed me being in love," he looked at Eala and smiled, "and I wondered was that the reason we were brought together, it wasn't. They showed me sending you away in groups of three, in four different directions. I didn't know then that you were to be the Messengers of the Gods, but now I do. Now I know you will be the watchers, the guardians, the messengers and in many cases, you will be the saviours as you carry my message to all corners of earth. Your efforts will help man to protect himself from the unseen and unknown evil that's coming." He returned to sit at the table,

"Over the next few days you will be given the power and skills to let loose vengeance upon those you find bringing The Darkness, but I must caution you on why you must do this sparingly and wisely because 'He' will be watching. He seems to be always watching. Use you Light and identify any threat, eliminate the threat before it can develop to endanger your task." He paused and looked around at the ashen faces and started to speak again.

"We now know Lucifer has been unleashing the serpents, at first in twos, and now in large numbers. We know that Hades, Ares and Athena secured the gates of Hell preventing any more serpents from escaping but this will soon fail, I've seen it. Lucifer is the most cunning of them all and I know his minions will evolve as the years pass. We know the serpents have been biting beasts of the fields and creatures of the oceans. They've started biting men, killed them but they'll soon learn how to bite without killing.

These bites will instead slowly spread the poison of fire, a new form of evil, bringing a terrible darkness throughout the ages. Hell will use those poisoned men and women as its conduits of terror," he looked across at Magni and got a nod of approval,

"You, my friends, have been given the gift of immortality and over the next few days you will gain many more. These gifts will help you to easily identify the 'evil one' in anyone bitten by the serpents of Hell. Eala, Mulan, Oba and Panya will be the messengers, carrying my message to those they find worthy. Boys, you will be their guardians but will also have the power to pass on the message when required. You all will have the power to bring back balance to any village, town or city you visit just by whispering this message,

'Go now, tell your children to tell their children's children for all time, that one day, they will be called upon by the gods and they must answer.'

Those who receive the message may not take action, their children may not take action but one day, their descendants will. They will be known as The Carriers and will answer the call to form the greatest army to ever have existed, and from among them will grow great leaders who will assist in defeating the evil of Hell. You must keep travelling, seek out the evilness and bring the Light back to as many as possible. You heard what the Ancient One said, 'Many souls are worth saving'. Save them, always remember that." He paused again, took a deep breath then said,

"You are already being trained by the greatest Warrior Gods and there are many more skills to be learned. They will teach you how to anticipate the tactics of the evil ones. You will suffer, some more than others and there will be many failures especially as Lucifer and his demons evolve. You will travel unseen for millennia under the protection of the Helmet of Hades.

Lucifer's armies will seek you out but your invisibility will always assist you to be one step ahead. I see many disappointments, especially towards the End Times, but by then the armies of Asgard, Olympus and the Astrals will all be ready to assist," He then addressed Magni,

"I see now what you see and it bothers me. I feel him crawl under my skin. He's after something I have but I can't see what it is, it's the one unknown that weakens my plans." Eala at this point felt a little queasy, she stared at Jacob feeling she knew what Lucifer was after but chose to say nothing. Jacob stood again and circled the table,

"In a few day's you will leave, three at a time." He looked at the girls and said, "As I said earlier, each of you will have two protectors." He turned to the boys and said, "I've been very hard on you; please don't hate me, but I'll be even harder on you over the next two days. I need to be sure you will be so well trained that the protection of the girls will be in no doubt. Although you will be invisible to man there will be times when you will become visible just as Fafner did during the battle of Dublin, this is when you will be vulnerable. 'He' will be waiting, he will use this time to target you, this will be the time he will unleash his legions to the location you are in and his attack will be relentless. He will try to destroy all you have achieved and prevent you from bringing the Light back to that area, he will be ruthless and merciless." He paused again before imparting his final thoughts,

"The Gods of both Asgard and Olympus, the southern pantheon and the Indus Gods will all be sleeping during your travels. The Astrals will remain awake, especially in the western lands for they are the guardians of the natural world. Watch out for them, they will always answer your call. The ancient source Light will be carried safely in your hands. Use it wisely, be careful. Don't let down your guard as we may not be there to rescue you.

The third age is about to be placed in your hands and in three days you will begin changing the path of man."

He then asked if there were any questions, reservations or fears. No one spoke for a while until Modi said, "Jacob, I'm impressed. I wish you were by my side during the cosmic wars."

Garuda found the courage to speak, "Everything you said seems well thought out and sounds great, why is it I feel so nervous? Why do you speak of our future successes and then throw in so many failures. Is the success of our journey not set in stone?"

Baldor spoke up, "You said I will bring the Light to the dark lands of the north. If we all carry the Light, why are you emphasising mine?"

Jacob replied, "Your Light is the same as all others but my vision shows you leading an exodus in the far north, a rescue mission, but I can't see why?"

Faer sheepishly raised his hand before lowering it again. He was unsure until Magni said, "Speak up, it's now or never."

"This might sound selfish and I don't mean to be," he said after clearing his throat, "that day in the lagoon, when we first met, we all sensed something, a strange calling. We knew our lives were going to change forever. We could have run away but something held us there. When we met Poseidon, your mother and then Zeus we knew then there was no going back. Many of us had our own hopes and dreams, things that meant and still mean something to us. We toiled in the fields and worked the waters. We had families and looked forward to our futures with, one day our own families; little children running about our feet. For me, to complete my life and especially since I turned fifteen, all I ever wanted was to be a father, just like my father and his father before him. Can this happen for us now?"

Jacob didn't know what to say, this never crossed his mind. Oba and Panya then spoke up and said they too always looked forward to the day when they would be mothers. Eala attempted to stand, she was noticeably uneasy while shifting about on her chair.

Magni intervened and reminded them of immortals who had children; he assured them that if it was meant to be it would happen. He told them that if it happened they would have the support of the gods and will be assisted at all times. He then asked them to put these thoughts from their minds and concentrate on the task before them.

Jacob thanked them and was about to call an end to the meeting when his expression changed, he slowly descended into a trance-like state. The torches in the room flickered, at first slowly then wildly. A slow tremor rumbled beneath their feet before gathering strength causing the columns in the temple to violently shake. Jacob's mouth slightly opened, uttering a sinister laugh causing Odi to summon the Hammer. Magni and Modi leapt to their feet; looked around but could see nothing. The eight boys took up defensive positions around the girls relying solely on their under-trained and unused martial art skills. There were no weapons. The Hammer arrived and failed to penetrate the doors, now magically sealed by an unknown force.

As powerful as this force was, it was unable to do any real damage because Olympus was heavily protected. Jacob remained sitting with his hands resting on the table. His mouth moved violently showing he was fighting an internal battle. At times a deep guttural sound was uttered until finally Lucifer broke through. The haunting laugh grew louder showing Jacob was now totally possessed. "Fools, you fools, you think you can defy me," said Lucifer in a rasping voice. "Through Jacob's I've seen and heard all your plans and now know what I must do. I'll be waiting at every crossroads, every bridge, every valley, on every mountain. You cannot hide from me. I will defeat the Light and bring back The Darkness. The Ancient One will rue the day he banished me."

Out in the gardens Zeus leapt to his feet and then quickly ran towards the temple with many of the Warrior Gods running closely behind. Raphael was closer and first to arrive. He used the power of an Archangel to smash through the door allowing the Hammer through. Odi raised his hand and the Hammer answered, he looked about, but couldn't see a target. He looked back at Jacob and saw him glow, it was the light of Raphael and he was using it to expel Lucifer. The Light grew brighter and suddenly a black mist rapidly flowed from Jacob's mouth before exiting the temple and crashing through the protective shield. Jacob collapsed to the floor recoiling in pain, "He hates me!" he screamed, "I don't know why. He's determined to destroy me."

Zeus by now had arrived and was furious his temple was breeched. He summoned his guards only to be told there was no perimeter breech and what happened seemed to come from within Jacob. After confirming Jacob was fine, he left to check the perimeter himself.

Jacob was shocked Lucifer now knew his plans but couldn't understand how he possessed him. He sat back at the table and looked around for Eala who was now surrounded by a very dim Light, one he didn't recognise. He wasn't troubled, it looked protective and he felt no threat. He did wonder if it was trying to tell him something or was it trying to hide something from him. After relaxing and focusing back on his friends, he looked at them and could see they were in control. He thought of his speech and was satisfied his plans would work even with Lucifer's threats. He said his farewells, and made his way to his room where he fell into a deep sleep.

Several hours later Odi arrived to find Jacob standing at the window looking out across the meadows, "Hope you're OK?" he asked.

Jacob just nodded, and then said, "Odi, this is all too much for me, I'm having difficulty coping. It was too easy for Lucifer to enter my head, how can this be?"

"You need to get over yourself," said Odi moving to stand beside him, "don't you realise how powerful you are? You are destined to be the King of Kings, do you not think that what happened was part of a plan? Evil cannot enter the temple, it may be able to breech the shield and enter the realm but never the temple. The only way it could enter the temple was if the Ancient One allowed it happen. I believe it happened to show us what we are dealing with. Lucifer thinks he's smart. He thinks entering Olympus makes him more powerful, he's not. He's been lulled into a false sense of power."

"I hope you're right," replied Jacob. "Everything was so real."

"Enough of Lucifer," said Odi while wearing his renowned smirk. "You know when something is best served cold? Well, it's payback time."

"What are you after?" asked Jacob, closing his eyes, fearing the worst.

"Fear not brother," said Odi, "those times when I entered your head without permission, I saw your friendships. I saw the parties and the girls. I saw how happy you were. I also saw the places you visited, places where the great artists, writers and sculptors lived. I want you to show me why it's so important to save them. Take me to the time of the renaissance. Will you do that for me?"

Jacob relaxed; he knew exactly where to bring him. He put in place a plan for them to leave the temple for about forty minutes allowing them to spend at least two whole days in the realm of man.

Just then Thor and Maria entered the room, and knowing their sons so well, they saw they were scheming. Maria entered Jacobs head and saw what he was planning, "This time," she said, "I'm not going to worry, or complain. You'll just ignore me. Go; make sure you look after each other."

Thor couldn't help worrying; he sought out Magni and told him to keep an eye on the twins and to make sure he travels with them. Magni ensured Modi was also aware of the twin's plans.

Chapter 21

Magni and Modi arrived to the bedroom and soon fell into a troubled sleep. Jacob was already in bed, he knew he was being watched. He also knew his brothers were not quite asleep. He too pretended and when he thought it was safe he stretched across and lit a nearby torch. Odi then woke and they started to talk about the events of the day. Magni's troubled mind caused him to twist and turn, still being very annoyed at how vulnerable he was earlier that day. He eventually woke and listened to the boys talk about Eala and Panya and the fun they were having together. He then heard Odi remind Jacob about their planned trip. When Jacob called on the Light, he jumped from his bed, interrupted him yelling, "Not so fast, you're going nowhere without us." He woke Modi insisting all four of them travel together, fully armed and ready for any attack that might happen. Jacob and Odi protested as this was a safe and random trip to the city of Florence in the north of Italy.

An unseemly row developed as Jacob and Odi made their feelings known, their shouting and objections went almost to the point of insulting Magni. Magni had enough, he grew in stature to his colossus form, looked down on his younger brothers bringing the fear of Odin into both of them. "You're going nowhere without us, never again will I stand in a different dimension unable to assist my brothers in a fight against an unyielding evil. We're going with you and there's no more will be said."

"There is a lot more to be said," yelled Jacob standing up on his bed, trying to get eye ball to eye ball with Magni, he hadn't yet learned how to become a colossus, "You're not coming, that's my decision so go and get a life." Modi and Odi nearly collapsed; no one has ever stood up to Magni and survived."

Magni was secretly impressed; even so he had to assert his seniority. He gripped Jacob by the shoulders and raised him so that they were now definitely eyeball to eyeball, "What part don't you understand?" he bellowed gripping Jacob even tighter, "We're going with you whether you like it or not, do I make myself clear?"

"You're not going to win this one," said a defeated Odi. "Best let them come."

Jacob had no intention of letting them go, he winked at Odi indicating he had a plan. He placed his hand on Magni's shoulder and quickly stretched down to grab Modi. He blinked and dropped both of them in Asgard. He returned to Olympus, grabbed Odi, blinked and travelled through time to arrive in the heart of Florence during the High Renaissance.

Florence was beautiful at that time of year. The streets were so clean and the buildings well kept for it was a rich city. The Medici family were at the zenith of their power and were patrons of the greatest artists and sculptors. The rich and famous of the time always included this city in a new fad that was developing in Europe at that time, which would eventually grow to be called, 'The Grand Tour'.

Odi was fascinated by the works he saw while in one back street studio, Jacob recognised the works to be by Michelangelo. They visited many other studios, including one that specialised in inventing. There were also paintings including one that was being worked on while they were there. It was the studio of Leonardo De Vinci and he was painting a most beautiful lady, her name was Lisa. Jacob knew of the artist, "Now that I really see her, I have to say, he didn't do her justice, yet this painting becomes one of the most famous and sought after paintings in the world."

"She is beautiful! I could stay all day just watching her. In fact, I could stay just watching this master at work." said Odi.

"Who's there?" said Leonardo, "I hear voices."

The boys went quiet and continued to watch Leonardo put the finishing touches to his work. "This is one painting for which he will certainly be remembered," said Jacob.

"Jacob," said Odi, "that studio we visited earlier, Michelangelo's. When we were there I felt Panya's presence. Did you?"

"No. But I did feel something. Let's investigate."

They arrived back to the studio just as a very excited Michelangelo was announcing a new commission to his apprentices. It was the sculpting of a colossal seventeen foot tall statue of David, to be installed on the buttresses at the east end of the Florence Cathedral.

Jacob and Odi listened to Michelangelo discuss the kind of model he required, how he had visited many workshops and private houses, even called to the military barracks in the hope of finding one man who would fit the image of what he wanted, all to no avail. The apprentices knew he was the consummate perfectionist and wouldn't commence the work until he found his model. One apprentice suggested he travel to Rome, a city of many, many thousands, in search of a model. Michelangelo agreed and made his way to his room to start packing.

On leaving his room he was surprised to see two tall, almost identical youths, standing near where his apprentice's were working. He rubbed his eyes, thinking he was seeing things. He quickly established no others could see them. He approached them, showing no fear, and placed his hand on

Odi's arm. The boys were confused as nobody was supposed to be able to see them. The apprentices sniggered, thinking their teacher was losing his mind, they watched him talk and gesticulate as though in an animated conversation. Little did they know that Michelangelo had found his model, not one but two handsome and muscular youths, who were both perfect for what he had in mind.

"How can this be?" asked Michelangelo, "I see you, yet no one else can. Are you angels?" Odi said,

"We're not angels," replied Odi, "we're travellers. We've come to see and admire your works."

The apprentices were sent home allowing Michelangelo to sit, uninterrupted, negotiating with Jacob and Odi for one of them to model. He chose Odi because his blond, red tinged hair made him stand out more than Jacobs dark hair did.

Jacob knew what was coming when Michelangelo asked Odi to stand on a nearby large stone plinth. Michelangelo blended sand and grit together to create a mix used for sculpting templates, while Odi climbed the plinth. Jacob bit his lip, trying to prevent a laugh escaping, he knew what the statue of David looked like and couldn't wait to see Odi's face when asked to remove his clothes.

"Odi," asked Jacob, "do you know what the statue of David looks like?"

"No, never heard of it," said Odi shaking his head.

"I've seen it, I used to think it looked familiar, but I never thought it was based on my identical twin brother." He bit his lip again. Then it happened, Odi's face was priceless, he protested but Michelangelo was very persuasive. Jacob was now doubled up, holding his abdomen, trying not to betray the fun he was having.

Odi was proud of his body and generally had no fear of revealing it in public, but he had limits, "There's no way I'm stripping if he's watching me," he said pointing at Jacob, "he's planning to tell everybody, to make a fool of me. He'll embellish it so much I'll never be allowed live it down."

"Why so scared, War God," said Jacob trying not to smile. "You seem to forget that we're identical twins. Everything you've got, I've got."

Odi thought for a moment, shrugged his shoulders and then suggestively disrobed. He stood there, the body of a god, proud of everything he had until he looked across at Jacob who had raised his arm and allowed his little figure to dangle. Odi responded by raising his hand and sending his version of that very well known, single finger response. They both laughed before Jacob said, "I need to go. I'll be back in a few minutes."

Jacob blinked and travelled to the twentieth century where he searched for an eight foot copy of the statue of David. He found one, conjured up the money and bought it. He used his powers to transport the statue back to Olympus where he placed it on a protruding plinth beside the steps of the temple. He placed it well before the gods were due to arrive for breakfast. He returned to Michelangelo's studio to find a four foot finished template being admired by Odi and Michelangelo. Odi admired his physique and all Michelangelo could say was, "Magnifico!"

All three then sat for many more hours talking about the gods and the coming battle with The Darkness. Michelangelo was told of how he will be remembered in history, how his sculpture, the Pieta, will adorn St Peter's Basilica in Rome. How his statue of the Angel will sit in the Basilica of San Dominica in Bologna and how his Sculpture of Bacchus will be taken from Rome and brought back to Florence. Michelangelo interrupted, "No. no. I've never sculpted Bacchus."

"My apologies," said Jacob, "you will create his statue, in the year 1516. It'll be based on an image of my cousin, Dionysus." Jacob then told him, "Your greatest painting will commence in 1508CE and be completed in 1512CE. This painting will tell the story of man starting with Genesis and will be painted in the Sistine chapel using depictions of the heavens shown to you by us."

"Where will I find time?" asked Michelangelo.

"There's always time," replied Jacob, "old age is a gift given to you. My visions show a funeral procession, Rome to Florence, it's your funeral, the year is 1564CE."

"That's many years from now," said a surprised Michelangelo, "there's much to do."

"And you will do it all," replied Jacob. "In the future there will be much discussion about a work you will create in 1530CE. It's the statue of Apollo, my greatest idol. Some think is Apollo, others David."

Jacob indicated that it was time to go. He walked to the centre of the studio and called on the Light. He was joined by Odi and just as they were about to depart Michelangelo stopped them, "Twelve hundred years ago an ancestor of mine, who lived near the ancient city of Palmyra, was approached by an angel and given a gift. My ancestor never understood what the gift was but made sure that the story of the angel was passed down through the generations and after our meeting today I now know it was the gift of Art."

"Did this angel have a name?" asked Jacob.

"Her name was Panya." was Michelangelo's reply. A wide smile crossed Odi's face.

"Panya's my friend," said Jacob, "she was sent by me to sow the seeds of greatness among man. She's moving towards the ice lands of the north and by now she should be in the Rus lands. Her gifts will help mankind fight The Darkness. She will be responsible for man loving your art and they will defend and protect it. The works of the great artists, the great composers, the great playwrights and the great sculptors will give man so much pleasure and keep them in the Light. It will also bring those moving towards The Darkness back into the Light."

Jacob continued, "I'm a God of Olympus, a Time Lord. Walk with me and meet your ancestors." He blinked and took him to walk through time, "see your father and your father's father. See your kin as we walk through time. Look at the columns of Rome, see the beauty of Greece, cross with me as we walk on water and reach the sacred lands, it is there where Olympus rests. Feel the power of these lands as we walk to the hills above Palmyra. Look into the cave and see a boy, he is but five years old, his name is Michael. See how my friend Panya comforts him and how Baldor and Thanases protect him. Now look at the ceiling of the cave. Take in the beauty of the paintings created by Michael's father. They are your ancestors, from them comes your gift of art."

Jacob then returned him back to Florence. Odi was ecstatic, his feelings for Panya were growing and to hear how after so many hundreds of years she was still travelling, this raised his spirits. The boys then left and returned to Olympus.

"Now to face the music," said a nervous Jacob, "wait here and don't move. I need to go back to the precise time I left Magni and Modi in Asgard, bring them back to the exact time I blinked them away and pray they won't have realised what happened."

He didn't get his way, just as he returning to the temple he was sent tumbling across the room by a forceful punch. It was Magni and he wasn't happy. "Do you think I'm a fool?" he yelled, "Do you think we don't know what you did? We are gods just like you. You were warned not to do anything stupid and what do you do? You ignore us. You are a target of Lucifer and your recklessness will allow him capture you."

"He had my protection," said Odi who suddenly realised he should have kept his mouth shut.

"Your protection?" yelled Magni, "I'm really pissed with you. Your protection didn't help when you were attacked in Dublin or in the village. Did it?" He grabbed Odi and went to punch him but was stopped by a more powerful hand. It was Thor who had just arrived into the room as Jacob brought Magni and Modi back. He held Magni until the anger abated and then whispered, "If you want to have a good laugh at their expense you need to go to the front of the temple."

Magni looked at his father, he was confused but his curiosity got the better of him. He angrily made his way to the main doors with Modi briskly walking behind him. On exiting their jaws dropped at the sight before them, it was about to gift them the greatest amount of fun in their ongoing teasing of poor Odi.

They walked to the front of the eight foot statue and when they saw the face they immediately recognised it to be either Odi or Jacob. The jokes just kept coming until they saw Jacob and Odi on the top step. Magni said pointing at the statue, "I'm trying to find the word but I'm having difficulty, is it small? No, it's TINY. You can't be a brother of mine."

"What have you done?" asked an embarrassed Odi, "How could you?"

"It was supposed to be a gift," replied Jacob, "I like it. After all it also looks like me." Odi was furious until he felt two arms wrap themselves around him. It was Aphrodite who held him tightly. She nibbled on his ear and then whispered just loud enough for Magni and Modi to hear, "Hello big boy."

Magni was disgusted. There was no point in continuing to tease because the sculpture was now endorsed by the Goddess of Love. Odi swaggered slowly towards, and then passed his two brothers with a smile that went from ear to ear. He was trilled knowing he'd got the better of them. Jacob then took the statue to a more appropriate position in the ornamental garden and arranged for the gardeners to place flowers and shrubs around it. Zeus and Odin arrived and admired how perfect it was. Jacob hid when he saw his mother and grandmother arrive. Maria just shook her head. At that point Jacob felt a red flushness cross his face, an embarrassment brought on knowing his mother hadn't seen him, or Odi, naked since they were babies. Odi arrived as Maria was leaving and walked by her with a smirk on his face. Jacob joined him and they both admired their physique. Their friends arrived and Eala was first to comment, "Looking good Jacob, exactly as I remember."

"That's not me, it's Odi," replied Jacob.

"Are you sure?" she said, "If it's not you, you're certainly identical in every way." There was a lot of muffled laughter.

Jacob wanted to swagger but thought better of it. He then got serious and told the boys to prepare for their second day of training.

Chapter 22

Early the next morning when Jacob arrived into the meadows the boys were already waiting. "Good," he said, "plans are slightly changed for today. I'll be running with you for the first hour, after that I want Faer to take control, spend time learning to master the sword, and hone your martial arts skills. I trust you to follow Faer's instructions while out in the meadows. When you return to the temple you'll be under the supervision of Ares and as a result I believe you will end this day as true warriors of Olympus. They left on their run.

Meanwhile, Magni joined Ares and asked him if he would be interested in a three round sword fight, he felt he was getting a bit rusty and needed a good workout. Ares willingly agreed. Magni was the one Warrior God he never beat. They made their way to the amphitheatre as word spread throughout the temple that a friendly fight was about to start.

The amphitheatre soon filled and then the banter between Ares and Magni began. Ares raised his shield and charged towards Magni who deftly somersaulted at ground level and landed behind him. They circled each other looking for the slightest weakness but to no avail, they were equals and had to find other strategies. Magni made the next move, landing his sword across Ares' shield allowing Ares to stretch out his arm just far enough out so as to return his sword, pounding it flat side on Magni's back sending him to the ground face down. Ares rushed forward placing his knee on the small of

Magni's back securing his sword under his neck. It was round one to Ares. He held out his hand and said to Magni, "I now see how rusty you've become; in the past you'd never have allowed that to happen, maybe you should be the pupil, not the teacher?"

Magni picked up his sword, and rapidly rotated it to loosen up his muscles. He took up a forward thrusting position, ready for anything Ares might throw at him. He was determined to win this round resenting the comment about training with the boys. Ares circled, probing gently and looked for weaknesses, but found none. Magni never budged. A few more moments passed when Magni stepped back and the closer Ares got, Magni kept stepping backwards. When a large space developed between them Magni made his move. The slid his shield along the ground causing the Asgard Gods to get uneasy, they knew Magni was about to unleash a fencing onslaught that no opponent could beat. He raised his sword using both hands and swung it wildly from left to right, stepping forward in determined strides causing Ares to get a little confused. Ares gathered himself together and prepared his defences. He threw his shield in a sliding motion, timed perfectly to land under Magni's right foot sending him again to the ground. This time Ares misjudged and missed Magni's back allowing Magni to turn and place his sword between Ares ribs next to his heart. Round two went to Magni.

During the second round the boys arrived back from their run and took seats to watch the last round. They saw part of the second round and were getting very anxious as Ares looked all pumped up and would probably give them a hard time.

Jacob was sitting with his arm around Eala's shoulder. She had her hand on his leg. Odi sat with Panya and the more they talked and laughed the more his feelings for her grew. He asked her to meet him near the lagoon, after dinner that night, a suggestion she willingly agreed to. Jacob saw the closeness develop and entered Odi's head and this time Odi was happy for him to be there. He wanted him to know he had a date for that night. Jacob was happy for his brother and wanted him to have a love like he had.

Round three began with a continuous and relentless attack on each other that lasted for half an hour. Ares used his shield not only for protection but also as a weapon. He pounded it off Magni's head when the chances arose. Magni was no angel either, he used similar tactics. The swords never got near either of them.

Their skin was covered in sweat and grit collected as each one fell, frustration gathered and neither was prepared to concede. Ares sought the inner strength of a god of Greece but even that didn't help. They were both equal. Ares became more determined and unleashed a powerful attack sending Magni reeling backwards towards a nearby column. Magni's back was to the pillar when he felt the tip of Ares' sword rest against his neck, "I think round three is mine," said a smirking Ares.

"I'm not so sure?" said an equally confident Magni.

Ares' face changed from glee to panic when he felt the sharp point of Magni's sword slightly tear his skin just between his ninth and tenth rib.

Zeus intervened, "End this now," he said, "There are far more im portant issues to be dealt with."

Magni and Ares bowed slightly to each other and agreed that maybe the next time there would be a winner. Magni then offered to assist with the boys training that day.

The boys, on hearing Magni's offer became more apprehensive and their fear was noticed by Apollo, "Why look so scared?" he asked and when he got no reply he suggested, "Stand back and look at each other, do you notice anything?"

The boys stepped back, looked at each other and to a man they said they didn't notice anything. Chiron stretched across and felt Girish's upper arm, squeezing it gently. Girish instinctively tensed up, allowing a huge muscle to rise. The boys again looked at each other and this time they clearly saw how strong and muscular they'd become, huge muscles had developed not only on their arms and legs but all over their bodies. "You may have been spending five or six hours training in the Olympus realm," said Chiron, "those hours, at times, can be the equivalent of months of training back in the realm of man."

The boys relaxed and went to face Ares and Magni knowing, that by the end of the day, they will have learned many new skills. Magni and Ares worked as a very skilful team, showing no mercy knowing mercy wouldn't be shown by any adversary. Their training was intense but when over the boys didn't feel as sore as yesterday, but still they asked Jacob to use the water to soften their muscles and relieve their aches and pains.

While the boys were training the girls were with Hephaestus for the first fitting of their robes and capes. The elves had designed the most exquis- ite cotton and silk gowns with matching capes that were light, and braided in gold. The jewellers were still working on their necklaces, ear rings and bracelets, promising to have the jewellery ready just before their departure. Maria, Aphrodite and Dione were also present.

Eala was first to be fitted and while undressing she was unaware Jacob was hiding in the shadows, watching and enjoying the view. However, he was caught by Maria who promptly ran him, telling him that this was ladies time. As he ran away he shouted, "Tell Hephaestus I'll be back later to see how the weapons, clothing and shields are progressing."

Jacob went to another of his favourite places, the grassy knoll, near one of the waterfalls at the side of the lagoon. While there he lay watching the white, puffed up clouds float by, before drifting into a restful sleep. He awoke several hours later to find Odi lying a few feet away.

"Hi," Odi said, "to use one of your Dublinisms, 'I'm bricking it', I've never been so nervous about meeting anybody as I am about meeting Panya later tonight. I've feelings for her, and for the first time I care too much to risk making a mess of it."

"I love you brother," said Jacob, "and I'm happy for you, but I'm afraid I can't help you with this one. You'll have to find your own way. Remember she's leaving in two days." Odi just nodded showing his disappointment. He left for his room leaving Jacob to head back to the workshops where Hephaestus was waiting on him. Baldor was there, already dressed in the imperial clothing and weaponry of an Olympus guardian and warrior. The cream tunic was perfect and came to just below his knees; tied with a belt that matched his boots. His scarlet cape hung from his shoulders using golden clasps in a Celtic design, it dropped behind him almost to his ankles. His dark brown ankle boots were tied in place using cord woven by the cave worms of Crete. The golden fitted breast armour carried the Valknut symbol of Asgard surrounding the Olympic flame of Olympus. The matching helmet was not unlike those worn by the kings of old and it was adorned with the feathers of the golden eagle.

The Santorini Nymphs then presented his weapons, a sword and a dagger made from gold plated titanium. They also created a spear suitable for use as a staff and a light bearer. Jacob saw there were ten swords, daggers and spears and asked who the two extra sets were for. The Nymphs then presented one set of weapons to him saying the other was for Odi.

The Nymphs assisted by placing the belt and scabbard around Baldor's waist and buckled a smaller belt just below his knee which held a scabbard for the dagger. The sword was then placed in his hand to ensure it was the perfect fit. Baldor then placed the sword in the scabbard. The shield shapers of Asgard presented a golden shield and placed it on his left arm. Hephaestus placed the spear into his right hand.

Jacob stood back and looked on Baldor in awe just as Merlin and Apollonius arrived. They too looked at Baldor and nodded in admiration. Merlin approached him saying, "You're not quite ready yet."

Jacob was confused, he felt he had covered everything required to create a powerful guardian. Apollonius reached into his pouch and took a small clear crystal, and after securing it in a specially designed recess just below the tip of the spear said, "Now you're complete. You and your fellow guardians will each carry a crystal, allowing the ancient source Light to guide and protect you on your journey. Use it wisely and it will be your friend. It will blind the serpents, but always remember it alone won't defeat The Darkness but it'll give you time."

Jacob stood back and alongside Merlin, Apollonius and Hephaestus they admired how Baldor looked. He was now a most powerful immortal, a Warrior God of both Olympus and Asgard.

The bell tolled for dinner summoning the gods to the temple. Jacob had earlier asked Zeus for permission for the round table to be placed in the Great Hall which was readily agreed to. He felt he should spend the last two nights with Odi and his friends, instead of with his family.

As usual the Olympus kitchens produced the best of food and wine, so much so that Dionysus was getting worried. The constant dinners and the young Asgard Gods were draining his cellars and he wasn't sure if he could arrange enough replacements for the following night's final dinner.

When dinner ended, Jacob took the opportunity to tell the boys about what was required on their third and final day. He insisted they begin with another hour long run through the meadows, followed by learning about horses and art of horsemanship, with Pegasus as their teacher. He sniggered when telling them they were likely to have blisters in sensitive places after riding to the furthest reaches of the Olympus realm. He assured them that by the time they returned they will have learned all the skills of the Horse Lords. He reminded then before the afternoon was out they will have learned the art of negotiation from Chiron and all about medicine from Apollo. The final lesson just before dinner will be about the tactics of war and it'll be given by Athena and Ares.

He turned to the girls and said while apologising for his lack of attention over the last few days. "Your part in this story is to plant, using the Light, the seeds of greatness in the mind of man. You are not to be distracted by what the boys will have to deal with. You'll be seen as angels and as goddesses. Your beauty will be spoken of and written about in the great stories. You will be visible to a few oracles and wizards and will always be protected." He told them they will be the ground layers and comforters of man.

Eala reached across and placed her fingers across his lips and said, "Enough, prophet of doom. Tonight let's celebrate all that we have achieved. Let the boys brag about their huge muscles and their fitness prowess. Let us sing and dance, for tomorrow will be another tough day." Jacob began to open his mouth when Odi stretched across and placed his hand completely across his mouth saying, "Brother, shut it."

Jacob slumped back in his chair and shrugged his shoulders. It was then that a little bit of boasting began. Girish stood, rolled up his sleeves and tensed his muscles. All were impressed until Thanases stood and removed his tunic. His long, blond, full and wavy hair reached his shoulders. He tensed and produced the most awesome muscles, the likes of which even the gods had never seen before. Odin gestured to Magni and Modi, "Look, he is of Norse descent, he is of Asgard, he stands as a Warrior God. Jacob has chosen him well, look after him, I see him leading the Norse Lords."

Chapter 23

Jacob excused himself and left the table, the hustle and bustle of the temple bothered him when he was anxious and the quietness of his bedroom always helped to revitalise him. He'd only just settled when Magni, Modi and Odi arrived, they saw he wasn't impressed and he made his feelings known. Jacob normally loved their company but this night he just wanted to be alone. Magni was having none of it and insisted he rejoin the family in the Great Hall. He reluctantly agreed and as he was walking towards the door all heard, beep, beep….beep, beep…. beep, beep….beep.

Magni grabbed a spear from the wall and took up an attack position. Jacob froze and then got excited. Odi knew what it was and told Magni to relax. Jacob ran towards his bed and fumbled around until he laid his hand on his iPhone, not believing it still had a charge. He opened the cover and found himself on face time. It was Shane who yelped excitedly on seeing him, "Scobie, where've you been, it's been months. I called every day, as much as ten times, you never answered. Why?"

"It's only been five days!" said Jacob

"No, are you mad?" replied Shane, "Jacob, it's been six months. I miss you, Scobie, we all miss you." Odi sat next to Jacob.

"Hi Odi, I hope you are looking after my buddy?"

"Of course I am," replied Odi, "we're inseparable."

"That's the way Jacob and I used to be until everything changed, I don't like these changes." said Shane.

"I'm sorry bud," said Jacob, "it's easy to forget how time here glides by so much slower than where you are, my five days must be the same as your six months."

"Everyone is still talking about what happened in Temple Bar," said Shane. "The funerals went on for weeks. The world is going mad. They never stop talking about you and Odi. There are more sightings of dragons. Dragons! Can you imagine? They won't leave me and the boys alone. I wouldn't be surprised if this call is been tapped."

"I don't think you should concern yourself about being tapped," said Jacob, "there's not much time left. The Darkness is coming, it's getting closer. NASA should have, by now, detected stars dying all across the galaxy. Whole areas of space should be turning black with no light coming from anywhere near there."

"We're not been told anything about that," replied Shane, "but now it makes sense as to why, all around the world, so many people are inexplicably being killed. It's suspected they've witnessed strange things happening and are being prevented from revealing this information to the public. Scobie, I'm frightened, I don't want to die. We need you to come back, please help us."

"There are plans," said Jacob winking at him, "I'll tell you about them at another time, not now, as you just said, tapped. How are the boys? Are they OK?"

"No, they're not," replied Shane while getting emotional, "they're still traumatised. Al has withdrawn into himself, he won't come out with us; he goes to school then rushes home, staying in his room."

Just then Magni came into view, and Shane reacted, "Who the FUCK is that? Jesus he's big, he looks like a Norse God."

"That's our elderly brother," said Odi before receiving a clatter to the back of the head.

"How old?" Shane asked.

"Since soon after the beginning of time," replied Jacob.

The door opened and Eala arrived, she ran to hug Jacob and then kissed him on the cheek.

"WHO…IS…SHE?" asked Shane. "Where did you meet her?"

"She's the love of my life. I plan to spend eternity with her. We met in the lagoon outside the temple."

"It's about time. I was beginning to think…" sniggered Shane.

"Ah, ah, ah, don't go there," interrupted Jacob,

"So you're the famous Shane," exclaimed Eala, "it's nice to put a face to the name. He never stops talking about you, so much so, that sometimes I think he would rather be with you than me."

Maria and Thor arrived. Maria got excited when she saw Jacob chatting on his iPhone. She grabbed the phone to be met with her usual greeting, "Hi Gorgeous."

She welled up while rubbing her fingers across the screen, she always felt like a second mother to Shane, he was always in her house and she loved his cheekiness. She joined Thor and brought him into view, "Say hello to Jacob's dad."

"Jesus," exclaimed Shane, "are all the men in your life that big? No wonder I'd no chance."

"So you're my competition?" said Thor just as the signal started fading. There was just enough time for Shane to plead, "Scobie, don't forget us, we need you, help us." The signal was lost.

Jacob threw the phone on to his bed and stared at Odi, he then looked at Eala. Both sensed his distress and knew he was planning to do something. They followed him to the Great Hall where he requested a private meeting with Zeus and Odin. Odi and Maria joined him and encouraged him to speak.

He began, "Since Olympus came back to life many of you have got to know me, some of you have already found out how stubborn I can be," he looked across at Magni but got no reaction, "I'm not happy and I'm worried about my friends in Dublin. They've an idea of what's coming but not about how bad it's going to be. Right now I'm conflicted so I'm seeking your advice. Just remember every bone in my body tells me I should go and prepare them."

He stopped Maria from speaking then continued, "The one thing I've learned since arriving in this temple is that everything to do with the gods is part of a grand plan, even my falling in love with Eala. It's with great difficulty I've accepted her departure and that's because of that same plan. Shane's call wasn't an accident; it too is part of the plan so I'm going to Dublin even though it breaks all the rules. I'm sought your advice out of respect, but I need you to trust me."

He was interrupted by Odin who said, "You and Eala are both immortals and will be together again, time to immortals means nothing but breaking the rules of Olympus is different. Those rules have served the gods well and shouldn't be disregarded so easily."

"I know we're immortals, but we're young immortals and time means everything to us. Everyone knows I respect rules but when rules are no longer fit for purpose, especially with the advance of The Darkness, those rules have to change." Zeus said nothing; all saw him bite his lip.

He turned to his family, "You all saw Shane and heard his pleas. He's my closest friend and he needs me. I'm going to help even if I break the rules

because it's the right thing to do. My visions show my friends, when prepared, being of great assistance when the battle begins,"

"You're not going," yelled Magni pounding his clenched fists on the
table. "Rules are rules and they must be obeyed. How can you help them
when it's you that needs more training? Man was given the means to defend
himself; they can figure this one out for themselves."

"I think you forget, over the last few days I've been trained by the greatest War Gods," said Jacob looking at each of his brothers in turn, "most
importantly I've been looked after by three great and caring brothers. I can
defend myself, you know I can. I'm going."

"You should know better," said Magni shaking his head. "Remember
what happened when you and Odi were attacked by the serpents and Dark
Angels?"

Modi intervened, he stretching across to grip Magni's arm, "You're
wasting your time, and you know you are. He's more stubborn than you ever
were, you're not going to win this one, let him go and we'll deal with any
consequences."

"We must trust Jacob," said Merlin, "he believes he must travel to Dublin so we must allow him. We cannot have a god go into battle carrying a
great worry and fear. We must let him allay that fear. Have you forgotten
how one day in the realm of man is but a short time here in Olympus? He'll
be back in thirty minutes and all our worries will have passed,"

Magni was furious at the intervention of Merlin but was pragmatic
enough to realise that he wasn't going to win this battle. "What's this desire
to go to the aid of Shane?" he asked, "our most sacred laws state that we
must never interfere in the realm of man. They must face the Ancient One
alone. Why do you give us this worry?"

Jacob said, "Why do you worry? As I've already stated, I've been trained by the greatest war gods including you."

Magni softened, "It happens to be part of what older brother's do. We'll always worry about our younger brothers."

"Whatever about me," said a now exasperated Jacob, "why would you worry about Odi, he's a War God and is powerful enough to beat the living daylights out of you."

Magni clenched his fists, he was having trouble containing himself, "Don't rile me," he said through gritted teeth, "you won't be able to handle me. Having said that, I know you're going to defy me, so I'm asking for one concession."

Jacob asked, "What is it?" to which Magni replied, "Take Fafner and Baldor as guardians." Jacob thought for a moment and agreed. Zeus didn't look happy; he just left and went to sit in the gardens.

Fafner and Baldor headed to the workshop where they were met by Hephaestus, who gathered together their robes and weapons. They quickly dressed and returned back to the temple where they walked in side by side. Those present were speechless and congratulated Hephaestus on his wonderful designs. Odin and Zeus gave their blessing, especially on seeing the way the revered Norse Valknut symbol, surrounded by the laurels of Olympus was etched across the breastplate.

"It pleases me," said Odin, "to see my symbol of power, courage and devotion surrounded by your symbol of victory."

"I agree," nodded Zeus. "The combined symbols can only be a good omen. Hephaestus has excelled himself this time. That armour will provide such strong protection."

In the meantime Jacob returned to his room to fetch his jeans, his trainers and a white t-shirt. When he arrived back to the Great Hall, he looked so different. Many of the gods never saw modern clothes and were impressed with how well he looked. Jacob stood between Fafner and Baldor. He sought reassurance from his mother and was delighted when she walked over to embrace him. He waved at Eala and blew her a kiss, he called Magni over and while raising his arms to embrace him said, "I'm sorry, you are the greatest. Odi would never be able for you, not in a million years. Please forgive me."

"Already forgiven," nodded Magni. "Just be careful."

Jacob then placed his hands on his guardian's shoulders and together they bowed to Odin. Jacob then blinked and all three disappeared.

Chapter 24

They maintained their invisibility as they walked through the gates of Jacob's old school. All around them, hundreds of pupils were using the playing fields but there was no sign of Jacob's classmates. They walked up the avenue and made their way towards the main door where Jacob used his magic to open the doors allowing them access into the entrance hall. Jacob went to the reception desk and accessed the computer to find the location of the transition year classrooms. He located the rooms and established which one Shane was in. On reaching the classroom and after opening the door he heard one of his classmates quip, "Must be Jacob."

The classmates nervously laughed while watching the doorknob rotate back and the door close. Shane was overheard saying, "I wish it was." At that point Jacob materialised.

Shane, Al and Davie leapt from their desks and ran to hug him, only to be met with the appearance of two imperial guards of Olympus, both with swords drawn ready to protect a grandson of Zeus. The boys froze as the swords and daggers rested on their Adams apples. Jacob raised his arm and defused the situation. All three again jumped towards him and it got very emotional. He had trouble separating from them knowing they needed more time. He gave special attention to Al aware that he was struggling the most, "Al, buddy," he whispered, "I know you're suffering and how frightened you are but you need to find your strength because what's coming will be much worse. What happened in Temple Bar was going to happen even if Odi and I weren't there. I'm here to help you prepare."

Jacob looked around and saw there were nineteen pupils and one teacher in the classroom. He enquired about those who were missing and was informed by the teacher they were killed in the battle of Dublin.

Jacob closed his eyes and in his mind travelled back to the battle. He searched everywhere and eventually found the missing pupils huddled together. He watched in horror as the serpents found and attacked them, he then saw the white mist leave them. He opened his eyes and told the class that the four boys didn't succumb to The Darkness; they went into the Light.

Two boys at the back of the class stood to verbally attacked Jacob; they were close friends of the boys who were killed. They accused him of bringing the evil from wherever he came from, and wondered if he was bringing the evil again today. They were so angry their voices began to break. Jacob allowed them vent and didn't react. When they calmed he said, "I've something to tell you and I want to explain myself."

"I'm not sure you should be here," said the teacher, "for all we know you and your brother were responsible for what happened in Dublin. Everything is still raw and the grief is everywhere. Are you aware there's a worldwide search going on for you?"

"I will not take responsibility for something I didn't cause but I will apologise for this intrusion. I suggest you sit and listen to what I have to say." The teacher and pupils sat and waited.

Jacob began, "I didn't have to come here today but every bone in my body screamed out to me that I should warn you about what's coming. I fear that what the future brings is the end of mankind. You are my closest friends and I care about you so I'm prepared to help. There were fierce objections to me coming here, fearing the dark one would locate me, but it's a chance

I'm prepared to take. I don't fear him because I've been trained by two of the greatest War Gods, Ares and Athena. I'm under the protection of the Asgard Realm, led by my brothers Magni and Modi. I'm also protected by the power of the elves, and the wizards Merlin and Apollonius. Look at my guardians and see their power, they will keep all evil from me. Lucifer has been released from his cocoon, we know he has risen. He expelled the God of the Underworld and ruthlessly took over Hell. Almost immediately he sent his serpents into the realm of man. His plans are simple, create terror, and defy the Ancient One. He is working with The Darkness. We temporarily stopped him but even that was too late, as hundreds, possibly thousands of his serpents have been released, waiting for their time to join a full scale attack. From their hiding places they've been doing their evil work. Over the last two thousand years they've been biting the ancestors of tyrants, and the evil they planted has now travelled through their bloodlines. Just look at your history books and you'll know who I'm talking about. These tyrants carry the mark of the serpent, just like the mark of Cain. We know Lucifer will break through our defences but we don't know when. We know he will unleash more Dark Angels, just like the ones you saw in Temple Bar, alongside them will be millions upon millions of souls, ones who have been turned evil since the beginning of time. He will also resurrect the fallen angels, those who were his allies during the first war. They will be the most lethal of adversaries and will be ruthless in their onslaught. Their whole purpose will be to gather as many souls needed to feed the hunger of Lucifer, and they will show no mercy. When this happens it will be the start of the greatest battle since the creation."

There was absolute silence. Nobody knew what to say. Just as questions were about to be asked two pupils left their desks and stormed towards the door, they accused Jacob of scaremongering and spreading a load of rubbish, they were joined by another seven. They didn't reach the door. Jacob raised his hand and commanded the door to slam shut; it did with the loudest bang. He used his powers to secure the latches on the windows, ensuring no one could leave.

"Why can't you see the changes happening around you?" he asked while approaching the two with the strongest objections, "Listen to the rumblings rolling beneath your feet, do you not hear them? He's coming and will destroy you. He's at his most powerful when people like you reject the Light. I need you to stand with me in defence of that Light."

All but one of the boys wavered and retook their seats, the remaining boy attacked Jacob. It was Jake. "My best friend was killed that night," he said while grabbing Jacob by the neck, "we were friends since we were babies. My life is empty without him and you caused it."

"If I and my brother gods weren't there," replied a gasping Jacob, "you, and all my friends would be gone. What happened in Temple Bar was the first attack on that scale, and we believe it was set to draw us out. They changed their strategy when they saw how we defended ourselves." Jake tightened his grip causing Fafner to raise his sword, preparing to decapitate him.

Baldor slightly backed away, sensing something, not sure of his feelings. With his sword vibrating in its scabbard he went on alert, he extracted his staff and called on the Light. When it arrived it sent a brilliant white glow around the classroom, highlighting the 'mark of the serpent' on Jakes shoulder. He increased its intensity, causing Jake to slam against the wall. His shrieks of pain were so loud they unnerved all those within earshot, but Baldor held his nerve and continued to increase the intensity of the Light. The writhing and shaking showed he was possessed by a very powerful entity causing Fafner to become more concerned. He extracted his sword and took a defensive position, preventing any expelled demon from gaining access to Jacob.

When the demon was finally expelled it stood in the classroom as an eight foot tall Dark Angel. His wings spread out showing the pupils the horror and power of Hell. On seeing Jacob, the Dark Angel smirked and in a rasping and sinister voice said, "Ah, King of Kings, yet still a boy. He'll be pleased you've let your guard down."

As the angel started fading, Baldor reacted and attacked. With his sword raised high, he leapt forward and with the swiftest of movements sliced the angel's head from his shoulders. The teacher and pupils were now cowering at the back of the classroom as Jake lay unconscious on the floor.

Jacob now had a dilemma - What to do with the black mist? He summoned his Light, hoping to prevent the mist from leaving the room. He used his Light to surround the mist, successfully stifling it, causing it to disappear into nothingness and preventing a warning from reaching Lucifer. He then used his power to incinerate the body of the Dark Angel, causing it to turn to ash before sending it into the nothingness.

Jacob then used his power to enter Jakes body, encouraging him to recover. When he recovered, he sat up, looked around and then burst into tears, "I've been trapped in Hell for the last six months. I've seen things, terrible things. I knew what I was saying was wrong but I was powerless to stop it."

"Be happy you've been released from the grip of Hell," said Jacob trying to reassure him, "when you recover I'll need you by my side."

Jacob turned to the others, "It's time for you to make a decision," he waited for a reaction then continued, "I'm offering to take you to Olympus, there I can prepare you to assist in the defence of Earth; will you come with me?"

"It's not my place, but I have to speak up," said Fafner apologising for intervening. "You know your grandfathers rule. No mortals may enter Olympus."

"I know the rule but everything has changed," said Jacob acknowledging Fafner's concern. "Zeus must also change. I'll plead my case when I'm back in the temple. I know he won't be happy but I expect him to support me, even humanity will have a part to play when the battle of the End Times begins."

He turned back to his classmates, "What you saw in Temple Bar is nothing compared to what's coming, for two thousand years the gods have been preparing for the battle against Lucifer. We've been sowing the seeds for your defence all over the world. The ancient gods, everywhere, are waiting for my call. There has been opposition to helping you because so many men, especially the ones in power, can't be trusted. Time, and time again, man has succumbed to evil but I lived for sixteen years among you, I know there is goodness and am prepared to defend it."

Jacob went quiet; he shifted his head from left to right as though searching through his mind. He slowly went into a trance. Baldor and Fafner got concerned and moved closer, drawing their swords again. They needn't have feared. All Jacob sensed was the presence of a deity of the Light.

It was a goddess who materialised. She glided gracefully through a hazy white mist. Her fair hair, woven with colourful flowers, gently flowed to fall below her shoulders. Her headband was embedded with precious stones and interspersed with oak leaves made from gold. She wore a pleated linen robe covered by the finest lace, made from silk and pulled together by silver threads. Her eyes were calming and her luscious red lips cradled an inviting smile. All around her, a brilliant white light pulsated showing her majesty. There were no necklaces, bangles or rings; there was no need for jewellery.

"I am Danu," she said looking around the classroom yet focusing on Shane, "I am Goddess of these Sacred Lands and right now, I rest alongside Eala, Faer and Fafner."

"I wondered who it was who sits on the fourth throne," said Jacob while turning to smile at Fafner. "Hey, dragon lord, you and the lady Danu are in two places at once."

Fafner laughed, "I know! I sensed it."

Danu turned to him, "So much younger than the one that sits by my side." She then leaned across to place her hand against Jacob's cheek, "Grandson of a dear friend, we finally meet. Eala always spoke of you. Just before the stone came and took her, she thought of you and shed one last tear; the tear of a goddess. She knows what's coming. I too know what's coming.

She turned back to the pupils, "I've come to beg for your help, you are of my realm and right now that realm is in great danger. The dark one sowed the seeds of corruption bringing on the Great Hunger; even all those deaths didn't quench his thirst for revenge. He hasn't forgotten, and will never forgive the one who rescued me from the fires of Hell. Listen to Jacob, train with the gods, wait for the white horses and be ready when you receive a calling from the Stone of Destiny. It's from there you will lead my realms defence of the Light. You won't be alone, a goddess will return, one who has given her name to these beautiful lands. She will come to be by your side, tell her of me,"

She was again distracted by Shane, "My Lord," she said slightly bowing. "We meet again,"

"We've never met," replied Shane. "How could I forget someone so beautiful?"

"In you I see his face, the face of a Celtic War God, once close to me. Do him proud." She then faded and disappeared. Shane was taken aback and although confused, he shrugged off her comments.

Jacob was about to speak again when Shane said, "You know I'd follow you anywhere, even to Olympus."

"Now, now, Shane," sniggered Jacob, "is that a God crush?" While everyone laughed Jacob got more serious and asked again if they would join him. Jake said, "I too will go with you." Al and Davie were next; then the remaining boys agreed to follow him.

"I've never transported more than four at any one time, seven will be a challenge but I'm going to try, who's first?" Shane of course was first, joined by Davie, Al, Stevie, Jake and two other boys. They formed a circle causing Stevie to quip, "A mini rugby scrum?" The boys laughed but didn't get a chance to make any further comments because Jacob blinked and they all materialised in the temple next to where Odi was anxiously waiting. Jacob acknowledged him then disappeared again.

Shane greeted Odi who was in total shock on seeing what Jacob was up to. He sensed his two grandfathers were close by and ushered the boys over to a side annex. Within seconds another group arrived and again Odi brought this group to the same annex. He was getting alarmed as there were now fourteen mortals in the temple.

It was on Jacob's third attempt when the teacher intervened, "How can you do this? Where are you taking them? What about their parents?"

"I can't waste anymore time, I need to go now, there's only one day left for them to be trained. If it makes it any easier for you I can erase your memories of me being here, allowing you to deal with the police and the parents." He suggested he leave the room and told him that by the time he was through the door his memory would be erased, therefore protecting the school from an attack by Lucifer and his armies.

Jacob arrived back in the temple with the remaining boys, Fafner and Baldor. He was visibly nervous knowing that when his grandfather found nineteen mortals in the temple there would be hell to pay and possibly a very large explosion, putting all their lives in danger. He gambled on the trust Zeus had gained in him and prayed Magni would assist but didn't expect the reaction he got from Odi who reacted by slamming him against the wall, "What have you done," he screamed, "you know the rule, it's a golden rule, Zeus will unleash his bolts."

There was no time to plan, Zeus and Odin had arrived and the look of shock on both their faces was indescribable. Zeus's lightning bolt fell from his arm into his hand and he was about to release its power when Jacob leapt out and pleaded for both his grandfathers to trust him. Zeus's anger caused tremors throughout the temple but Jacob kept pleading, "I had no time to request permission, I had to make a quick decision as there's only one day left to train them. Give me a few moments." He ran out to the gardens look-ing for Magni.

Magni and Ares were pacing the length of the ornamental pond unable to relax until Jacob had returned safely to the temple.

"Magni, Magni!" yelled Jacob running to join them, "I need you in the temple. Zeus has produced his bolt and is threatening to kill my friends."

"Your Friends?" asked Magni with a look of concern, "Don't tell me brought mortals into the temple? Have you learned nothing?" He leaned across and clattered Jacob across the back of his head. He was furious but when he saw the passion in Jacob's eyes he knew he had to act. He and Ares ran to the temple.

When they arrived all nineteen boys were now in the presence of Zeus and Odin. It was a tense few moments but Odi stood between them and his grandfathers, offering what little protection he could give, he also hoped Odin wouldn't allow Zeus to take any action that might kill his favourite grandson. Magni was taken aback and turned to Jacob, "Did you bring half the school? How many are there?"

"Nineteen," replied Jacob.

Magni faced Zeus and his grandfather, "He's young, impulsive, and his heart is in the right place. What he's planning is sound and I would have done the same thing. Allow them stay, Ares and I will take charge of their training and ensure they understand the secrecy of Olympus.

Zeus said nothing, turned and left, he wasn't happy but knew he had to trust the plans that were being prepared. Jacob followed him, "Grandfather, I'm sorry for breaking your most sacred rules but Hell or The Darkness will not respect any rules, I've seen it. I felt there was no choice and I trusted my instincts. I need to know you trust me. The Lady Danu pleaded for my help." Zeus still didn't say a word; he just dismissed Jacob with a flick of his hand.

Jacob slowly made his way back to the Great Hall, he was despondent wondering was his arrogance so ingrained that he felt he could so wantonly disregard the rules of Olympus. He felt a voice enter his head, "I too can enter your head and leave at will," It was Zeus, "after all I'm God of Gods. I left because I sensed the presence of evil while looking at your friends. Looking into their eyes I saw all but one walks in the Light. Beware Jake, the poison holds him, and you're being deceived. Lucifer has him and through him will watch your every move. You know what must be done; be careful, be discreet, and make it quick."

"I'm embarrassed," said Jacob, "how did I miss this? I feel ashamed for letting you down."

"That's easy," said Zeus, "you're dealing with the greatest deceiver. With every mistake you make, you must always remember, the secret is to learn from them. Go now and assist my friend Danu. Do what must be done, make me proud. "

Jacob was delighted his decision to bring the boys to Olympus was now endorsed but he was devastated knowing he had to kill Jake. On entering the Great Hall he was aware Odi was in his head, "Don't be distracted. Leave Jake to me. He will not see the vastness of Olympus." Odi met with Magni and alerted him to the situation,

"I too will be watching," said Magni. "Do it at the second beam of the pergola, if you fail I will be waiting at the end, He will not make it to the meadows."

Jacob was upset, he liked Jake. He entered Odi's head and asked if there was another way. Odi was firm, "No, Zeus has spoken, if he saw no other way, there is no other way. Remember brother, Jake is no longer your friend, he's been taken by the great deceiver. His time is up."

"When it happens," suggested Jacob, "do it in public, make it look like an accident, I'll take his body back to the school woodlands and leave him under the fallen trunk of an old tree. It will be considered an accident."

It was getting late and the boys were given three rooms at the far end of the temple, far enough away from the nearest exit. Magni positioned himself out of sight, but close enough to keep an eye out for Jake. His suspicions were well founded because during the night he observed Jake leaving the room and heading towards the Great Hall. Magni followed him, wondering what he was up to. He didn't need to take any action.

Jake slipped passing one of the pillars; he fell against a large and heavy vase causing it to topple and knock him down three steps. The vase landed on his back crushing his spine and breaking his neck. Jacob and Odi as well as most of those staying that night heard the crash and rushed to investigate. There was widespread shock when they arrived. Jacob and Odi quickly established that Jake was dead and they were relieved, killing someone who had been unwillingly taken by Lucifer was not something they wanted to be involved in. Magni stepped out from the shadows and in Jacob's and Odi's eyes he was immediately under suspicion. Odi approached him, "In the temple? That's sacrilege. Please tell me you'd nothing to do with this!"

"Don't ever ask that question again," replied Magni.

Odi backed away. Jacob knelt beside Jake's body, placed his hand on his shoulder and then blinked. He arrived in the woodland beside the school, and left Jake beneath a recently fallen tree, knowing he would be found the following morning.

Shane and the boys were upset, another of their friends was dead, Shane asked, "How come you couldn't save him? After all you're supposed to be gods."

"He broke his neck and crushed his spine," replied Odi, "he severed his life force; all we can do is bring him home so his family can grieve. Jacob will stay until he's found, he will protect his dignity."

The boys grieving troubled Maria, they needed to be strong for their training plans the following morning. She stood among them, staying close to Shane and Al in particular. She closed her eyes and allowed her Light to shine. Its power spread, bringing her calmness to each of the boys. Everyone then returned to their rooms.

Eala and Panya were last to leave for their room, they were waiting for Jacob to return. They waited for several hours and gave up. Walking towards their room they heard a slight rustle in the shadows, it was Odi. He was waiting on Panya, hoping their date was still going to happen. It was, and they left for the grounds hoping not to meet other gods. He already let Jacob know it was the first time ever that he actually had real feelings for a girl and wasn't sure how to act appropriately with someone he liked in that way. He offered his hand and she gladly accepted it. He talked and she willingly responded. He felt a bond develop and worked hard to suppress his playboy instincts fearing any false move would ruin the magic moments they were now sharing. He asked for a kiss and she readily obliged. Her lips against his sent incredible sensations throughout his body awakening his suppressed instincts. He wanted her so much his hands went from her back to rest on her hips gently pressing her closer to him. His mind drifted taking him to times he had with beautiful women but those memories didn't make him feel the way he felt right now, until he thought of Jacob and lost the moment. He suggested returning to the temple, hoping she would agree to meet him again the following day. She agreed.

After leaving her to her room he left to sit on the steps of the temple. Every thought of her caused breathtaking sensations to race through his body. At times he wanted to strip and run naked through the meadows but thought better of it. He went to his room and found all three of his brothers were asleep. He excitedly woke Jacob, "I know what their like, the butterflies. They're amazing; I won't be able to sleep."

"At last," sighed a tired Jacob, "you finally spent some time with her."

"She's awesome, now I understand." They talked for a short while longer and then fell asleep.

The next morning the sun seemed to rise a little earlier. Baldor and Fafner were already waiting and were soon joined by Girish, Jomo and Thanases. On reaching the workshops they found Faer, Garuda and Jahiri were already there. All eight met with the elves for the fitting of their robes and armour, and after the fitting they returned to the steps where Jacob's school friends where waiting.

Baldor was in charge, he led the group in a very intense warm-up before taking them out for their hour long run through the meadows. Sixteen of Jacob's friends kept up but two struggled, they gave up after twenty minutes. Baldor tried everything to encourage them but his efforts failed.

"You must understand," said Shane after approaching him, "we attend a school that encourages its pupils to play rugby, we practice every day, that's why most of us are able for this training, Conor and Joey are more into reading and studying, they don't like sport. We call them Nerds; you must go easy on them."

"Jacob knew this when he chose them," replied Baldor. "They need to understand that the Darkness won't distinguish between warriors, doctors, scientists or...Nerds. It will destroy all before it. They must train." Shane said no more, he rejoined the others up ahead.

After awhile they reached the lagoon where they went for a swim in its soothing waters. While in the water they discovered they now had the ability to spend lengthy periods swimming along the seabed without having to surface for air. They also learned their muscles had grown giving them the power to keep up with the darting fish. They were curious how this could happen so quickly, they decided to wait and ask Jacob.

Conor and Joey finally joined them to be met by a torrent of abuse. They didn't care, they felt different. They too had enlarged muscles and felt stronger. Shane took hold of Joey's arm; then said after squeezing his muscle, "Another hour and you'll be as big as the rest of us." They all laughed until Thanases stood and flexed his arm and leg muscles. "That's put me in my place," said a chastened Shane. A light breakfast then arrived.

After enjoying breakfast they prepared for the return journey to the temple, this time the run included the use of the beams in the pergola for a series of pull ups. Joey and Conor surprised everybody with their sudden prowess at acrobatics, especially their abilities at twisting, rolling, turning and spinning.

On reaching the temple they felt even stronger but Baldor wasn't satisfied, "More needs to be done," he said insisting they run to the folly and back again. "Another hour in the meadows will do you no harm," he said with a smirk, "when finished, meet with Magni and Ares, only then will you be ready to learn the art of swordsmanship."

While the eight guardians left to meet with Apollo and Chiron the boys completed their final run. They made their way to the amphitheatre where Magni and Ares were waiting. Hephaestus had already arranged for eighteen specially designed swords to be forged and ensured Hades gave them invisibility.

The training began using the eight basic angles of attack, and using those angles they were taught to always seize the offensive rather than wait for the right time to counter-attack. They learned the five strongest defensive moves starting with an overhead attack and a rising vertical attack. Their training included ways to protect themselves from downward cuts or thrusts as well as high horizontal movements. They quickly mastered the art of parrying away cuts directed at their legs by dropping the sword downwards giving them enough space to absorb any impacts. They also learned to swing their swords across their bodies protecting themselves from attacks coming from the left or right. After three hours Ares and Magni felt they could teach them no more.

Apollo, Chiron and Jacob were watching the final moments of the training session and were very impressed by how quickly the boys became masters. "Magnificent," said Apollo after joining them. "Holding a sword so mystical and invisible to others should be a great honour. Always keep it by your side. It will warn you when a serpent is close by. In that very moment your swords will become one with you by taking control of your arm. Remember that they are the only weapons which can defeat a serpent and you've been taught to be ruthless."

Jacob knew they had questions and proceeded to explain why their muscles had grown in such a short time. He explained how time travelled so much slower in Olympus than it does in the realm of man. "One hour in Olympus," he said, "could be as much as a week, a month, even six months on earth."

The boys knew their time to leave the temple had arrived. They changed back into their school uniforms and waited for Jacob to embrace them before returning them home. He returned them in groups of six, constantly reminding them that many months may have passed since they disappeared.

Their arrival at the school gates didn't attract any attention until they started walking up the avenue towards the main doors. It was during lunch break and all years were in the school grounds. At first there was shock, then excitement. What the pupils were looking at were eighteen missing boys who no longer looked like what they did before disappearing. They were taller, more chiselled, more muscular, more confident. The principal arrived, "Where've you been? It's been three months, and not a word. Are you aware there's been nationwide and international searches, looking for you." The boys didn't respond. The principal called the Gardaí who quickly arrived. Their parents were contacted and they too arrived, each one showing great relief.

Back at the temple Jacob was pleased his plans were now in place and believed there was no more to be done. He decided not to allow any more changes or thoughts of the battle interfere with the dinner and the after-party he had put together. When dinner was over he was delighted it went down so well, the kitchen staff had excelled as usual, and a great meal was had by all. Dionysus was relieved his cellars had coped.

Jacob, being a party animal, arranged for the greatest party ever witnessed in the realms of the gods. He brought the most renowned DJ's from Ibiza who blasted out anthem after anthem. He ensured the lighting systems reacted with the music. The younger gods never experienced such beats and rhythms; they just drank and danced the night away. Jacob's friends were used to village festivals and kept the excitement going by performing a selection of their traditional dances.

At the back of the hall Maria watched everyone enjoy themselves, she was joined by Jacob who said, "Remember grandfather saying how glad he was when we arrived, how we brought a light back into Olympus, a light he had long forgotten? Well, after tonight I bet he'll be glad to see the back of us." They both laughed.

Before seeking Eala he arranged for Maria to return the DJ's, and the equipment, back to Ibiza and wipe their memories when the party ended. He went searching and found Eala dancing with Fafner and cut in. They danced together never taking their eyes from each other and after a while he used his eyes to signal for them to leave for the gardens.

"I know a place," he said taking her hand, "it's a secluded bench where we won't be interrupted."

"I know that look," she said briskly walking beside him, "that twinkle gives you away, you're after something."

"Me. After something?" exclaimed a shocked Jacob, "Never! I'm shocked you'd think I'd scheme like that."

They reached the bench and after sitting they enjoyed the sound of the trickling water from a nearby water feature, before admiring the beauty of the star lit sky. He gently kissed her sending pleasant sensations throughout both their bodies. Their passion grew and they briefly parted as they undone their clasps, straps and buttons. They went in for another deep open mouthed kiss when Jacob briefly opened his eyes, a split second that killed his passion.

Eala backed away, "What's wrong," she asked, "have I upset you?"

"No, no, It's not you," he said pointing towards the statue. "Kissing with Odi watching doesn't do it for me."

"Where is he?" she asked, not realising he was pointing at the statue, "I'll kill him."

He again pointed at the statue, "His bits are almost in my face," they both laughed.

"Aah, poor Jacob," she said while pulling him up to stand, "let's go to the lagoon, I know something else that can be 'in your face' and bring back your passion." The words were barely out of her mouth when he was carrying her, over his shoulder, towards the lagoon.

They reached the beach and decided to walk in the shallow waters where they kissed again and the passion reignited. They moved further along only to find Odi lying on a nearby grass verge with Panya in his arms. They were deep in a very passionate embrace causing Jacob to panic, "We need to leave, we need to leave right now. I'm too close to Odi and will automatically end up in his head….. It's too late, Oh no…I can feel everything, he's close."

Just then a light shot out across the cosmos. "Did you see that?" asked Eala.

"I did," panted Jacob, "That was some bright light."

They backed off and continued towards the sand dunes where they spent a most enchanting, loving and passionate night together.

Chapter 25

Jacob was first to awaken just as dawn pushed the stars aside. The first rays of the rising sun struggled to break through but when they did it was like an explosion of colour shooting across the heavens. Vibrant colours designed to uplift the saddest of souls.

A feeling of despair had welled up in him bringing on a sick feeling. He looked at the still sleeping Eala longing for her journey to be cancelled, but he knew it wasn't to be. He woke her and after hugging they made their way to the Great Hall. They walked slowly, holding on to every last second. On reaching the Great Hall they joined Odi and Panya who were already sitting in a quiet corner. All those at the other tables exchanged stories and bantered about last night's party, whereas Jacob and Odi were too upset and in no mood to talk.

After a while it was time. Jacob nodded to Odi indicating that he was to take the boys to the workshop to collect their robes and armour. Odi did what was asked but didn't stay with them. Maria brought the girls to their room and left them preparing for their departure.

After breakfast many of the gods left to stand in silence on the patio surrounding the temple. On a number of nearby small hillocks several gods took up positions for a better view. Magni, Modi and a very subdued Odi stood silently on the nearest mound, close to where Jacob would open the portal. Thor and Maria stood alone on the next hillock. Zeus, Odin, Hera and

Dione stood near where the road split to travel in three different directions. Pegasus and Chiron stood on the next hillock and finally Dionysus, Eros and Apollo stood on the highest one. They all took their colossus form and waited. The Astrals and the Archangel Raphael joined the remaining gods on the patio.

Jacob at this point was the only god still in the temple. He waited for his friends to arrive and when they did he was taken aback, what a sight. Eight immortal warriors dressed in the finest garments that Olympus could provide, and four beautiful girls who were unbelievably stunning. Their full length gowns with hooded capes helped them present as the goddesses they were to become. Their jewellery shone and glimmered in the stunning light of the morning sun. Filtering through the windows, that light made them look like angels. Jacob just stood there, still staring in disbelief, especially at Eala. When he finally spoke, he said, "Always remember, you are immortal, never to tire, never to feel the cold, never to burn under the sun. You will never need to eat or drink, but you should at every opportunity. Remember, for two thousand years the gods will be asleep, but the Astrals and the Archangel will be near at all times." He then reminded them of their task and wished them well.

The first to leave the temple was Panya and she was escorted by Baldor and Thanases. While standing on the steps she appeared as a most regal, and beautiful women, her aura showing her to be a true Messenger of the Gods. Her gown and fur-lined cape rested perfectly to surround her hour-glass figure. Her jewellery and headband contained so many diamonds, the refracted light, when split, enhanced the spectrum of rainbow colours surrounding her. Her guardians stood each side of her.

Thanases stood as a rugged good looking youth who exuded confidence, holding his head high. He looked athletic, agile and muscularly powerful. His blond, shoulder-length hair framed a perfect face and his piercing blue eyes drew in all those he met. His robes and armour enhanced that appearance. Resting under his right arm was his helmet and on his left he held his shield.

Like Thanases, Baldor also stood as a good looking youth. He didn't exude the same confidence, but he certainly held his head high. He was equally as athletic and agile but not as muscularly powerful. He too had shoulder-length blond hair and piercing blue eyes.

Jacob embraced all three, holding the longest grip for Panya. He said very little when opening the portal for the first time. As they stepped through he bowed and wished them well.

They turned right and moved towards the crossroads making their way towards the ice lands of the north. Odi's heart sank especially when she forlornly looked back at him, revealing a single tear trickling down her cheek. As she walked away he tried to imprint in his mind this last memory, her ice blue coloured gown, her matching fur-lined cape, her jewellery, especially the magnificent diamond encrusted hair band filled with clear crystals he knew to have been mined in the volcanoes of Italy. For the first time in his life he too allowed a tear to trickle down his cheek. He didn't care that his brothers were watching, this time they didn't tease him. They felt for him.

Jacob turned back to face the temple waiting on Oba, Jomo and Jahiri to arrive. When they did, they too oozed power. Oba stood there wearing a yellowy white gown designed to deflect away the constant glare of the southern sun. She didn't wear as much jewellery for fear the sun would threaten to reveal her using the jewellery as a conduit. Instead she wore the brightly coloured Geles head wrap of the Yoruba peoples. Like Panya, she too stood as a powerful Goddess of the Light.

Jahiri and Jomo stood each side of her, looking very powerful, each wearing the robes and armour of Olympus warriors. Jahiri looked like a true African god, sculpted to perfection. He had the height and striking good looks of the Maasai. His dark, semi braided hair framed a chiselled and youthful good looking face that lit up each time he revealed his brilliant white smile. Jomo was equally as tall but not as striking. His hair was tighter and his face rounder. He too had a smile that would brighten any day. His eyes were spellbinding, the kind that was able to reach deep into anyone's soul. He was stronger and broader than Jahiri and each time he flexed he revealed his muscular and titan-like shoulders.

On reaching Jacob it was obvious they were nervous. Jacob embraced each of them in turn, hoping to take away their fears. He gave them more time and cautioned them, "Where you're going there are ancient gods, some not seen since the beginning of time. Most will assist; some will feel threatened but they will support you." He opened the portal for the second time allowing them to begin their walk along an old dusty road destined to take them deep into the south.

Jacob turned back and saw that Mulan, Garuda and Girish were already on the steps of the temple. They were the one group he knew were to suffer the most and it concerned him. He looked at Mulan and was in awe. She was smaller than the other messengers but when she tied her hair, in a tradition Chinese bun, she almost matched their size. She was beautiful, of mixed western and oriental appearance. Her fair, almost white complexion; highlighted her almond-shaped eyes and the angular curve to her mouth. The cream coloured Kimono she wore was simple, straight-seamed and secured by a gem encrusted braided sash. The sleeves were long and flowing with vibrant colours. Her cape was a darker shade, almost taupe. Her head band contained an assortment of gems mined in the high mountains of the Indus peoples and when they glowed they showed that she too was a true Messenger of the Light.

Garuda stood to her left and presented as a formidable warrior of Olympus. His robes and armour didn't take away from the fact that he was of the Indus. He was good looking, tall and muscular. His thick, coal black hair, framed his brownish-yellow complexion. His deep brown eyes and inviting smile showed his gentleness.

Girish too presented as a formidable warrior of Olympus. He wasn't very muscular but it was obvious by the way he stood that, when required, he had the strength and speed to make him equally as imposing. Like Mulan he had deep set, almond-shaped golden brown eyes. His thick black hair was tied up in a pony tail contrasting perfectly with his sallow skin tone showing he descended from the Far East.

Jacob embraced each of them in turn, and then opened the portal for the third time allowing them exit. They turned right and walked to the crossroads where they turned towards the East.

As each group left, they always looked back one last time, happy to see the gods raising their hands to wave them goodbye.

This was now the time Jacob dreaded the most, he refused to turn and face the temple. He knew Eala was waiting on the steps anxious to get going.

"You can't put this off," said Odi after entering his head, "turn and face her, let her know how much you love her." He had difficulty turning but when he did he saw a beautiful, statuesque vision. She stood on the top step wearing a fitted silky white full length gown, covered by a gold braided cape. The gown accentuated her curves making it difficult for him to avert his eyes. As she approached she seemed to glide causing her slightly curled fair hair to dance in the light wind. The diamonds in her necklace sparkled, capturing sunrays before beaming them in all directions. When she reached him, he took her into his arms holding her tightly. They both closed their eyes taking in the beautiful feeling of their bodies resting against each other one last time.

Faer and Fafner stood close by waiting on the portal to be opened. Like the guardians that left earlier, they looked formidable, both standing over six feet tall. Fafner was muscular, particularly his upper body. His face was surrounded by hair that was thick, dark and wavy, split in the centre and growing to just below his ears. His eyes were deep blue and he had a smile that disarmed those he met. Faer wasn't as broad or muscular but was more handsome. His face tanned and his eyes a paler shade of blue. His hair cropped shorter and parted to his left.

The time came for the portal to be opened for the last time and when it did, Fafner and Faer stepped through, and waited for Eala to say her goodbyes. Jacob still had difficulty letting her go; he continued caressing her face and hair, kissing her gently as though it was to be the last kiss ever.

Fafner stepped back through the portal to take Eala by her arm saying it was time to go. Jacob wanted to kill him but knew he was only doing what was asked of him. When they were through they turned right and made their way to the crossroads.

Jacob watched her walk away and decided to walk along the inside of the shield, never taking his eyes from her. As she walked she seemed to be moving that little bit faster, causing him to run to keep up. Occasionally she'd look back, stop and wait for him. Time and time again they'd place their hands on the shield as though still able to touch each other. They even tried to steal another kiss.

Fafner sensed the devastation, he was warned this might happen and knew he'd again have to intervene.

Chapter 26

Despair and grief took Jacob as he ran up the nearest hillock. From there he watched Eala turn left towards the west. When she went out of view he ran to the next hill and when he found her he again never took his eyes from her. His heart raced as he ran up the following hill hoping to see her again. He was so blind to what was happening around him he didn't notice the briars and thorn encased branches that were ahead of him. He ran through causing his tunic to be ripped from him. As he ran, the extended branches retracted and shot back lashing across his chest, and then as they continued back into their original position they extended forward again and on their return they lashed his back. He didn't care, he didn't feel the pain. All he wanted was to see Eala one last time. His blood continued to trickle down his chest and back as he reached the highest hill. From his vantage point he saw her again, time had moved on and she was out of her robes, wearing looser and more comfortable clothes, so were the boys. He watched them disappear again and waited until they climbed the next hill. Time and time again he called her name but she never responded. He pounded his fists off the shield, trying to get through but it was sealed. What he didn't realise was Zeus and Odin were holding the shield firm, preventing any portals from opening.

He continued watching as Fafner and Faer faded into invisibility and knew Eala was soon to join them. He kept calling her name while pounding off the shield hoping she'd respond, she didn't. He fell to his knees in despair, landing on sharp pebbles causing him more pain. Odi attempted to join him but was prevented by Magni who felt Jacob had to go through this on his own. Maria was devastated. This was the first time she couldn't come to her beloved son's aid. Her tears fell as though the gates of a powerful dam had just been opened. She then buried her head into Thor's chest.

Jacob's heart was broken but through his grief, he kept calling and then softly he whispered her name. He let out one last call and she stopped, turned and raised her right arm as though to wave goodbye. He gasped, and then froze. He saw her left arm resting on a now very large bump. Odi was in his head at that very moment and saw everything Jacob saw, he also felt everything Jacob felt. Jacob had difficulty standing but managed, he leaned against the shield and let out the most heart wrenching call that the gods would never forget. "Eeeeeaaaaalllllaaaaa," he yelled.

Odi struggled to escape Magni's grip. He managed to raise his right arm and put it around the back of Magni's neck. He found the strength to bend forward, far enough to drag Magni over his shoulder and knock him to the ground. At the same time he announced to the temple, as loudly as he could, "She's pregnant, that's what Lucifer is after. He's after the baby of a god."

Odi ran as fast as he could but Jacob was still too far away. He used his powers to summon a nearby white stallion who allowed him grab his mane and jump on his back. The speed at which they travelled allowed Odi reach Jacob in just a few moments. "This happened to us," said an inconsolable Jacob while burying his head into Odi's chest, "we were robbed of both parents. Now they're robbing me of my baby."

Just then Kalen arrived. He encouraged Jacob to stand, "Your babies will be under the protection of the elves and will not be found. Hell is not that powerful. They'll sleep until you come for them and will still be babies when the End Times battle is over. They will see you as their father and Eala their mother." Jacob just stared and then asked, "There's more than one?"

"There are three," replied Kalen.

Jacob placed his two hands to his head while pacing back and forth; he couldn't believe what he was hearing. He looked towards where Eala last stood but she had now faded, she was gone.

He continued pacing, trying to prevent himself from losing control. "You knew?" he yelled.

"We didn't," replied Kalen, "when Eala turned, like you our oracle saw the bump. Images of three babies appeared, two boys and a girl."

Raphael arrived, "This changes everything," he said expressing the concern of the Archangels, "Lucifer will slaughter the innocents just like Herod did thirty one years ago. He won't stop until he destroys the male baby of such a powerful god as you. We wonder does he already know there is a girl and wants her as his consort? We believe the elves are the best protection and failing that, the Archangels will be close by."

Jacob wasn't reassured. "Lucifer is the most cunning and dangerous of them all," he said, "I'm not convinced Eala and my babies are safe."

Apollonius arrived insisting he show his future. He placed his hand on Jacob's forehead and used his staff to call on the Light. The Light came and showed Jacob the End Times. He saw two lakes and a hidden cave. He saw four thrones, one with the stone image of Eala. Outside, he saw the cave being protected by the wolfhounds of Na Fianna and the mountains guarded by the golden stag. He saw the Elf lands and three babies being well looked after. He saw a man, sword in hand, bloodied, and with torn clothing, walking through a forest into open fields, walking across raging rivers and calm lakes, walking towards the cave, being stalked by the golden stag. He saw the elves arrive carrying three babies. He saw Eala run from the cave and sit with her babies and as the man kneels before her. He saw he was the man. He was now convinced.

Odi talked Jacob into coming back to the temple and as they walked, arm in arm, Jacob paused, "Odi, I saw the four thrones. Fafner, Faer, Eala and the Goddess Danu, they were all there. I saw the wolfhounds and the golden stag, they still stand guard."

Getting closer to the temple Jacob sensed Odi getting anxious, he had discreetly looked up and saw Magni standing with his arms tightly folded and his teeth grinding against each other, "He's going to kill me, isn't he?"

"Not if I've anything to do with it," replied Jacob.

Even in his hour of grief Jacob couldn't help himself, when he reached Magni he said, "I saw what Odi did, I think we all saw it. You have to admit it was some move. I bet you didn't see it coming?" he smiled while placing his arm protectively across Odi's shoulders, "I did tell you he could beat the living daylights out of you." They all laughed and continued towards the temple.

"If what I saw is real love," said Magni pushing Odi away from Jacob, "I want part of it. You are both so lucky to have found each other." They entered the temple but all was quiet and sombre.

Jacob excused himself, wanting to be alone. He hugged his mother and went to his room. He lay on his bed thinking of Eala wanting to be there for her. It was tearing him apart that she was going through the birth alone. He thought that at least his mother and father were able to share the beauty of a birth when he and Odi were born, before they had to separate. He cried himself to sleep, and as the torches diminished he went into a deeper sleep. He entered the dream world where he was transported forward to a little village near the north of Greece, in the land of Macedon. He walked among the villagers and listened to them ridicule a young girl who claimed an angel and two soldiers were living in a cave near the lake. The angel had given birth to three babies.

Jacob wanted so much to speak to the little girl but he was in the dream world and couldn't be seen. He transported himself back by two days and located the cave where he saw Eala struggling through her labour. He watched the Elfena assist with the births and watched as Kalen arrived. He was intrigued when Kalen crossed the cave and whispered while standing next to him, "I know you're here."

Jacob got emotional again as each baby arrived, he wanted so much to hold them. He smiled watching his babies open their eyes and was startled as they slightly bowed to him. They could see him and as he looked into their eyes he again knew they were safe. Eala looked around, feeling his presence. Their love for each other was breaking through all the barriers placed before them, she knew he was with her and smiled as she too looked into her babies eyes. She could see Jacob looking out at her and Jacob could see Eala looking out at him.

Kalen and the Elfena took the babies promising they would be safe in their realm. Jacob walked behind Eala and with his hand resting on her hip. She sensed him and was comforted by that fleeting touch. The babies were wide awake as Eala handed each of them over to the elves before kissing them goodbye.

Jacob too said goodbye, and all present saw the slight indentation appear on each of their cheeks as he stretched in to kiss them. Eala struggled to the cave entrance hoping to get one last glimpse before the elves finally disappeared into their realm.

The first rays of the rising sun climbed towards the cave, sending a brilliant crimson coloured-ray of light through the spirit of Jacob, making him visible to Eala. She held her arms forward but they just went through him. She asked was this a dream and he just shook his head. She struggled towards a small cave pond, being fed by a trickle of crystal clear water, filtering down from the mountain above. She sat on a ledge, where just beneath was a thermal spring that heated the trickling water. She closed her eyes and relaxed. Jacob used all his might to break through his dream but he failed. He called on Poseidon for help and immediately felt the powerful arm of his grand uncle rest on his shoulder. He placed his hand in the pool causing a gentle ripple to rise and caress Eala's legs and arms, bringing her great relief. This gentle motion put Eala into a deep sleep taking her to the same dream world.

On entering she was met by her beloved Jacob. They ran to each other, holding each other in an embrace that resonated throughout the cosmos. They brought themselves back to their long and magical walk through the Olympus realm, to their time swimming in the lagoon, but mostly to the times when they just held each other. They talked about their babies and of how happy they were that both of them were together for the births.

"Have you thought of names," asked Eala, "while here we should name them together,"

"I could sense their powers," said Jacob. "They will be Gods when their time comes, they should be named after their powers."

"Yes," agreed Eala. "In that case our daughter should be called Helena; she will be a Goddess of the Light and a torch bearer for the gods. She will bring brightness into the darkest of places. She will also be known as the Goddess of Rescue."

"I'd like my first son to be called Demetrius," said Jacob. "He will be the greatest mystic of them all, a god protector of the Astrals and a lover of the earth."

"How will we together pick a name for our youngest son?" asked Eala

"Somehow I feel you've already chosen one," replied Jacob.

"He's strong," she said, "I see him as a pillar of strength for all whose lives he touches."

"Well then," said Jacob, "it's decided, his name is Obelius, God of Olympus."

This magic time was not to last. Eala felt herself being tugged back into the real world. Jacob also felt himself being called back to his world. He opened his eyes to find Odi standing over him. "Who were you hugging?" he asked.

"Eala," replied Jacob, "we met in the dream world and held each other so tightly I know we'll never lose that beautiful and magic feeling of pure love. Our babies are born and together we named them. Helena, Obelius and Demetrius are their names. I was able to kiss them. Their eyes followed me around the cave. Odi, they're safe in the realm of the elves. I'm now ready to move on."

Odi and Jacob talked about how their lives were now complete, they were happy for each other especially now they'd both found love. "I'm kind of jealous of you, now that you're a father," said Odi. "Since meeting Panya, I want to have children of my own. I suppose the good thing is? She's been chosen to travel north which means the chances for us getting together has increased. When things settle, I intend returning to Asgard to fulfil my destiny, I'm hoping she'll be part of it."

"Does that mean you'll be loyal to Panya?" asked Jacob,

"In the hours I spent with her I've learned what real love is all about." replied Odi, "There's no way I'd mess that up."

"What about our elderly brothers?" said Jacob, being suspicious that his brothers are pretending to be asleep, "They seem to always play hard but never have time to find true love."

"That pair?" laughed Odi, who was also suspicious, "Who'd want them?"

"I suppose, when you've trained for war all your life, there's no time for love," Jacob was now certain they were listening. "I've learned to love both of them," he said while sticking two fingers down his throat pretending to be sick, "I love the way they try get one up on us for us to somehow come out on top. Sometimes I think they like to let us believe we're winning, but it's actually them who are light years ahead of us. I always feel safe and secure knowing that they have our backs but I'm warning you, don't tell them I said that."

"I heard that," said Magni while getting up to join them.

"I too heard what you said," said Modi. The four brothers sat all night just talking.

⁖

The following morning Jacob went to the Great Hall and wasn't surprised to see it so empty, He knew the elves had left, he saw them at the birth of his babies and knew they couldn't be in two places at the same time. He was aware Raphael had left for the west after attending a long meeting with Zeus and Odin before midnight. This left the Asgard Gods, the wizards and Homer as the only visitors still in the temple. When Zeus arrived he summoned Homer into his presence and asked if he was happy with the stories he had accumulated. He suggested he only write about the gods of Olympus, other realms have their own poets. Homer agreed and was then transported back to his own time where he put the finishing touches to 'The Iliad' and 'The Odyssey'.

Odin, Magni and Modi finished their breakfast and prepared to join their imperial guards in the meadows. For Odin it was a sad parting, Thor had chosen to remain with Maria and Odi made his decision to stay with Jacob. He wasn't happy but knew it was for the best. He, Magni and Modi then left the temple and made their way towards the northern Ice lands of Asgard.

Zeus sat on his throne, and from there acknowledged each god as they said their farewells. Each one turned and waved at Jacob before mounting their plinth to slowly turn back to stone. Thor and Maria walked together to bow to Zeus, then hugged their sons before mounting a plinth, specially designed for both of them. They held each other in an eternal embrace as the stone came and took them. Jacob and Odi bowed to their grandfather and watched as he, Poseidon, Hades, Chiron, Dione and Hera walked towards their plinths to begin a long and peaceful sleep leaving Odi, Jacob, Merlin and Apollonius alone.

Merlin gestured for Odi to mount his plinth and when he did the stone quickly came. Jacob, while watching his brother turn to stone said, "The statue of David really is his likeness but I know the difference," he turned to the wizards, "David was a shepherd before becoming a King. Odi, my amazing brother, was a prince of Asgard, before becoming a God."

Jacob then mounted his plinth, fixed his cape, and held his sword for support. He turned to face the east as though waiting for the rising sun, and then the stone took him. The wizards climbed the steps, turned and faced back into the Great Hall. They raised their staffs and the torches extinguished. The windows clouded over ensuring sunlight could no longer penetrate the temple, bringing a calmness allowing the gods an eternal rest.

In the meantime, deep in the darkest recesses of Hell, in a cavern overlooking the volcanic lakes, the very place where the fallen angels and the lost souls faced their never ending torment, was the throne of Lucifer. He sat there, presiding over, and relishing the constant sounds of torture, and the piercing screams coming from the victims of his serpents of Hell. He revelled in the continuous gasps for air as each soul reached for relief knowing none was forthcoming. He paused for a moment, twitched as his head slowly rose and a broad smile of devious delight crossed his face. He just uttered one word,

"Baby"

The End

Jacob
Walk of The Messengers
Eamon Blake

Throughout the ages there were many heroes, and the common thread weaving its way through their lives was honesty, bravery, chivalry and the protection of the weak. Nothing exemplifies this more than the heroism the four Messengers of the Gods and their formidable guardians showed while delivering Jacob's message during their journey of eighteen hundred years.

Jacob - Walk of the Messengers - is the second in an exhilarating series of five books, and this one tells the story of those same messengers and guardians. How on every road they walked, every river they crossed, every mountain they climbed, they were met by an onslaught of brutality from the forces of Hell that was relentless. With each attack their confidence grew and their skills enhanced, and as the years passed they continued to mature to become powerful gods in their own right.

Will they survive the relentless attacks by the forces of Hell?

Will they succeed in their task of creating the mightiest army ever assembled?

Will Jacob keep his promise and intervene when all seems lost?

Jacob
War of the End Times
Eamon Blake

For centuries, there've been epic battles fought across vast battlegrounds. There've been empires that rose and then fell to the sound of powerful armies using weapons designed for mass killing. None of that compares to what is put together for the battle between the forces of the Light and the servants of Hell.

Jacob - War of the End Times - is the third book in a riveting series of five and tells the story of a monumental battle that threatens the very fabric of all existence. Apart from open battlefields, it also takes the reader into villages, towns and cities to witness the destruction of all infrastructures that makes those cities function.

Defence of the Light is led by Jacob, and using the power of the Gods, he brings together those of myth and legend. He also calls upon the overwhelming might of the Carriers, the millions of Carriers assembled over the centuries by his messengers.

Opposing Jacob is a massive army of pure evil led by Lucifer, the Prince of Hell, and Cain, the first murderer. Both of whom are being manipulated by the stifling shadow of The Darkness.

Does Jacob possess the strength to successfully command the armies of the Light?

Will humanity survive the relentless onslaught from the forces of evil?

Will the well-planned tactics of the Olympus and Asgard War Gods be enough to defeat Hell?

Jacob
Children of The Gods
Eamon Blake

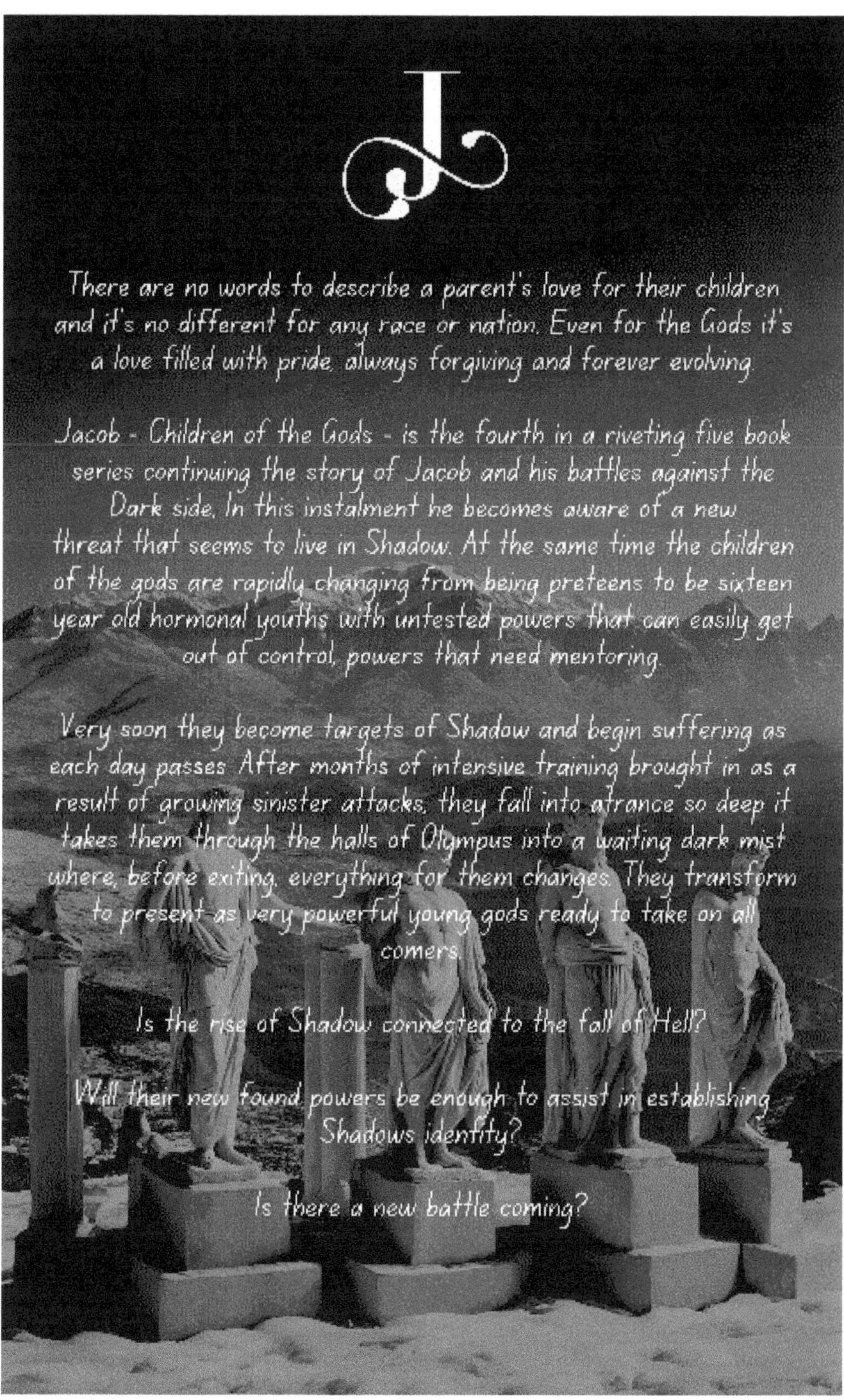

There are no words to describe a parent's love for their children and it's no different for any race or nation. Even for the Gods it's a love filled with pride, always forgiving and forever evolving.

Jacob - Children of the Gods - is the fourth in a riveting five book series continuing the story of Jacob and his battles against the Dark side. In this instalment he becomes aware of a new threat that seems to live in Shadow. At the same time the children of the gods are rapidly changing from being preteens to be sixteen year old hormonal youths with untested powers that can easily get out of control, powers that need mentoring.

Very soon they become targets of Shadow and begin suffering as each day passes After months of intensive training brought in as a result of growing sinister attacks, they fall into atrance so deep it takes them through the halls of Olympus into a waiting dark mist where, before exiting, everything for them changes. They transform to present as very powerful young gods ready to take on all comers.

Is the rise of Shadow connected to the fall of Hell?

Will their new found powers be enough to assist in establishing Shadows identity?

Is there a new battle coming?

Jacob
Battle for Olympus
Eamon Blake

A mysterious and frightening shadow has been skulking its way through all the realms of myth and legend. Its sinister presence is always followed by an attack of such evil violence that few survive.

Jacob - Battle for Olympus - is the last in a riveting five book series. It concludes the story of his battles against the Dark side. In this instalment he finally establishes who Shadow is and quickly learns it can only be defeated with the assistance of the Ancient One.

Jacob's heart breaks on learning of attacks by Shadow on the Dragon, Elf and Yeti nations and is devastated when he discovers many of his friends and allies have been killed.

When Asgard is destroyed he concludes that Shadow's plan, just like that of The Darkness, is to destroy all that has been created by the Ancient One. This emboldens him to awaken the defenders of Olympus who have, since long before the time of Zeus, been sleeping deep in the caverns below the temple.

Can Jacob rescue the remnants of those of myth and legend?

Will the Ancient One come to Jacob's assistance?

Is the Battle for Olympus to be the battle to end all wars?